Crossings

A Harry Reese Mystery

For a glossary of period terms, biographies of the characters, and a complete chronology, please visit:

streetcarmysteries.com

Crossings

Robert Bruce Stewart

Street Car Mysteries

Florence, Mass.

First Print Edition, May 2013

ISBN 978-1-938710-06-3

Street Car Mysteries

streetcarmysteries.com

To those who've made the daily crossing

For a crib sheet with characters, a short glossary, and a map, please visit:

streetcarmysteries.com/crossings

1

It all began just after I arrived home Tuesday evening.

"Harry, you'll never guess what Dorothy told me today."

"She admitted she was sent here to poison us?"

"Don't be cruel, Harry. She tries. The result is no sin of volition." She was interrupted when Dorothy herself came in from the kitchen with a plate of carbonized meat, perhaps pork, and deposited it on the table. After we thanked her and she had made her exit, Emmie resumed. "She told me the previous tenants had been killed in their sleep."

"It was an accident. They fell asleep without turning the gas off properly. I told you about it months ago. And Dorothy wasn't even here at the time."

"Well, the Eckerts' maid told Dorothy that the others in the building suspected it was something more sinister."

"Just what are you up to, Emmie?"

"I'm not up to anything, Harry. I'm just surprised you brought me to an apartment that had a pall over it."

"I rented the apartment precisely because of the pall over it—the landlord offered me the first month free. And I brought you here so I could pay the past-due rent with the dowry you led me to believe I had coming." I said this just as Dorothy made another entrance from the kitchen. Like the Eckerts, I knew there were two ways to keep your servants happy: pay them a living wage, or provide them with the sort of gossip their friends will find entertaining.

After Dorothy had left for the evening, Emmie raised the subject again.

"Mr. Ahearn is the chief suspect."

"The janitor? Suspected of what?"

"Murder, of course. Murder of that young couple who died in this very apartment. He could have loosened the gas pipe, then tightened it before the police arrived."

"I'd be careful, Emmie, repeating rumors like that. Besides, I've never known Ahearn to have any luck with leaky pipes."

"Oh, I don't believe it was him. What motive would he have had?"

"Maybe they forgot to give him his Christmas tip. I guess I had the best motive."

"You? Did you know them?"

"No, but I got a free month's rent out of the tragedy."

That closed the subject until later that night. Three times Emmie woke me up asking if I was sure the gas was off, and three times I told her it had never been on. I knew this was all part of an act. Emmie isn't the nervous type. In fact, she has a fascination with the sordid—particularly murder. She scours the newspapers for sensational crimes, and has even taken to attending trials. Our meeting, engagement, and marriage all occurred in an eight-day period punctuated by two murders. The truth was, if Emmie honestly believed there had been a murder, she'd be as happy as a clam.

There is another, far more troubling, facet of Emmie's character. She lives under the misapprehension that I'm easily manipulated. Taking these two traits together left little room for doubt. She was up to something. And the next morning she lost no time getting back into it.

"You know, it's funny your saying you had a motive to murder that poor couple."

"Why is that funny?"

"Because the Lowerys already believe you have some sort of illicit occupation."

"Who are the Lowerys?"

"Third floor, rear. Dorothy...."

"I don't want to hear what their maid told Dorothy, Emmie. I've never even met the Lowerys."

It was then that Emmie finally showed her hand. There was an opening in the Margaret and she thought we should take it. The Margaret was a sort of upscale house of flats just down Vanderbilt Avenue, on the Plaza.

"We have plenty of room here, Emmie. And we can't afford a place like that."

"It might be a bit of a pinch, but can we honestly continue to live here? With a murderer possibly still in the building?"

"There is no murderer, Emmie."

"Well, leaky gas pipes then. And the neighbors spreading rumors about you."

"I know how to handle that." Dorothy had just arrived, so I set right to it. "What's that Lowery fellow's name?"

"You mean Martin Lowery, Mr. Reese? Up on the third floor?" I had Dorothy hooked.

"Martin Lowery, yes. And how old would you say he is?"

"Oh, he's older. He has a time getting up the stairs."

"Walks with a limp?"

ROBERT BRUCE STEWART

"Yes, a bad limp, Mr. Reese."

"Well, that's interesting, because when I was a boy up in Utica there was a Martin Lowery who was run out of town after some dalliances with women of the altar guild."

"Church women, Mr. Reese?"

"Yes, it was quite a scandal. And you know what's very odd?"

"What's that, Mr. Reese?"

"He walked with a limp." I paused for dramatic effect. "Of course, that was twenty years ago. I wouldn't recognize the man now."

"And you think it's the same Martin Lowery?"

"Oh, I'm sure it's just a coincidence, Dorothy. That's probably a common enough name."

Dorothy went into the kitchen and Emmie gave me a smile.

"Well, Harry, I'm not sure that will make our stay here any more agreeable."

"Probably not, but now the neighbors will know I'm not someone to be toyed with."

I bring up all that simply to explain why I had difficulty taking the subject of death-by-gas seriously when it arose later that morning. There's no disputing that time spent with Emmie can be quite diverting. But it's equally true that it leaves one unprepared for normal human intercourse. It's as if you are exempt from the laws of physics while in her presence. Then, on leaving it, gravity brings you down with a jolt.

At the time, I was working for the Gotham Insurance Bureau, across the river in Manhattan. The Bureau was a sort of insurance information office that allowed insurers to find out if an applicant already carried similar

4

insurance in suspicious amounts, or had a predilection for making well-timed claims. When something looked odd, and there was a potential for profit, the Bureau would offer the services of its investigators. The offices were on William Street, a few blocks up from Wall Street, where much of the insurance industry was headquartered.

Like everyone else, I was making a reasonable show of looking busy when the boss came up in the elevator. He had another fellow with him and summoned me into his office. That was about 10 a.m. on Wednesday, April 3rd.

Keegan, the owner of the Bureau, opened things by introducing me to Lewis Redfield, of the Sovereign Mutual Life Insurance Company. Redfield was a large, well-fed man, but too short to be accused of having a commanding presence. In another setting he might have looked ridiculous, but standing beside Keegan, who was even better-fed and shorter, he looked almost normal.

We all sat down and Redfield told us that an agent his company did business with had committed suicide—with gas. Well, that's when I put my foot in it. I gave a little chuckle—barely audible—but loud enough to incite quizzical looks. Quick as I could, I turned it into a sort of bronchial cough and they let it go at that.

"Was there something suspicious about his death?" Keegan asked.

"Well, he was young, healthy, and reasonably successful, so suicide seemed odd," Redfield answered. "But the police seem sure that's what happened. He lived and worked in Brooklyn. His name was Huber and he died in his office in Williamsburg. But it isn't his death that really concerns us."

"Someone else died with him?" I asked.

"No, no. You see, Huber had written a number of policies for us, and our man who oversees outside agencies, Byron Perkins, thought it a good idea to make sure the policies were all on the level. He concluded they were. There was one claim on a recent policy, but the death was accidental, nothing Huber could have spotted when he wrote the policy. Then two weeks after his suicide, another claim came in on one of Huber's policies. This one wasn't even a month old. And this fellow also died in an accident. And both men lived in Manhattan."

"Couldn't it just be a coincidence?" Keegan asked.

"Yes, I hope it is. But I want to know for sure."

"What do the police say?" I asked.

"They say there's no connection between the two accidents, and no apparent connection to Huber. But that's one of the things that troubled Perkins. How did Huber meet these fellows? Why did two men living in Manhattan go over to Williamsburg to get a life policy?"

"So you just want to be reassured that there's an innocent explanation?" I asked.

"Yes, exactly. Maybe they were friends of an uncle, or met Huber on a train."

"Or maybe it's something not so innocent and the reason Huber committed suicide?"

"That's the fear, of course. And if it is that, I want to know about it as quickly as possible."

Keegan instructed me to help in any way I could. He also made it clear I would be on his payroll and there was no chance of a bonus on this job. When we were sent to investigate potential fraud cases, we were usually given a per diem and the promise of a bonus as an incentive. If we could provide the proof that allowed the insurer to avoid paying a claim, we'd receive five, or maybe ten, percent of whatever we saved them.

Redfield and I left for his company's offices, just a few blocks up William Street. He introduced me to Byron Perkins, Sovereign's Superintendent of Agencies, who led me to his office. Perkins was a rather tall fellow with a little too much nervous energy. He had several files laid out on his desk and began filling me in on the details. The whole time he spoke, he was continually flipping a letter opener.

William Huber was 26, had been to college, and had had a successful agency for the last three years. His death had occurred about three weeks earlier, on the 13th of March. His father was Conrad Huber, a prominent real estate lawyer in Brooklyn's Eastern District. They shared an office in Williamsburg, on Graham Street, just off Broadway. Much of William's success could be attributed to his father's associations, but Perkins felt he must have also put a lot of work into the business. Huber's was an independent agency—he could write policies for a number of insurers—but most of his life policies were with Sovereign. Perkins had cultivated a close relationship because he felt Huber was destined to expand and take on much of the business in the Eastern District. He knew nothing of Huber's private life, however, and conjectured that maybe a failed love affair was the motivation for the suicide.

The two policies that had caught Perkins' attention were both written earlier that year, 1901. Robert Barclay was a stock broker downtown and lived on East 58th Street. He was found dead on February 12th. He was 36 and already had a policy for $2,000 through another agent when Huber wrote one for $15,000.

"$17,000 doesn't seem excessive for a Wall Street broker," I said.

"No," Perkins agreed. "But Barclay wasn't the typical Wall Street broker. And why didn't he go back to the agent who wrote the original policy?"

"Maybe he'd left the business?" I asked.

"No, Barclay bought a $1,000 policy on his wife just last December through the same agent. And how did Huber meet Barclay?"

He sat there flipping the letter opener as if he were waiting for me to answer his question. So I asked one of my own. "Did his wife know about the $15,000 policy?"

"Oh, yes. She remembered Huber coming by a couple times, and the doctor visiting for the physical."

"How did Barclay die?"

"He fell in a hole being dug for a new building on 4th Avenue. It was late and apparently he was drunk. After Huber's death," Perkins explained, "I looked through the claims on his policies over the last year, and Barclay's stood out. First, because the death occurred so soon after the policy was written. And second, because it was the only one outside of Brooklyn. Almost all the rest were written in the Eastern District: Williamsburg, Bushwick, and Greenpoint—with a few elsewhere in Brooklyn."

"Maybe they just met at a club, or had a common friend," I said.

"Yes, of course. And there was no reason Huber should have anticipated Barclay would get drunk enough to fall like that. He had passed the physical fine."

There was another awkward pause and more flipping of the letter opener. "What happened next?" I asked.

"Then we received a claim on Christopher Farrell, another of Huber's recent clients. He was a 43-year-old drummer who lived with his wife on West 19th Street. The policy was for $5,000, a reasonable amount for a reasonably successful drummer. He was killed when he tripped on a platform of the 6th Avenue L, fell onto the tracks, and was decapitated by the next train. The accident occurred late on the night of March 22nd, just three weeks after the policy was written. And it was ascertained he had been drinking heavily."

"I see. Any one bit of it might be easily explained, but you've got a lot to swallow when you put them together."

"Yes, precisely."

"But you haven't found anything definitely suspicious?"

"Nothing. The signatures all seemed to check, the physicals, the police reports."

"And Huber's records?"

"All in order. Any payments he received were passed on. At least for our policies." He paused and then went on. "But there is something else that's suspicious. You see, we paid the policy on Barclay off, but I've held up payment on Farrell. And his wife has barely raised a peep."

"What has she been told?"

"Just that we need to verify some facts. But usually a widow is damned insistent."

"Maybe she has other things on her mind?"

"Sure, maybe."

"Well, I suppose the best way for me to help you would be to fill in the blanks: why did Huber kill himself and how did he meet Farrell and Barclay."

"Yes. If there're innocent explanations to those questions, we can live with the rest of it."

Once I had all the names and addresses, I set off for the Roosevelt Street ferry, just beyond the bridge. This was the quickest way to Williamsburg, and it came with a pleasant river cruise. I felt like a truant. I preferred being on my own this way, but had spent the last six months working regular hours on a project for Keegan. This was a time when insurers had begun writing burglary policies in large numbers and the grafters were quick to adapt. And while society generally frowns on fraud, if it's an insurance company at the short end, society contents itself with something closer to a sly grin. Insurance companies have to look out for themselves. That's why Keegan had three of us writing a monograph with the winning title *A Treatise on the Prevention and Detection of Fraud for the Underwriters of Burglary Insurance.*

The ferry landed at the foot of Broadway, just above one of the sugar refineries and just below the tower for the new East River bridge that was then under construction. At the time, the huge metal towers on opposite banks of the river were all there was of the bridge. The eastern tower dominated the Williamsburg riverfront, looking something like a flattened version of Eiffel's.

I took the L down to Graham Street and found the building where the Hubers had their offices. William's father was in but on the telephone. When he finished, he led me into his office and I explained who I was and why I was there. The conversation was an awkward one, of course. If his son had done anything wrong, the family would want it buried along with him. I had to use a line about clearing his son's name because of rumors that were circulating. But you don't build a successful real estate practice by being gullible. He told me he had no idea why William would take his own life, and yet he had no reason to believe it was anything but suicide. His son was successful and well-liked, with innumerable friends. He instructed me not to attempt to interview his staff, and above all, to stay well away from his wife.

I wasn't likely to get any family secrets from him, but he did show me his son's office and left me to look around. I had no trouble finding his copies of the policies on Farrell and Barclay. Barclay's was written on the 2nd of January and Farrell's on February 28th. He wrote life, fire, and accident policies, and also a fair number of business policies. Most of the life policies were with Sovereign, but two were with other companies and I noted them. I went through his desk and then his correspondence, but saw nothing that would explain his suicide.

His calendar had notations on pretty much every page, even most Sundays. The majority were calls he made on clients, but I saw none to the Farrell or Barclay residences the previous winter. Evenings usually had a meeting or outing penciled in. Like most successful agents, Huber was a joiner. He was a member of the Broadway Merchants Association, the Broadway Board of Trade, the Grand Street Board of Trade, the Union League, the German-American Municipal League, and the Y.M.C.A. He was a Mason, an Elk, and in two rival societies of Foresters. On the walls were certificates from the Deutscher Orden der Harugari and the Seawanhaka Boat Club, and a diploma from Hamilton College. I made a list of these on the chance he met Farrell or Barclay at some meeting or other.

It was a small office, with large windows looking out over Graham Street, and a gas heater set in a corner. This is where he was found dead. I'm not a philosophical type, but I felt a connection to William Huber. He was just a year younger than I was, and we were both in college at the same time, not a hundred miles apart. So I felt motivated to explain his death. Of course, the prospect of a bonus would have been a far better motivator.

The cop who had investigated Huber's death was a sergeant at the Stagg Street station just a few blocks to the north. I never liked dealing with the police, but I particularly didn't like dealing with the police in New York. And it wasn't simply because they were all corrupt. It seemed as if the laws were purposely written just vaguely enough, and with just the right number of contradictions, to allow for the arbitrary enforcement that cops thrived on. And their badges gave them free rein to be as brutal as they liked. Add to that the fact that they *were* all corrupt and you have what one of their own number described as the largest gang in New York. The only thing that kept them in check was all the infighting over the spoils.

Things went pretty much as I expected. Sergeant Corwin was an older fellow with an unlighted cigar that never left his mouth. He treated me as if he had just learned I was the one who had defiled his daughter. I couldn't blame him for not wanting someone poking his nose in his business, but he didn't need to be so damn surly about it. The only real news I picked up was that the coroner had determined William definitely died of asphyxiation due to gas inhalation, and that his body was discovered by his brother John, who worked at a law firm in Manhattan.

From there, I went back to Broadway and took the L down to Palmetto Street, where the Hubers had a house, just past Bushwick Avenue. It was a respectable place, but nothing opulent. The old man's prohibition didn't extend to servants, so I rang the bell and when a girl answered I tried to question her some about William. No go. The only thing more annoying than a gossiping servant is a discreet one. She offered to call her mistress, but I decided it would probably be unwise to establish just how successful old Conrad could be at making my life a hell on earth. I tried some of the neighbors and found out nothing more than that William was a fine boy who treated his parents well.

By then it was almost five o'clock and I remembered I had told Emmie I'd pick up her mother at Grand Central. Of course, I thought I'd be working at William Street and meeting the 5:40 would be a piece of cake. Now I was on the far side of Brooklyn. I had to take the Lexington L downtown, transfer to cross the bridge, and then transfer again on the other side. I didn't get to the station until after six. Emmie's mother was nowhere to be found. I combed the station and had three people paging her. Then I phoned home to tell Emmie.

2

Emmie greeted the news that her mother was alone and at large on the streets of Manhattan with a strange gurgle, followed by a few choruses of "Oh, Harry, how could you?"

Then, having had her fun, she confessed that her mother was there with her. Emmie had met the train herself. It was past eight when I got home. Thankfully, Emmie's mother had kept a plate warm for me. I know one is expected to dislike one's mother-in-law, but I had always gotten on well with mine. She was completely conventional, but often in unconventional ways. For instance, she had been brought up in a traditional New England Congregationalist household and still attended church regularly—Catholic Mass, that is. And she converted not because she married a Catholic, but rather married him after her conversion because he was a Catholic. And it wasn't the theology that drew her. It was the show. She viewed a High Mass the same way a sophisticate views grand opera. Her visit, quite intentionally, coincided with Holy Week. She hoped to attend four Masses in four days, culminating in Easter at Saint Patrick's.

The next morning, Emmie and her mother were dressing for the morning show at Brooklyn's own St. James Cathedral when I left for William Street. At the office, I made inquiries into the life policies William Huber had written with the two companies other than Sovereign. No claims had been made. After that, I telephoned his brother John, who agreed to meet me for lunch. Mrs. Barclay was next on my list. I reached her at home and she said I could stop by anytime that afternoon. There didn't seem to be a telephone number for Mrs. Farrell, so I took the L up to 19th Street, hoping she hadn't left town.

She was there, alright. And just getting up, from the looks of things. The apartment was in a third-class sort of building, and I got the impression housework wasn't high on Mrs. Farrell's list of priorities. Nor was personal hygiene. She looked like someone who had indulged to excess, and then had her supply cut off. Maybe drink, maybe something else.

I told her I was investigating Huber's death, not her husband's. But she was still plenty suspicious. She said she had never met Huber, that her husband must have signed the policy elsewhere. But she did remember the doctor's visit. I asked her about her husband's habits—did he go out with friends, play the horses, etc. She pled ignorance, but pointed out Farrell was a drummer with a three-state territory and was almost always on the road. Then I ran down the list of Huber's fraternal organizations. She was sure her husband hadn't belonged to any of them.

"His only clubhouse was the nearest saloon," she said, then gave a sorry little laugh.

"Did he have one he visited regularly?"

"No, he wasn't particular," she said. "When will I get my money?"

I assured her it would be any day and then headed back downtown to meet John Huber at the old Delmonico's on Beaver Street. He was a fairly short fellow, shorter than me anyway, about 30, smartly dressed, and looked just the way an up-and-coming Wall Street lawyer should look. I got through the condolences and then explained why I was looking into the case.

"What would satisfy the people at Sovereign is an explanation of why your brother killed himself," I said. "I assume you're convinced it was suicide."

"I suppose you know I'm the one who found him. It certainly looked like suicide. He was on the floor. It looked as if he'd been just sitting at the desk, then fell out of the chair when he became unconscious. I turned the gas off, opened a window, and dragged him to it, but it was too late."

"The gas was on all the way?"

"Yes, the heater had three jets and they were all on."

"So it wasn't an accident."

"No."

"Why did you think he'd been sitting in the chair?"

"There was a bruise on his head. The doctor said it must have occurred when he fell out of the chair."

"Did he leave a note?"

"Oh, yes. Didn't Father tell you?"

"Your father didn't confide much of anything."

"There was a slip on the desk that just said, 'Tell Mother I'm sorry.'"

"Was it odd he didn't mention your father?"

"No, I don't think so. He knew how much it would hurt Mother. And he was right."

"And there's no question it was in his hand?"

"It was his scribble, alright."

"So it was suicide," I agreed. "But why?"

"That I haven't been able to explain. He was doing well with the agency. Father bragged about him. He seemed to be enjoying himself, too. Of course, William always seemed to be enjoying himself."

"If money isn't a problem, love usually heads the list."

"Yes, I thought of that," he said. "You see, I've been looking into it myself. He was always seeing several different girls, off and on. I've talked with them, and they all seemed to see the relationships as he did. Sally Koestler, she's a childhood friend of mine and William's, said she would have known. They travel in the same crowd."

"But he wasn't intimate with her?"

"Well, I wouldn't say he'd never been intimate with her. But if she had any idea why he killed himself, she'd tell me. And she was probably William's closest friend."

"Did he have any conflicts with other men?"

"You mean jealous lovers?"

"That, or maybe business conflicts."

"No, William charmed everyone. He was impossible to pick a fight with."

"So, he was successful in business, content with his love life, got on with his parents, and I assume was the picture of health. Did he have any faults?"

"Sure, he had faults. You visited the office?"

"Yes, but I didn't learn much."

"But you saw the diploma from Hamilton on the wall?"

"Is it a forgery?"

"No, not a forgery. William graduated, alright. But then some evidence of cheating came up. They called him in and he confessed. So they rescinded his degree. The sad thing is, he could have easily avoided it."

"You mean by not cheating?"

"Well, that, of course. But I mean when they called him back. Were you in college?"

"Yes. And yes, I know pretty much everyone cheated on something at one time or another."

"Exactly. All he had to do was say, 'Look, you caught me. But I can give you the names of half the members of the graduating class who also cheated.'"

"Inform on his fellows?"

"But he wouldn't have had to. They couldn't afford a scandal like that. They never would have called his bluff."

"You must make a good lawyer," I smiled. "Do you still live at your father's, too?"

"No, I have a place on this side of the river."

"Then how is it you were the one to find your brother at the office?"

"The day before was my birthday. I went home to celebrate it with the family. Sally was there. But William didn't show up."

"And that was out of character?"

"Yes, at least not to have telephoned. We ate, had the cake. But Mother was becoming increasingly nervous. So Sally telephoned some friends. Then she and I went out looking for him. We went to all his usual haunts, stopped by friends', anything we could think of. Finally, around one in the morning, I took Sally home in a cab, then went back to my parents'. Mother and Father were both up. I didn't want to just sit there waiting, so I offered to go check the office. Father had called there repeatedly, but agreed I should check it. He gave me his keys and I walked up to Graham Street."

"You didn't take the L?"

"They run so infrequently at that time and I didn't want to wait. I suppose the walking eased the anxiety some," he said. "I smelled the gas as soon as I reached the second floor. The rest you know."

"What time was it when you found him?"

"About four that morning."

"Have the police found out anything?"

"No. Father basically told them to end the matter and they did."

"And no one had noticed a change in your brother? One day he's happy-go-lucky, next day he kills himself?"

"I only saw him once or twice a week. Sally said he had seemed a little down recently, but he told her it was some minor business setback. Mother worried over him constantly, and Father probably isn't sensitive enough to have noticed. And William wasn't one to burden people with his worries."

As we were leaving, I asked him about Farrell and Barclay, but he hadn't heard of them. Nor could he explain how his brother might have met them. Then, as we were walking along William Street, he stopped and invited me to join him that evening.

"I'm going to meet Sally later. There's a place we haven't visited yet, the Hotel Le Roy. Apparently, William spent some time there. I don't think anything will come of it, but you could meet Sally."

"My mother-in-law's in town, but I might be able to get away later."

He suggested I meet them first at one of the German dance halls in Williamsburg. I asked him if he could bring a photograph of his brother, then went off to the Bureau.

There was a message from George Tibbitts, a Manhattan police detective who had looked into the deaths of Farrell and Barclay. I telephoned him, but he was out. Then I headed uptown to meet Mrs. Barclay.

The Barclays lived on East 58th Street. The doorman directed me to a fourth-floor apartment. The name on the door was Edward Howell, but the woman who answered the door identified herself as Mrs. Barclay and led me into a little study.

Before I met Mrs. Farrell, one theory that had crossed my mind was that William had had some romantic interest in the two men's wives, set up the policies, and then killed their husbands. I didn't get very far with it, and on meeting Mrs. Farrell I laid it permanently to rest. But Mrs. Barclay was another matter entirely. She was in her late twenties, blonde, and looked like one of Mr. Gibson's models. I'm not saying I'd kill over her. I probably wouldn't get anywhere with her even if I did. But if a fellow had a predilection to murder strangers— and received a little encouragement—she would be the one he'd kill for.

I fed her the whole condolence business and she thanked me. Then I told her about Huber and how I was trying to find some connection between him and her husband. I went through my list. She said she thought her husband was an Elk, but wasn't altogether sure. She did remember meeting Huber, and the doctor coming by, but she couldn't remember when either had occurred. She had no idea where her husband had been the evening of his accident, as she had been out of town. But she did provide a short list of his friends. When she had to go into another room to find the name of her husband's firm, I realized that while Mrs. Barclay may have had the looks of a Gibson creation, she was unlikely to be caught spouting one of the clever lines the girls are noted for.

I remarked on the name on the door and she said Howell was her sister's husband, and that they'd been sharing the apartment for the last several months. Then I tried to delicately inquire about her husband's vices. He drank some, she said, and sometimes too much. Then I brought up gambling and for the first time she got a little nervous.

"Lots of men gamble, Mrs. Barclay. It's nothing to be ashamed of." My phony comforting seemed to work.

"Oh, well, yes. Rob did gamble some. He played cards, poker."

"Did he go to poolrooms? Or visit the race tracks?"

"He went to the race tracks," she said emphatically. Which I took to mean he spent a lot of time in poolrooms. Then she started crying and suggested I had better leave. Her tears seemed genuine, but whether she was crying over her husband's death or just my questioning her about it wasn't clear.

I went back to the office and tried Detective Sergeant Tibbitts again. He said he'd stop by the Bureau around ten the next morning. I gave Keegan a brief update and then left for the King's County Court House over in Brooklyn. There I was able to see a copy of the coroner's report on William Huber.

There wasn't much to it. Death was due to asphyxiation by gas. He'd been dead about four hours when the doctor arrived at the office, which was about 4:30 that morning. There was a bruise on the forehead that had occurred sometime before death. As John Huber had mentioned, the conclusion was that he had lost consciousness while sitting in the chair, fell forward, hitting his head on the edge of the desk, then slid out of the chair. From the courthouse I took a car home.

It was early, but I thought if I was going to try to get away later in the evening, I had better put some time in as attentive husband and son-in-law. When I arrived at the apartment, Emmie was out and her mother was explaining to Dorothy how much dust could accumulate under a carpet. I was immediately put to work moving furniture and rolling up rugs—a just punishment for my good intentions. When Emmie came home we reassembled the living room and got dressed for dinner. We had tickets for the Montauk, where E. H. Sothern was playing Hamlet. I still hadn't quite decided if I was going to abandon Emmie and her mother at the theatre. But I wasn't anxious to see Mr. Sothern's interpretation of the brooding Dane.

I had recognized the name of the place John had mentioned. It was a Raine's Law hotel that had attained a certain notoriety. There were hundreds of so-called hotels in Brooklyn, but only a few dozen were legitimate hotels. The Raine's Law was a liquor law passed by the state that restricted the sale of alcohol in all sorts of ways. Hotels, however, were allowed a number of exemptions. Within a few years of the law's enactment, the number of hotels shot up dramatically. But nearly all were faux "hotels"—as closets, storerooms, and even stables were said to be for the use of guests.

Then stricter definitions were written on what constituted a hotel. Most of the new hotels complied, in one way or another. So now there were thousands of modest hotel rooms without any real guests. American ingenuity being what it is, it wasn't long before uses for these rooms were found. This gust of creativity may not have increased the disreputable activities of the citizenry, but it did bring more of them into public view. Which, in turn, provided an opportunity for the scolds to crack down.

In the fall of 1900, the Committee of Fifteen—a group of very proper, mostly wealthy, prudes—came into being. Then the newspapers got into the act. It was around this time that the *Brooklyn Eagle* ran a story about how vice was flourishing in the Eastern District. It recounted all sorts of goings-on: sexes and races mixing freely, women of suspect character singing badly and dancing the can-can, etc. To the ill-trained eye, these activities might be mistaken for signs that the clientele was innocently enjoying itself. But to the scolds, they were signs of society's descent into a state of animalistic behavior.

Needless to say, the depiction presented by the *Eagle* appealed to Emmie's tastes. To her, it was the equivalent of an *Appleton's Guide to the Eastern District*. When I declined to escort her to the establishments enumerated, she gave me the full treatment. You've never really encountered a cold shoulder until you've felt Emmie's. It took weeks of outings, dinners, and shows to get me back in her good graces. So you can see why I was determined to keep her in the dark about the Huber case. Any, or all, of the three deaths *may* have been murder. And now I'd be accompanying the brother of one of the dead men to the vice dens of the Eastern District. The attraction this would have had for Emmie is incalculable.

While I was checking our coats at the Montauk, I found a bribable usher and instructed him to page me and deliver a message. As soon as we had taken our seats, the boy was calling my name. I waved him over and he told me a Mr. Keegan had telephoned and said I was needed at once. I made my apologies and left as quickly as I could.

Later I would regret not inventing a more plausible ruse. It's difficult to imagine an urgent situation involving an insurance treatise.

3

The Teutonia was a typical German dance hall, a big open room with a bar off to one side. There was a band playing a schottische and I saw John Huber out on the floor. When the song ended, he led a petite blonde over and introduced her as Sally Koestler. She was probably about 20, but had a girlish aspect that obscured her age. We went to their table and John handed me a small photograph of himself with his brother.

"I told Sally all about our meeting," he began. "She's anxious to help, too."

"Is this the type of place William spent his time in?" I asked Sally.

"Oh, sure," she said. "If you're from Williamsburg, and German, you naturally spend a lot of time in the halls."

"And he also frequented places like the Hotel Le Roy?" I asked.

Sally had become distracted by the arrival of some acquaintances on the far side of the room and it was John who answered. "No. Not frequented. But Sally and I have been everywhere else. Someone said he'd seen William at the Le Roy a couple times."

Another fellow approached the table and John introduced him as Casper, a friend of William's. He sat down and shortly afterward John and Sally went off to the dance floor. I explained why I was there and asked him about his thoughts on William's suicide.

"It's a puzzler," he said. "I've come to the conclusion

there's some dark mystery behind it," then added quickly, "but don't tell those two I said that."

"Why not?"

"Oh, they've spent a lot of time asking people about William, but I think if they ever found something, a real reason for him to have killed himself, they'd be crushed."

"John told me about William's troubles with his college."

"Did he? Well, it was kind of an open secret. I don't think many people thought less of William for it."

"And you can't think of what his dark mystery might have been? He had no real vices?"

"I didn't say that. He had the normal vices. Gambled some, you know."

"Gambling gets a lot of people in trouble," I said.

"Yes, I guess that's true. But he wasn't habitual or anything. Once in a while he might stop by a poolroom, or a group of people he was with might end the night at one of the casinos."

"Can you think of anywhere in particular?"

"Not really—there are poolrooms all over, and they come and go. But I remember being in Minden's Hotel with him."

"You mean out on Ocean Parkway, at Gravesend?"

"No, he has another place right here in Williamsburg. Where the ferries dock at the foot of Broadway. It's not fancy. I'm not even sure it's still open—it was raided last year."

John and Sally came back and she coaxed Casper into taking her back out on the floor.

"Casper mentioned William gambled some," I said. "Doesn't that seem a possible source of his trouble?"

"I suppose normally it would. But if William ever got

in trouble he'd just go to Father and he'd bail him out."

"Maybe your father told him enough was enough."

"No, I doubt he could deny William anything. And if that *had* happened, Mother would have told me."

"Have you checked any of the gambling spots?"

"I thought about it, but what would be the point? Who's going to tell me anything?"

It had gotten on to about ten o'clock when Sally, John, and I finally made our way to the Hotel Le Roy. It was just a few blocks away, at the corner of Rutledge and Broadway. The Le Roy was a large, but otherwise typical, Raines Law hotel. It had a men-only barroom in front, and in the back a women's parlor, which we reached through a separate "family" entrance. A colored man was playing a piano that straddled the wide doorway between the rooms. There were a couple dozen women and a few score of men about the place. The women were very young and very friendly. Races and sexes were mixing scandalously.

There was some impromptu dancing going on and Sally suggested she and John join in, but he demurred. She definitely stood out among those of her sex, or rather, they stood out from her. Sally was dressed for an evening of innocent, and proper, dancing. The girls of the Le Roy had a more liberal interpretation of what was proper, and what constituted dancing.

I made a foray to the bar but had trouble enough ordering beer without entering into an interrogation of the bartender. I struck up a conversation with a fellow beside me and learned that this was a pretty normal evening at the Le Roy. I also learned that it was owned by Michael Minden. Apparently the man liked to cater to a wide clientele. His place in Gravesend was a favorite of the well-heeled horse set.

I went back to the table, where John and Sally appeared to be having an awkward discussion. They became silent as I sat down, making it just a little more awkward. It wasn't clear why John had agreed to come at all, as he spent his time trying to shield Sally from the spectacle. Or, perhaps more accurately, to block her from joining it.

In the meantime, the piano player gave us the usual sentimental parlor tunes, with some strikingly unsentimental lyrics. And while he didn't have much of a voice, he certainly knew how to brighten up Stephen Foster. It was nearing midnight and it was obvious we weren't learning anything about William, so I told them I'd need to head home soon. John was of the same mind and, with some persuasion, Sally agreed.

"Is home nearby, Sally?" I asked.

"It used to be. But we've moved out now, over below Prospect Park."

"That's my neck of the woods," I said. "I'd be glad to escort you home."

"All right, thank you."

I wasn't sure if I had interfered with some plans of John's, as he looked a little pained by the idea. But I actually had a motive in mind. I hadn't had a chance to speak with Sally alone all evening and I wanted to ask her about the night William died. John said he had taken Sally to her home around one a.m. Then he stopped by his parents' house, and soon left for William's office, arriving around four. The times were vague, but there seemed to be quite a gap between dropping off Sally and finding William.

After saying good-night to John, we walked over to Lee Avenue and caught a Nostrand Avenue car. It was a long trip to Albemarle Road. We talked some about William, and she told me much the same story as John. She also mentioned the gambling, and the girls.

"I've heard he was popular with the women," I said. "But was there anyone in particular?"

"William was never particular. He went through a Hell's mint of girls. If he was ever serious about any of them, he didn't let on to me."

I had the impression that if there was any jealousy on her part, it was of the fun he had, and not of the women he favored. I asked her about the night of the suicide. She said she had arrived at the Hubers' about seven. And John was already there.

"What about his father?" I asked.

"He was there, too."

"Why hadn't William come home with him?"

"His mother asked that. Mr. Huber said William was out when he left. He kind of snapped at her, as if he was angry she asked."

The rest of it conformed to what John had told me. She couldn't remember exactly what time she had arrived home that night, but thought it closer to two than one. The trip took us about 40 minutes. A cab would have been faster, maybe 30 minutes. Sally's family had one of the showy suburban houses in a new development. I brought her to the door, and then walked over to Flat-bush and took a car home.

Emmie was reading in bed when I came in. I was smelling like the Hotel Le Roy and seemed destined for a reunion with her frigid shoulder. But as soon as the lights went out, she chuckled to herself.

"Care to share the fun?" I asked.

"I'm on to you, that's all."

"On to what?"

"Oh, I saw you talking to that usher. And then he paged you from five feet away. That wasn't very subtle, Harry."

"Well, Emmie, if you want to know the truth, some of the boys were giving a smoker for Hendrickson. He's getting married in a few weeks. I was just afraid of hurting your mother's feelings with an excuse like that."

"You really are an awful liar, Harry. You've been given a case, haven't you?"

"A case? What makes you think that?"

"Oh, I can tell. Your mind's been on something. And it wasn't Mr. Keegan's book on burglary insurance."

"Well, that doesn't mean I've been given another case. Maybe I'm seeing another woman."

"You're on a case and it's something you don't want me to know about, so it must be an interesting one. Another woman...." She just gave another chuckle.

The next morning, I made a point of leaving the apartment at my normal time. Not that anyone noticed. Emmie had already left to do some shopping, and her mother was giving poor Dorothy another lesson: how to remove the grime between floorboards with a thin knife. I walked up to Bergen Street and got on a car headed for the Atlantic Avenue ferry. This was the route I usually took to work, which was well known to Emmie. So I was only mildly surprised to see her on the same car with me. She must have waited at the stop before mine and when she saw me arrive, boarded the next car. She had a book in front of her face, but held it in a way that only drew attention to herself. She got off at the stop before the ferry landing, and I saw her watching as I got on the ferry. I hoped this would be enough to satisfy her, but when I got to Whitehall, I stopped and bought a paper and waited for the boat to empty.

Sure enough, she had been on it. She walked quickly toward the office, as if to catch up to me. But I was behind her and just as we turned up William Street I came up beside her.

"Emmie, dear. What a surprise!"

She jumped a good three feet—then made some nonsensical explanation about having been shopping in the neighborhood. I had had my fun, so I didn't press the point. I gave her a kiss and went up to the office. Detective Sergeant Tibbitts showed up about 10:15. He was a tall, sandy-haired fellow, about my age, with a typical cop mustache. But he was unusually pleasant for a cop, almost friendly. He didn't owe me any money, so I assumed he wasn't feeling himself that day.

"How is it you heard I was working on this?" I asked.

"Someone at Sovereign Mutual called someone at the front office. I was told to fill you in on the deaths of Farrell and Barclay."

That explained his agreeable attitude. The one thing New York cops respected was wealth and they always showed a particular deference to large corporations.

"There isn't much on Farrell," he said as he opened a file. "No witnesses, no reason to suspect anyone."

"It's not simply these deaths I'm interested in, but what connection they might have to the suicide of a Brooklyn insurance agent." I then described William Huber and his death. "What I want to find out now is, how did Huber meet those two?"

"Well, I can tell you what we know." He picked up the file, paged through it some, and read aloud whenever he came across something of note. "Farrell was a drummer for a shirtwaist company.... His territory was New Jersey, Pennsylvania, and New York above the city. He had a few circuits he did regularly, each one lasting a couple weeks.... Here's something: the dates the company had him marked as being on the road didn't match exactly with what his wife told our man." He looked up. "Maybe he had something on the side?"

"In Brooklyn?"

"Who knows?" Then he picked up a second file. "Barclay had a more interesting life. He was caught running a bucket shop last summer. I worked that case, so when he was found dead, they gave me that, too. There weren't any witnesses, but I did have a suspect. His brother-in-law, Edward Howell. It seems he'd been carrying on with Mrs. Barclay."

"And they all lived together at the Howells' apartment?"

"When the bucket shop went down, Barclay served four months. His wife moved in with the Howells. I guess that's when it started. I never got a straight story out of any of them. At the time of Barclay's death, Howell had left the apartment and was living at his club. He insisted the affair was long over. And he had an alibi for the time of Barclay's accident: he was playing cards with some fellows, one of them a judge. Barclay's wife was staying at the home of another sister, in Baltimore, not that she was much of a suspect."

"Of course, Howell had the money to get someone else to do it."

"Sure, but I couldn't turn up anything," he said. "No one seemed too upset the guy was dead, so after a week or two, I moved on."

"What was Barclay doing after he got out?"

"Believe it or not, he went to work at Howell's firm, a brokerage, Haight & Jensen. As near as I could tell, they're legitimate. He worked there until his accident."

"Why would they hire someone who just served time?"

"He made a specialty out of catering to rich women. This Haight & Jensen wanted to get into that line. At least, that's what I was told."

"What about outside of work?"

"You have something in mind?"

"Poolrooms, maybe."

He pulled out a notebook and paged through that some. "Here we go. I talked to a fellow he worked with, he said they'd visited a place in Greenpoint a few times."

"Why would they bother crossing the river to find a poolroom?"

"It could be their regular place moved across the river when the anti-vice campaign heated up last year."

He gave me the name of the place, and described how to get there. I thanked him for his help, and he said to call him if I needed anything else. Then I walked him out to the street. There was no sign of Emmie.

Greenpoint was part of William's territory, the northern end of the Eastern District. There'd be nothing odd in his stopping by a poolroom there. I went in and told Keegan what I had learned and asked him about the poolroom.

"They'll be busy this afternoon—the horses are running at Bennings this week," he said. Gambling was a sort of hobby of Keegan's.

"I'd also like to call in some help—there are a lot of details to check."

"Detectives?"

"Yes, I know a fellow at Newcome's."

"All right, but tell them as little as possible."

I telephoned Dan Ratigan. He was an old friend who'd recently become a supervisor at Newcome's Detective Agency, which specialized in corporate work. The hoi polloi think the Pinkerton agency is the last word in detectives, and I suppose it is—assuming the work involves spying on streetcar conductors suspected of holding back fares, or strong-arming some underfed mill hands into feeling content. I gave Ratigan all the particulars I had on Barclay and Farrell and asked if his people could learn anything else. I told him I was trying to connect them to William Huber, who had sold them life insurance policies, but didn't mention Sovereign. Around 12:30 Emmie showed up. She said she'd been shopping and thought I might like to take her to lunch. The truth was, she was disappointed to find me at my desk.

"How lovely," I said. "I know just the place." I took her to a chop house over on Pearl Street. This was the type of place where middle-aged men sat at long, communal tables. I found one where we'd be sandwiched between two loquacious fellows discussing the nuances of steel-structure suspension bridges. Emmie didn't last a minute.

"I just realized, Harry, I barely have time to get home and get ready for Mass."

"Oh, that's too bad, Emmie," I said.

"Yes, Emmie, it's quite a disappointment," the fellow next to her added.

When I finished lunch, I took the uptown L to 11th Street and walked to the river, where there was a ferry landing. It was my first trip to Greenpoint, but the riverfront there was like the riverfront everywhere: docks, factories, and undefinable odors. The poolroom in question was right on Greenpoint Avenue, a couple blocks up from the ferry landing. Like most poolrooms of its ilk, it was sort of hidden in a rear room of a saloon.

There are generally two ways to gain entry to a poolroom: be an acquaintance of the man at the door, or just look like a sure-thing sucker. He'd never seen me before, but waved me in with a smile. One wall held a large slate blackboard where the various races were listed, along with the horses and the odds being offered. Today's board was given over entirely to the races at Bennings, wherever that was. Like most "poolrooms," there were no pool tables cluttering up the place. I made a bet and then made some small talk. I lost that race, made another bet, and made some more small talk. This time I won, playing the favorite, but the odds were so short I won three dollars on a five-dollar bet. At the track, the odds are lopsided in the bookmakers' favor, but in poolrooms they're a complete sham. For every ten dollars bet, the house kept three.

I found a local fellow who'd known William Huber, but he couldn't say if he'd seen him in this place. I did hit on something with Barclay though. After I told the story of him doing time for the bucket shop, the cashier remembered him.

"Sure, he was in here," he said. "And he was a regular when we were on the other side."

Just about everyone I spoke with seemed to remember a fellow named Farrell, but not surprisingly, each of them remembered a different Farrell. I lost another five dollars of expense money and then headed back across the river. Keegan was still in, so I went in to give him a report.

"My theory is that Huber met Barclay while visiting poolrooms," I said. "They both gambled and Barclay seems to have gone over to a place in Greenpoint. Farrell may well have gambled some too, and maybe he likewise crossed the river."

"And the reason for Huber's suicide?" Keegan asked. "Gambling debts?"

"Right now, it would be my guess," I said. "His brother insists it isn't the case, though he can't come up with anything else. But how do I establish a fellow had illegal gambling debts? They don't publish lists in the newspapers."

"Yes, that's a problem," Keegan agreed. "Let me make some calls this evening. I'll see if I can set up a meeting with someone who could advise us. Make sure you're in the office at ten in the morning."

Then I headed off for home. Emmie and her mother were just getting in from Good Friday Mass. Mother seemed to have had a good time, but Emmie was in one of her blue funks. It wasn't that she was upset with me for abandoning her and her mother the previous evening. She just felt I had let her down by—apparently—*not* being on a case. And in the not-too-distant background, there was the resentment she was nursing over my vetoing a move to the Margaret. She announced that after putting her mother on the train on Monday, she was going to visit a college friend down in Washington. I made the mistake of agreeing too readily.

4

The next morning, Emmie had planned to take her mother back to St. James for the Holy Saturday show. But at breakfast she suggested that perhaps Dorothy could accompany Mother while Emmie made the arrangements for her trip.

"Well, ma'am, I'll be attending Mass later with my mother and sister."

"Perhaps you could persuade them to attend at St. James instead?" Emmie wasn't going to be dissuaded. "It *is* the Cathedral. They do a very fine Mass, don't they, Mother?"

"Oh, yes," Mother agreed. "They have a wonderful choir."

"I'll tell you what, Dorothy," Emmie said. "Mr. Reese will pay for you to take everyone out for a nice luncheon after Mass. Why don't you telephone your mother and make arrangements."

I still hadn't caught on to what this was about when Dorothy returned to say that the deal was on. I took out my wallet and handed Dorothy three dollars. She looked at it briefly, then told us her two aunts would also be coming. I gave her another dollar. She was about to put it away, but stopped herself.

"Oh," she exclaimed. "I just remembered—today is supposed to be a fast day."

Apparently, the going rate for enjoining a servant to break fast was two dollars and fifty cents. I handed it over and then moved to the door before I could be cajoled into funding indulgences for her distant cousins. Emmie was there, with her coat on.

"We can ride across together, Harry. If you don't mind going over the bridge."

Now I was on to her. My encouraging her to take the trip to Washington made her realize I *was* on a case. One has to be very careful with Emmie. Every conversation is a game of maneuver. Make one unguarded remark and you find your flank has been turned.

We took a Park Row car up Flatbush. At Pierrepont, I said good-bye and left her on the car, then walked over to the bankers' ferry. This was the boat that ran between Montague Street and Wall Street. Emmie had gotten off the car and was about half a block behind me. But there were no more than two dozen men waiting for the ferry and there was no way for her to catch my boat without showing herself. She stayed back and waited for the next boat.

On the other side, I didn't wait for her but went right up to the office. Keegan showed up about 10:30 and told me he had found a fellow willing to help me with my investigations into Huber's gambling.

"Mr. Demming is an authority on the subject," Keegan informed me. "I asked him to meet us at your apartment at eleven."

"My apartment?"

"Yes, I couldn't very well ask him here. And it needed to be someplace private. Is there any problem with that?"

"Well, my mother-in-law is visiting, but she shouldn't be back until later. The other problem you know about."

"What other problem?"

"Emmie. You remember our adventure in Glens Falls?" I was alluding to Emmie's unfortunate visit to the race course.

"I remember having a very agreeable time," he said. "You have to be able to accept some losses in life, Harry."

"If Emmie were your wife, would you be anxious for her to make Mr. Demming's acquaintance?"

"Yes, that's a fair point," he conceded. "Well, give her some money and send her out shopping."

That showed how little he knew about Emmie. If you expected to send Emmie someplace, you had better first make sure that's where she desired to go. We went down to William Street, where Keegan had a cab waiting.

"Why do you keep looking behind us, Harry?"

"To see if we're being followed," I said.

"Who in the world would be following us?"

"Emmie. I've made her suspicious."

"You haven't been married a year."

"Oh, it's not that. Never mind." I'd learned by then that trying to explain life in Emmie-land to outlanders was a lost cause. We arrived at Vanderbilt Avenue and I tried to hurry Keegan upstairs. But you don't hurry a man who weighs in at three hundred pounds. By the time Keegan was on the curb, Emmie had come up in another cab.

"Oh, hello, Harry. Hello, Mr. Keegan," she said breezily. "Harry, why don't you pay my driver while I open the apartment and put on coffee?"

When I eventually got Keegan up to the apartment, Emmie was in conversation with a man in our front room.

"Harry, this is Mr. Demming," Emmie announced—as if she were introducing an old friend.

Demming was a stout man of about fifty-five, with long grey hair, and holding a tall derby in his lap. He looked like an affable Irish saloonkeeper, but was dressed more like a financier.

"Your janitor let me in, Mr. Reese. I hope that's all right."

"Yes, of course." I took their hats and coats and then went into the kitchen, where Emmie had gone for coffee. "I'm sorry for the intrusion, Emmie. Perhaps you'd like to go out shopping?"

"And leave our guests? That would be unthinkable, Harry."

"It's simply that we have some financial matters to discuss."

"Oh, I won't listen in, Harry. Don't worry."

I went back out, where Keegan was asking Demming about the races that would be starting up at Aqueduct in the near future. When Emmie came in with the coffee, I tried to change the subject by mentioning that she was going to Washington the next week.

"A wonderful trip in spring, Mrs. Reese," Demming said. "And the horses will still be running at Bennings." Then he gave her a playful wink.

She gave an innocent "Are they?" in reply, but the first cat had left the bag. Until then, I'd no idea where Bennings was. But I now knew why Emmie had chosen Washington as her destination. When she had gone off and made a show of busying herself elsewhere in the apartment, Keegan introduced the reason for our little meeting.

"Harry, why don't you tell Mr. Demming what you've learned?"

I did—at least as far as Huber was concerned. The

suicide was bad enough, but I wasn't going to discuss the coincident deaths of Farrell and Barclay with Emmie's ear to the door. Unfortunately, Keegan prodded me until I did so.

"Ah, that is a curious situation you have there, gentlemen," Demming said. "But the connection to gambling would seem rather tenuous."

"Yes, there's not much to it," I agreed. "It's just for the want of anything else."

"I'll be frank, gentlemen. I'm a little wary of being involved in anything that may be construed as slandering the trade. I do have my standing in the community to think of."

"I'm not sure what you mean," I said.

"It's just that with that self-appointed Committee of Fifteen running about, and all this loose talk about a war on vice," Demming said, "I wouldn't want anything I say to be put in the wrong hands."

"Mr. Demming," Keegan seemed genuinely taken aback. "I think you should know me better than that."

"I do, Mr. Keegan. And I apologize if it sounded as if I was questioning your own discretion. I simply want Mr. Reese to appreciate the risks involved. But no more need be said on the matter."

"Has this crusade driven poolrooms across the river into Brooklyn?" I asked tentatively. "To Greenpoint particularly."

"Oh, yes," Demming said. "You see, there's a continual dance going on between the operators of poolrooms and policy shops, the bookmakers, etc., and the authorities. It's very easy for a man opening a poolroom to reach an accommodation with the local police captain. He pays him a few hundred as an initiation fee and then so much a week. But as the poolroom prospers, the captain increases his fee. And, of course, he has to feed the patrolmen, the roundsmen, and the sergeants as well. The operator may decide to move his operation to a precinct where he can arrive at better terms—provided his clientele is loyal enough to follow him.

"At the same time, the police captain is under a varying amount of pressure to close down known gambling spots. So a peripatetic poolroom can benefit all concerned. That's why I compare it to a dance. Imagine a large ballroom with all the couples exchanging partners, first moving in one direction, and then another. When there is a new war on vice, it's a fast two-step. When all's quiet, a slow waltz. But the dance goes on, no matter what."

"How well you put that, Mr. Demming," Keegan said.

"Thank you, Mr. Keegan. This time, however, the pace hasn't merely increased, the dance itself has become far more complicated. And this is due to two things: Roosevelt, and consolidation. Roosevelt and the reformers broke the captains' hold on their precincts. In the past, a man would buy captainship."

"Like an officer in the British army?" Emmie asked. She had entered with a tray of stale cakes. Now she knew all about the case. The second cat had vacated the bag.

"Exactly so, Mrs. Reese. A captainship in the Tenderloin might go for $25,000. And once purchased, the captain's precinct was more like his fiefdom. Then the reformers came on the scene and jumbled everything, moving captains about willy-nilly."

"But what does the consolidation have to do with it?" Keegan asked.

"Well, before consolidation, you had the City of New York on that side of the river, with the police controlled from Tammany Hall. And on this side, you had the City of Brooklyn, with the police controlled from the Willoughby Street auction rooms."

"Auction rooms?" Emmie asked.

"Yes, old Hugh McLaughlin runs it all from Colonel Kerrigan's auction rooms," Demming explained. "Tammany, representing the larger of the two cities, assumed they would take charge after consolidation. Willoughby, quite naturally, had other ideas. For the last three years, they have been battling over control of the Brooklyn precincts. You may remember that last year Chief Devery, an old Tammany man, tried to transfer a number of the captains around Brooklyn. Ostensibly, that was said to be a part of the war on vice by keeping the police captains honest. In truth, it was an attempt to gain control of the Brooklyn precincts by Devery and Tammany. In the end, they were out-maneuvered by Willoughby and the order was rescinded.

"So now we have a particularly complicated affair: poolroom operators and police, Willoughby and Tammany, the reformers and the broad-minded. All changing partners and weaving about. To get back to your question, Mr. Reese, yes, it would be perfectly understandable that a Manhattan poolroom would migrate across the river to Greenpoint."

Emmie was being a little too attentive, so I led her back out to the kitchen, then returned and sat down again.

"That was an excellent précis, Mr. Demming," Keegan said. "And it brings us to the cause of William Huber's suicide. If we assume that his troubles were due to gaming debts, how would you suggest we verify the matter?"

"Well, Mr. Keegan, that would be most delicate. Approaching the likely holders of such debts would be futile. Even with my contacts, I would get nowhere using such a direct approach. I think you will need to learn who this man's friends were at these establishments. Perhaps people who went with him there, perhaps people he met there. It could take some time."

"Yes, of course," Keegan said.

"I suppose I could help by showing Mr. Reese where the places are. Then he could visit them on his own. I imagine he'll have a reputation in no time."

"As a full-time gambler?" I asked. "Under an assumed name?"

"Oh, I would use your own name," Demming said. "It's perfect, really. Harry Reese. A wonderfully prosaic name. No one would suspect anything of a man named Harry Reese."

Emmie gave herself away by giggling behind the kitchen door.

"Besides," Demming went on, "using an alias is much more difficult than you'd think. One slip and you bring the whole show down."

"It will be easy, Harry," Emmie said as she flew into the room. "I can help. I've already helped."

"How have you helped, Emmie?" I asked with a feeling of dread.

"Well, I've let it be known that you have an unusual profession."

"What are you talking about, Emmie?"

"Simply that many people already think you.... Well, that you are involved in the underworld."

"What have you been telling people, Emmie?"

"Directly? Nothing."

"What sort of profession do these people think I have? Gambling?"

"Some. Mr. Ahearn thinks you're in the green goods business. But he came up with that himself."

Both Keegan and Demming found it all very amusing.

"Well, Emmie," I said, "I think you've helped enough."

"Wouldn't it add to the authenticity if I were to accompany you?"

"No, Emmie," I said. "I don't think it would. Correct me if I'm wrong, Mr. Demming. But aren't these establishments men-only?"

"Yes," he confirmed. "I'm afraid that's true. Though...." He obligingly stopped himself when he saw my alarmed expression.

Keegan rose and said it was probably time to go. I brought them their hats and coats and at the door Emmie let the last cat out of the bag. She addressed Demming as Mr. Larabee. She quickly corrected herself and said it was simply that he looked so like a butcher she'd been to. I accompanied the two men downstairs and Demming suggested we meet the next evening.

"Will anything be happening Easter Sunday?" I asked.

"No, that's why it will be ideal for our tour."

I agreed, but had him write out a time and meeting place. I didn't want to take any chances with Emmie hearing the arrangements. I went upstairs and we had lunch.

"Did you pick up your ticket for Washington, Emmie?"

"Oh, didn't I tell you, Harry? I received a wire from Barbara. Her baby is down with something and she thought it would be a bad time for a visit."

Of course, there had been no telegram from Barbara, who was probably unaware she even had a baby. What Emmie meant was that a case involving gambling and multiple deaths trumped the races at Bennings. I asked her to repay me for bribing Dorothy, and for her cab fare. She readily agreed and went and got the purse that held her earnings from her newspaper writing. She handed me her last seven dollars with a smile.

There wasn't much I could do on the Huber case until the next evening, so I decided to go in to the office and see what my co-authors were up to. Emmie had no idea when I was meeting Demming, so I took it as certain she'd be following me. I walked along Sterling Place and caught the Fifth Avenue L. I saw Emmie get on the train in the car behind mine. At the bridge, I went down to the street and walked to the landing for the Catherine Street ferry, at the foot of Main Street. I had to wait a bit, but I saw no sign of Emmie. Then, on the Manhattan side, I spotted her coming out of the women's cabin. She had somehow managed to change her scarf and jacket. This newly acquired aptitude for quick changes troubled me some. I walked down South Street and cut across to the Bureau.

The Trow's city directory confirmed that there were no butchers in Brooklyn named Larabee. But there'd be no sense in confronting Emmie about it, as the story would just become more twisted. I found my co-authors, Little and Cranston, in our cramped office playing cards. We had more or less finished the treatise a month or so before. But we all had gotten used to the regular paycheck and had agreed to keep it going as long as possible. It was easy enough to find some report in the insurance press about a new fraud scheme involving burglary insurance, so the updating never ended. When Keegan was out of the office, as he was that afternoon, we occupied ourselves as best we could.

At five, I went home to find that Emmie and her mother were dressing. We were going out that evening for dinner and then to see Sarah Bernhardt at the Academy of Music. She was playing the lead in Rostand's *L'Aiglon*. I suppose it counts for something to be able to say I saw Sarah Bernhardt on stage. It certainly did to Emmie's mother. But honestly, playing a virile young duke is a bit much to ask from any fifty-year-old woman. Particularly one with a high, nasal voice. And the play itself left me cold. I don't know who it was who told M. Rostand that Napoleon's petulant heir would be a suitable subject, but he was not his friend. None of this bothered Emmie's mother in the least. Nor did the fact she knew not a word of French. As she pointed out, she didn't know Latin either and that was no barrier to her enjoying a good Mass.

That night, Emmie again tried to induce me to allow her in on the Huber case. But she wasted her efforts. The next morning, as we were dressing for Easter Mass, I brought up her previous work on my behalf.

"Emmie, am I right in thinking that when the people upstairs were speaking ill of me, they were just repeating rumors you had initiated?"

"The Lowerys? I only said they suspected you had some sort of illicit employment."

"Yes. But did that suspicion arise only after you had planted that idea in Dorothy's mind?"

"Oh, it wasn't like that. I just alluded to your work, in a general sort of way. And I did tell her about Mr. Schuler, back in Buffalo, and Robert Mason, and your friend Danny Sullivan being stabbed to death and thrown into the canal."

I felt a little bad for soiling old Lowery's name without cause, but it would do him good to learn never to repeat rumors. We arrived at St. Patrick's to find that they had restricted attendance for Easter Mass. But Emmie told the usher that her mother was the sister of a Monseigneur, and we were her escorts. She flustered him enough that he let us in. Even I had to admit the show was well worth her transgression. If you're going to sit through a long, Latin Mass, go to a place that doesn't simply pull out all the stops, but throws in a whole orchestra besides.

Later, while dinner was being cleared, I made my exit with barely a word. I was sure Emmie hadn't had time to follow me, but I waited a bit outside just to make sure. Although it was raining, as it had been since the night before, I had determined to take a circuitous route to my meeting with Demming. I went up to Myrtle and caught a train that crossed the river. Somehow Emmie made the same train.

At the bridge, I made as if to get off, but then sat back down. She did the same. At Park Row, I waded into the crowd at the L station, left by another stairway, and trotted uptown a few blocks, then over to the river and down to the Roosevelt Street ferry. There was no sign of her at the landing, or on the boat. This time I made sure by walking through the women's cabin and closely eyeing anyone that might have been Emmie in disguise. A little too closely, as it happened. One of the young ladies shouted for a policeman.

5

Demming had instructed me to meet him at the Carleton House, just a couple blocks below the ferry landing in Williamsburg. I made it there by five, and Demming showed up a little later. He pointed to the trophies and boating accoutrements about the place and said the Carleton House was the home base of the Seawanhaka Boat Club. I hadn't even realized I'd mentioned Huber's membership in the club. When the bartender came around for our order, we chatted some with him and I told him I had known William Huber from college.

"He was in quite a bit," he said. "He was what they call a social member. Meaning he didn't get on the water much."

I imagined John Huber had already talked to people here, but thought maybe I'd check back when there was more of a crowd. From there, we walked up Kent Street. It was still raining steadily, but that didn't seem to bother Demming. He pointed out Minden's Hotel.

"I was at one of Minden's places, the Le Roy, just the other night. But I didn't see any gambling."

"Well, you just didn't see it," he smiled. "Minden knows how to play the game. He has at least half a dozen places, all in different precincts—a couple in Manhattan, one out in Queens, and the rest here in Brooklyn."

"I heard this place was raided last year," I said. "Are you sure it's still operating?"

"That raid was Willoughby Street flexing their muscles. They wanted to send a message."

"So, Minden kowtows to Willoughby and he's back in business?" I asked.

"Yes, Minden and the police chief. Then all was forgiven. They even gave back the faro bank and the roulette wheel they'd seized, thank goodness. But now, rather than merely walking up stairs to the game rooms, you need to use a separate entrance. When you visit, be sure to check out that roulette wheel. A true work of art."

He showed me a couple more places on Broadway and then we went up the six blocks to Grand Street. There was another ferry landing here and another set of places catering to visitors from the other side. Then we caught a Metropolitan Avenue car and went out to Maspeth, just across the borough line in Queens. There were three poolrooms in six blocks, one owned by Minden. At the time, there wasn't much else in that part of Queens and I left with the impression that poolrooms were the principal industry of Maspeth. We took a car back to Kent Street and then another to Greenpoint. On the ride, I asked him about Emmie. At first, he denied having met her before. Then, when it was obvious I wasn't convinced, he offered an equivocation.

"Harry, I can assure you I know nothing about Mrs. Reese that should cause you consternation. And, I would add, you should be thankful you have a wife who can never be accused of being dull."

"There are times I crave a little dullness," I said. "I know Emmie seems amusing in small doses, but you have no idea what it's like day after day."

"Oh, I do, Harry," he smiled. "In her youth, Mrs. Demming was more than a match for young Emmie. Though I don't mean to sound boastful."

In Greenpoint, there were four poolrooms within

three blocks of the ferry landing, including the one I'd been to on Friday. The others I would never have spotted, but Demming pointed to the telegraph lines running to them. Not many cigar stores have a legitimate need for a Western Union wire. There was also one hotel, and Demming said he thought this might be a "resort," his term for a place with a roulette wheel and faro bank.

It had been raining continuously and by then we were both pretty thoroughly drenched. We took a car back down to Broadway and Demming said he needed to meet someone across the river. We said our good-byes and he told me to call on him if I needed any more help. On the ride home from Williamsburg, I took out a blank notebook and started writing the names of fictitious women, giving each a playful description, as well as an address or telephone number. I knew that sometime that night Emmie would make a search for my notebook, trying to find out where I'd been, and I thought I'd give her something to read.

It was half past eight when I arrived home. Emmie's mother didn't seem to mind that I'd skipped out on her last evening with us. But Emmie had determined the full treatment was in order, whereby she pretends not to notice my existence. She was sure she'd be able to wear me down one way or another, but I had an ace in the hole.

The next morning, I left the apartment before she was dressed and visited the janitor at the Margaret. The apartment Emmie coveted was still open, and he gave me the address of the agent. Then I visited our Mr. Ahearn. I told him I wanted to get out of the lease by the first and didn't want any trouble about it. He hesitated. So then I suggested that the cops were on to me and I wasn't sure how the neighbors would feel about a police raid. That brought him around.

Back upstairs, I had breakfast with Emmie and Mother, then left the house at a leisurely pace. Once I was certain I had Emmie in tow, I took a car up to the agent's office on Fulton Street. He called the Bureau to check on my employment, and then my bank. When I told him my wife was a friend of Mrs. Holt, who lived in the Margaret, he said that was reference enough. We agreed to terms and signed the lease.

It took me a bit to spot Emmie outside. She was hiding in a little florist's kiosk. I bought some flowers, which I presented to her along with our new lease.

"You know I can't deny you anything, dear," I said. As I began walking toward the Fulton ferry, I turned and added, "Better start packing—we need to be out of the old place in three weeks."

She looked at me dumbly. I relished moments like this. It was so rare I was able to turn the tables. The move was bound to occupy all her time for the next few weeks and I was sure she would have to give up following me around. You might be thinking to yourself, "How did he turn the tables on Emmie? Didn't she want to move to the Margaret all along?" And you'd be right, of course. But you must concede this: *I did it on my own terms.* And it was definitely the lesser of two evils. Besides, I was well used to living beyond my means. There was, however, one thing that troubled me. When the agent called our bank, he very clearly wrote down the figure "572." If we had a balance of five hundred and seventy-two dollars, it was certainly news to me.

After arriving at the Bureau I made out an only modestly fictionalized expense report, then decided my next step should be to check on Barclay's bucket shop. I phoned Ratigan at Newcome's and asked him how I'd get a list of names of the shop's other proprietors and investors. Maybe Farrell's or Huber's name would come up. Ratigan said he could get it, but it might take a few days. I also asked for an explanation of how exactly the shops worked and he told me to come by and he could give me some articles.

Newcome's offices were in the World Building, up on Park Row. At the time, this was one of the premier addresses in the city. Like all of New York's tallest buildings, it was near the Manhattan end of the bridge, in the neighborhood of City Hall. I walked up and spent the rest of the morning reading about bucket shops. In a nutshell, a bucket shop reduced investments to mere bets. Most of the shops presented themselves as stock brokers, but never actually handled real securities. Their clients were primarily people of modest means hoping to become the next Jay Gould. In an old-time bucket shop, you could "buy" a share of steel for a margin of as little as a dollar. Say steel was selling at $90. The bucket shop would take your dollar and mark the sale at some price slightly above $90, maybe 90¼. That 25 cents was their commission. If the stock fell to 89¼, you were wiped out immediately. If it went up to 92, you could sell, but again paying a ¼ point commission, so you'd receive $1.50, a fifty percent profit on your one-dollar bet.

Ratigan told me the bucket shops had been pretty well cleared out of New York. The legitimate brokers insisted on it. But they still popped up from time to time. He remembered Barclay's venture. As Tibbitts had said, it was geared toward women who were bored with going to vaudeville matinees and had outgrown playing the numbers at policy shops. Barclay's establishment did very well for a while, but eventually it collapsed.

"That's how they all end," he said. "You see, the bucket shop's business is really just a gamble itself. It's essentially a bet that the price movements of the securities are random. Or at least that their customers are too foolish to detect patterns. All it takes is a big bull market, when even fools can bet correctly, and they're wiped out."

I asked him to look into Haight & Jensen and see if Huber was a client, then took a car across the bridge and arrived home just in time for lunch. Afterwards, we escorted Emmie's mother to Grand Central for her 2 o'clock train. Once she had boarded, Emmie and I hopped on the downtown L. As we approached the Cooper Union, I pointed out Emmie's hair was coming undone. While she was occupied with that, I gave her a peck and left the train quickly enough that she couldn't follow. I walked down to the Houston Street ferry landing, bought a bag of peanuts, and got on the boat going to Grand Street in Williamsburg.

As was my habit when the weather was pleasant, I made my way past the carriages and wagons in the center of the boat to the bow. I liked feeling the wind off the water. When we were about halfway across, I felt someone going after the peanuts in my jacket pocket. I was sure it was Emmie, triumphantly announcing her presence, so I jumped about quickly to grab her arm. Instead I found the muzzle of an equally surprised horse. We agreed to split the peanuts.

I stopped in two different poolrooms that afternoon. Demming had suggested I not bring up Huber until I became more of a regular customer. So I just put down my bets and made small talk with the other dupes. When the last race at Bennings had come over the wire, I walked down to the Carleton Hotel and put in another appearance in the barroom. There was a different fellow behind the bar and I told him the story of having gone to school with Huber.

"He was in here, you know. That very evening."

"Huber was here the night he killed himself?" I asked.

"Yeah, well, early. Came in about five o'clock."

"By himself?"

"Yeah."

"Did he seem upset?"

"Seemed so to me. Sat in a corner by himself. That wasn't like him. Left here in bad shape."

"What time was that?"

"I couldn't say for sure. Not much past six. I told a cop about it, but he didn't seem interested."

He couldn't tell me anything else about that evening, so I just exchanged some small talk with him and some others before heading home. Emmie had placed the flowers I'd given her on the table and prepared a lovely dinner. She thanked me for conceding on the move to the Margaret.

"Not at all, Emmie. I just hope you'll be able to get all the packing done in time."

"That's no problem, Harry. I'll enjoy it."

The suspicion that my strategy of the morning had more or less backfired spoiled my mood some, but I still felt certain there was little chance I couldn't keep Emmie from following me. The next morning, Tuesday, I saw no sign of her. It occurred to me she was counting on me going to the Bureau and would follow me from there. As it was, my plan was to visit Sovereign Mutual that morning. Perkins had explained to me how the claims on Farrell and Barclay had caught his notice. But I wondered if there were others, maybe the year before. Perkins took me around to the Claims Department and introduced me to the manager, a fellow named Sanford Osborne.

"We've looked through the claims," Osborne pointed out. "There was nothing else that stood out."

"Well, I'm not even sure what it is I'm looking for."

He didn't hide the fact that he saw my going through his files as an affront. Of course, he didn't have much choice in the matter. But he was right about it. If anything, my search just reinforced how unusual the cases of Farrell and Barclay were. Huber had written about three dozen policies through Sovereign and the only other claims were on accident policies. And as had been mentioned to me earlier, every other policy holder lived in Brooklyn. There was something else common to the Farrell and Barclay policies. The same company doctor, Edward Dibble, had seen them both. There was nothing remarkable about that, but I made sure I got his telephone number and address before I left for the Bureau.

There was a message from Ratigan waiting for me and I phoned him back. He began with this summation, "Farrell was a slob." Then he basically documented the fact. He was a mediocre drummer, often drunk, and he was a philanderer, but with no regular woman on the side. He did visit poolrooms on the road and in New York, but not often. The discrepancy between his employer's and Mrs. Farrell's accounts of when he was on the road the Newcome's people attributed solely to Mrs. Farrell's feeble memory. There was nothing to indicate he'd ever even been to Brooklyn, but Ratigan pointed out it was difficult to prove otherwise. The facts on Barclay were pretty much what Tibbitts had told me. He was a sort of high-class confidence man who had been trying to gain legitimacy. Ratigan had noted the connection to Sovereign Mutual, so I went ahead and told him the whole story.

Next, I phoned Dr. Dibble. He was tied up most of the day, but said I could drop by his office at six o'clock. After lunch, I went back over to the first place in Greenpoint I had visited the previous Friday. Now I was a recognized sucker, so everyone was a little chummier. About halfway through the Bennings card, I went off to another Greenpoint poolroom. Here I was stopped at the door. I told the fellow the place had been recommended by some friends. I mentioned Huber's name, but that meant nothing to him. Then I tried Demming's alias, Larabee. Open sesame.

This place was just like all the others I'd visited, a telegraph operator in the corner, yelling out results at they came in, a man at the blackboard writing them down, and sometimes writing new odds. A cashier at a little table where you made your bet and collected your winnings. The only reason to visit one place over another seemed to be the same as for a saloon: you liked the company.

Unless, of course, you were in a line like Huber's and wanted to meet as many potential customers as possible. Spending an afternoon going from poolroom to poolroom, a man adept at small talk could make a lot of acquaintances. It could be Huber wasn't hooked on gambling, but just saw it in the same way he saw going to the Elks Lodge.

I actually finished ahead that afternoon—fifty dollars all together. It made me realize that I could end the week with a positive expense ledger if I wasn't careful. I caught the 23rd Street ferry to Manhattan and walked over to Dr. Dibble's office on Lexington. His nurse had me wait a bit, but then showed me into his little office. He was an older, pudgy fellow, with a red face. If you stuck a white beard on him, he'd make a good St. Nicholas. I had already explained the reason for my visit on the telephone, so I got to the point.

"I take it your work for Sovereign is just something you do on the side?" I asked.

"Yes. Many doctors do some work of this type to supplement their practice. They give me a name and then I make arrangements to meet the man at a mutually convenient time and place. Usually in the evenings at their own homes."

"And that's what happened with Farrell and Barclay?"

"I don't remember the details of how the appointments were made, but here are the notes of my visits."

He handed me a notebook opened to a page where there was an entry for Barclay, and a few pages later one for Farrell. The dates matched what I had. The rest was in doctor's hieroglyphs. I handed it back.

"So I take it they were both healthy?"

"Yes, Barclay certainly. Farrell was a little older, and certainly not a stellar physical specimen, but he checked out all right."

"Did you see any evidence that either was a heavy drinker?"

"Nothing alarming, but from his general condition I would guess Farrell drank more than he ought to have."

"Were their wives there when you visited?"

"Their wives?" He leaned back to think this over. "Mrs. Barclay, definitely." He smiled.

"Yes, she is rather memorable."

"And I believe Mrs. Farrell was there, but perhaps in another room. I really have a hard time differentiating, I go on so many of these visits."

"Did you know William Huber at all?"

"The name doesn't sound familiar. Was he another Sovereign client?"

"No, he was the agent who wrote the policies on Farrell and Barclay."

"Oh, I never noticed. They send around a form with a name, an address, and a telephone number. I make the appointment and examine the man. Then I fill out the form, sign it, and send it back."

"Were you surprised by how they met their deaths?"

"I was told they both died through accidents."

"Yes, but both were apparently intoxicated."

"I can't say it's noteworthy that one night a man drinks to excess and has an accident. I suppose it's a coincidence that it should happen to two men I visited a short time before. But what else can it be but a coincidence?"

I couldn't think of an answer, so I thanked him and headed back across the river for home. I'd planned on a quiet evening, but I could tell Emmie was anxious to follow me someplace. She'd discovered that following me to work in the morning was fruitless, but she was ready for any nighttime excursions. She had her satchel in the entryway, no doubt loaded with a costume change.

I thought I'd play to her expectations. After dinner, I told her I needed to go out. She said that was fine, as she had some packing to do. I went up and took the Fulton

Avenue L to Rockaway Avenue, then a car out to Ca-
narsie, and finally came home via Church Avenue. It was
after ten when she followed me in. And she didn't seem
terribly amused.

6

When I arrived at the Bureau Wednesday morning, there were two messages for me, one from Ratigan and another from Tibbitts. Ratigan had some information on the bucket shop for me, so I walked up to his office to see it. The principals of the bucket shop were Barclay and a fellow named Stauton. Stauton was the front man. He had inherited a legitimate brokerage but couldn't make a go of it. Barclay came along and suggested they exploit the firm's reputation with a more lucrative venture. They aimed for a more select clientele than the traditional bucket shop, and some of their clients may have believed they were actually buying and selling securities. Stauton had managed to leave town when the shop went bust and no one knew where he was.

The client list had sixty-odd names, but it was assumed to be an incomplete list. They were mostly women, with a scattering of men. I didn't see any Hubers or Farrells on the list. Of course, many were probably aliases.

"Is it any help?" Ratigan asked.

"Not really," I said. "I suppose these would be the same type of people who'd visit the races, or maybe a poolroom."

"Sure. Just a little more socially acceptable, especially for a woman."

"What did you learn about Haight & Jensen?"

"They've been around a long time. They're about as legit as they come. And there are no Hubers among their clients."

"If they're so legit, why would they hire Barclay? I was told they wanted to attract women clients. Still, it's an odd choice in a business where reputation is everything."

"Maybe that was part of it. But Barclay's brother-in-law is a member of the firm, so that might have had more to do with it. And there aren't many firms without some taint in their past. You have to keep in mind that on Wall Street cheating is just another form of cleverness, unless you have the bad luck to get caught."

I thanked him and returned to the Bureau to find Emmie rifling my desk. I watched her for a while, along with the other fellows. But when she started pulling out drawers and emptying them, I thought it best to intervene.

"Hello, Emmie. How lovely of you to stop by."

"Oh, hello, Harry. I was just looking for that letter I gave you to mail."

"A letter to mail? I don't remember any letter."

"Don't you, dear?" Then she looked in her bag and made a show of surprise. "Oh, yes, here it is. It's a letter to Aunt Nell. I realized I forgot to include something, and thought I had given it to you to mail."

This was a pretty typical Emmie explanation. I could poke all the holes in it I wanted, but I'd get nowhere. It would just keep getting more elaborate, and more illogical, until I gave up in exhaustion.

"By the way, Harry," she said. "There's a message from Detective Sergeant Tibbitts here."

"Yes, they're on to me, Emmie. Apparently Mr. Ahearn talked. I've decided to turn myself in."

Little and Cranston were sitting there open-mouthed. They'd both met Emmie before, but never seen her at her best. I escorted her downstairs and gave her a peck good-bye.

"I won't be home for dinner, Emmie." As soon as the words had left my mouth I knew what I'd done.

She was elated. "Won't you, dear?"

"You don't have to sound so happy about it, Emmie."

"Oh, I'll just be able to get more packing done if I don't need to make dinner."

I went back upstairs and called Tibbitts. We arranged to meet for lunch and then I spent the rest of the morning putting my desk back together. The restaurant he had named was on Thames Street. I took a circuitous route as a precaution, just to make sure Emmie couldn't follow. There are a lot of dark, cavern-like streets in lower Manhattan, but Thames Street is one of the darkest. And the place Tibbitts had chosen was on the dark side of the street. And the proprietors didn't go in much for illumination. When my eyes finally adjusted, I found him waiting.

"I hear you've been looking into Barclay's bucket shop," he said.

"I guess you were the source of the list of clients?"

"Yeah, I told you it was my case. But don't count on that for much. Places like that don't like to keep too many records."

"Yes, I know. It just seemed worth a try."

"What about the poolroom in Greenpoint?"

"That's a possibility. I'm looking into that, too."

"So you're thinking maybe this Huber went to the bucket shop?"

"Maybe. And if I'm lucky, maybe Farrell, too."

"Well, there is one person who might know."

"Who's that?"

"A girl. She was mixed up in the bucket shop, as a shill. She knows how to put on an act, visited the right card parties and teas. Dropped hints about making money at the bucket shop. She got all weepy in court and the judge let her off."

"Would she agree to help?"

"Sure, if I tell her to. I have an arrangement with her."

"What sort of arrangement?"

"Last fall we uncovered this divorce ring. It was run by a lawyer named Zeimer. Say a woman is sick of her husband. She goes to this lawyer and he has a girl who will testify she's been sleeping with the woman's husband. Sometimes she probably did sleep with him. Well, it comes to trial and this Zeimer gets ten years. The girl goes all weepy and the judge lets her off. It's the same damn girl using a different name."

"And no one noticed?"

"No one but me."

"And you've kept it to yourself?"

"Sure. That kind of thing keeps a pigeon loyal."

"Yes, I can imagine it would."

"I'll talk to her and set something up."

I thanked him and when we parted I went over to Roosevelt Street and caught the ferry back to Williamsburg. From there, I hopped on a Metropolitan Avenue car, the one that went out to Maspeth. I arrived at the Queens County Pastime Club just as things were getting under way. This was another one of Minden's places. It was larger than the other poolrooms, and the odds tended to be a little less unfriendly. Which I imagined was the reason people traveled the extra distance.

Next I went over to Germania Hall in East Williamsburg, just over the line from Brooklyn. When you walked in the door, a man handed you a card. This entitled you to membership in the Tammany Club, and you were now eligible to lay your money down with the other suckers. This place was a little smaller and the clientele more local—lots of Germans from Williamsburg. I had no trouble finding people here who knew the Hubers. I didn't ask specifically if they'd seen William there, just used the line I knew him in college and made my face known.

I had another winning day. I liked this work, and decided to do what I could to keep the case open as long as possible. Not that there seemed any danger I'd come across a solution soon. I took a car back to the river and went into the Carleton. The bartender there recognized me and introduced me to a couple members of the Seawanhaka Boat Club. I sat and played cards with them and brought up Huber. I didn't learn much, but one of the fellows had seen Huber with a particularly attractive woman a few times. Later, I ate dinner at the bar.

About eight, I sauntered over to Minden's Hotel. I went up the unmarked stairway and had no trouble gaining entrance mentioning the name Larabee. There was a faro bank, a craps table, and, of course, the roulette wheel. The room was large and dark, with a bar along one side. There didn't seem to be much of a crowd, but it was early. I placed a couple bets and made some idle conversation. There was a young fellow I took to be a manager who hovered about watching the tables and talking with the customers.

Another fellow addressed him as Al and asked him about business. "Kind of quiet tonight, isn't it?"

"Well, you know how it is," Al answered. He was a nice-looking fellow, with a quick smile and an easy manner.

"Yeah, I heard someone had the bad manners to raid you here last year."

"You know how it is."

"Sure. Is Bernie around?"

"Down at the Le Roy," Al said. "There's more action down there now."

I studied the roulette wheel to see what Demming had been talking about. It didn't seem like a work of art to me. The wheel was very slightly askew on its axis, so that one side of the wheel was always a little lower than the other. It seemed reasonable to conjecture the ball would be somewhat more likely to fall into a number on this side than the other. I made a couple bets based on my theory, but it didn't pay.

I took the L down Broadway to the Le Roy. The barroom was packed, but the gaming room I found upstairs didn't seem much busier than at Minden's Hotel. I spent some time chatting, lost some more of my winnings, and about eleven decided to head on home. I walked out of the Le Roy and ran into Sally Koestler. She and a small party were entering what looked like another German dance hall and she invited me to join them. The sign beside the door read Bayerischer Frauenverein Sorgenfrei. Applying my half-remembered college German, I roughly translated this as a club to relieve the anxieties of the women of Bavaria, the native soil of many of Williamsburg's Germans.

We entered a large hall, but there seemed to be nothing going on at all. From there, Sally led us into a smaller room, where some older women were playing whist. One of them looked over our group and then opened a door. Just beyond this door, there was a second, steel door. We went through and ascended a stairway, and at the top, yet another steel door opened at the sound of an electric bell. There was a little vestibule, and from there you entered a large room with a sort of mezzanine above. There was a band and a dance floor, and a bar tucked into a corner. Little tables and potted palms were scattered about, and there was no shortage of carved wood and marble. Though I didn't see any gaming tables, it seemed obvious from the precautions that this was a resort—just nothing like the others I'd been to, more akin to the tea room at the Astor. And the similarity didn't end with the tasteful interior. The clientele was almost all female.

We sat down at a table and Sally introduced me to her friends, three young women and a fellow named Charlie Sennett she seemed particularly chummy with. He was about thirty, tall and well-dressed, with a thin mustache. Then Sally, rather abruptly, led me away from the table and upstairs to the mezzanine. This is where the gaming tables were, but she didn't seem interested.

"Listen, don't mention to John you saw me here. He wouldn't approve, and I don't want any lectures."

"All right," I agreed. "Did William ever come here?"

"Sure, but don't tell John that either."

"All right," I said. "Did you and William come here together?"

"No, he usually had some cooler on his arm. William and I were just friends."

"Did you catch the names of any of these coolers?"

"I don't remember any names, but usually tall and blonde."

By then her friends had joined us, so I excused myself and wandered about on my own. The crowd was a little thicker up here, but likewise mostly female. I made a few bets on the roulette wheel and then was startled to hear a fellow call out a greeting to "Larabee." He was referring to the gentleman I knew as Demming. He greeted the other as Bernie. They spoke a while and then Demming came up beside me.

"Let's go downstairs for a drink," he said.

We bought drinks at the bar and took them to a table.

"You didn't tell me about this place," I said.

"Well, I didn't think I'd need to. But it is quite a resort, isn't it?"

"Yes. How did Minden pull it off? Not many women would risk it."

"Oh, more than you might guess. But why do you think it was Minden's idea?"

"Just a guess. I heard you call that other fellow Bernie, and I heard a Bernie mentioned at Minden's other resort."

"That was Bernie Bannon. He's Minden's right-hand man, a bookkeeper of sorts," Demming said. "Minden manages this place, but it's owned by the Frauenverein."

"A charitable organization?" I smiled.

"Oh, yes, it is indeed. They get half the take. The key to its success is that the ladies regulate the clientele. Unescorted men are forbidden. As is smoking, and anything the ladies consider ungentlemanly."

"I suppose this Bernie Bannon would know if William Huber was in debt?"

"Perhaps, but he'd never tell. By the way, what do you think of the roulette wheel at the place by the river? That was my design."

"Making it lopsided?"

"Making it appear lopsided. It gave you the impression that numbers on one side would be more likely to hit than those opposite, correct?"

"Yes."

"But in fact, the face of the wheel is carefully crafted and the numbers on the opposite side are more likely to hit. By a factor of 6 to 5."

"So you rigged it to make it appear to the gambler he has an unfair advantage, when it's actually working against him."

"Just so. You see, that's the essential ingredient of any bunco. The mark must believe he's the one with the edge. Once you convince him he's taking advantage of someone else, he'll go along with anything. The wheel here is far too crude."

"I didn't notice anything odd."

"Well, if you look closely, you'll see the man at the wheel jerk it slightly in one direction or the other before he spins it." He then explained how the wheel had a mechanism that allowed the slots of one color to be widened and the others narrowed. So if the suckers had more bets on red numbers than on black, the man spinning the wheel could make sure a black number came up.

"It sounds rather ingenious," I said. "Why did you call it crude?"

"Well, it's an old trick. And it's very easily detected on examining the wheel." Sally and her party had sat back down at their table and Demming nodded in their direction. "Who's your young friend? I saw you upstairs with her."

"Sally Koestler. She was a friend of Huber's. I happened to meet her outside."

"If you care about her, steer her away from that Sennett character."

"Do you know him?"

"Of him. He has an unsavory reputation in the fraternity. A gambler, a bookmaker. But a cheat, as well."

If that was meant to convey opprobrium, it seemed an odd choice of word for a man who designed crooked roulette wheels. We were both ready to leave, so we made our way through the steel doors and back downstairs. The whist game was still going strong and several of the women greeted Demming by name. As Larabee, that is. I was about to ask Demming who his escort was, when he introduced me to Mrs. Larabee, who I assumed to be one and the same as Mrs. Demming.

"Oh, Mr. Reese. How nice to meet you at last," she said.

I said something equally pleasant, but had to wonder what she meant by "at last."

"The Frauenverein was her idea, Harry," Demming boasted.

"Very ingenious," I said. She was a small, older woman, and looked as if she'd be more at home knitting stockings before a hearth than running a resort.

"Perhaps you could bring your wife to dinner some night?" she asked as we were leaving.

"Oh, yes, that would be lovely," I said—but without much conviction. Among people I least wanted Emmie to meet, proprietresses of casinos were ranked prominently.

7

It was late by the time I entered the apartment, and Emmie was in bed.

"You're really being childish, Harry," she said. "I thought we'd have a modern marriage."

"You mean one where a wife loses her husband's future earnings at the track and he finds it terribly amusing?"

"You're still punishing me for one tiny mistake I made months ago."

"I'm not punishing you, Emmie. I'm protecting you."

"Protecting me? Bah." She turned away and muttered, "Now I know how Mrs. Ertel felt."

"Who's Mrs. Ertel?"

"She's the woman who murdered her husband when he was unfaithful to her."

"I haven't been unfaithful to you, Emmie."

"Oh yes you have. You've betrayed my expectations."

"Wasn't the man Mrs. Ertel killed someone other than her husband?"

"Semantics. She lived with him as his wife." Then, just as I was about to fall asleep, she added, "Mrs. Ertel was acquitted."

I had several arresting dreams that night. In the morning, I tripped over the one box Emmie had managed to pack the evening before. Somehow, it had migrated to the foot of the bed. When I went into the kitchen, Emmie was there with Dorothy. Emmie's eyes were red from crying. And Dorothy was looking at me as if it was now confirmed: I was a wife beater of the worst sort.

We sat down to breakfast, and the tears started up all over again.

"You're so cruel, Harry."

Dorothy had gone to extra effort to serve me a meal that was even more unappetizing than usual. Both my flanks had been turned. If I didn't want to be routed completely, a strategic withdrawal was in order.

"All right, Emmie," I said. "You can help on the case, if you agree to show restraint."

"Restraint in what way?"

"Well, for instance, I don't want to have to look about every ferry I get on to see if you're following me."

"All right, Harry."

Her recovery wasn't immediate, but by the time she came back from dressing she was her usual self. We took a Park Row car over to Manhattan together. On the ride I told her most of what she didn't know. I described the poolrooms and resorts, but emphasized their all-male clientele. And needless to say, the Frauenverein went unmentioned. I asked Emmie to check the marriage and death records of Farrell and Barclay, getting whatever details she could.

"Why are they important, Harry?"

"I'm not sure they are, but we won't know until you check. And remember, Emmie. No following me. I'll be home for dinner and we'll discuss things then."

"All right, Harry. But can't we meet for lunch?"

"No, I'm not sure where I'll be."

Then we split up and I went down William Street, but when I got to the Bureau, I decided not to go up. I needed to think and I couldn't do that with Little and

Cranston in the room. So I strolled down to Whitehall and then took the ferry out to South Brooklyn and back.

The problem with this case was that there were just too many coincidences. If Farrell and Barclay were killed for their insurance, then either their wives killed them or, more likely, had them killed. But that didn't explain why the insurance would have to come from the same agent who lived across the river in Brooklyn. One explanation would be that William Huber was involved in some sort of scheme to relieve wives of husbands they'd grown weary of. But why use the same insurer? If the policies had been with different insurers, the case would have been closed with Huber's suicide. Huber must have *needed* to use the same company. Why? Because he needed someone else to go along with him. The doctor.

The one flaw with all of this was that while Huber had his faults, it seemed quite a leap from cheating on a college exam to participating in a scheme that led to multiple deaths. Of course, that made the gambling-debt theory even more likely. He needed money and somehow this opportunity presented itself. Maybe he was told the men were dying anyway and this was just the only way they'd be able to get insurance—if an agent and doctor covered up. He saw it as helping some widow. Then when he read about Barclay's death, he knew. He couldn't bear the guilt, and didn't want to shame his family by exposing it.

It was pretty contorted, but at least provided explanations. The alternative, that Huber just happened to meet Farrell and Barclay and then they both just happened to die in similar accidents—around the time he commits suicide—never was too easy to swallow.

Back on land, I went up to the office and phoned

Tibbitts. I was suddenly anxious to meet the girl he had spoken of the day before. There were certain parallels between the divorce racket he told me of and my hypothetical insurance racket. He was out and I left a message. Then I called Ratigan and asked him to check out Dr. Dibble. I went to lunch and came back to find a message from Tibbitts saying he was headed out again, but would be at his desk at six o'clock. Then I went up to Roosevelt Street. As I waited for the ferry, I scanned the crowd. I saw a woman a ways back who seemed to be likewise scanning the crowd, only she had opera glasses. When she finally walked off, she did so with a distressingly familiar gait. But I didn't see her get on the boat. They were stringing the first cables between the towers of the new bridge and when we landed I had to wade through the crowd of onlookers. Then I took a car back out to East Williamsburg and the Tammany Club.

I was a member now and saw several familiar faces. The small talk came easier and I had a long chat with a fellow who knew old Mr. Huber. It entailed listening to a lot of anecdotes about the old neighborhood, but eventually I brought the conversation back to William's death. This fellow's theory was a lost love.

I rode the car back to the river and then went up to Greenpoint to the place where they had remembered Barclay. I was one of the fraternity now and even got a few tips, one of which paid off at fourteen to one. I brought up William again with a couple fellows and one told me he'd heard a rumor it was gambling debts that brought him to suicide. But I had a nagging sense the rumor he was repeating might have started with my poking around these places asking about Huber's gambling. I may have become an impediment in my search for the truth, but at least the tips paid off. I was up $80 for the day. Feeling celebratory, I stopped by the Carleton House to buy a round or two for the fellows. Then, at six, I phoned Tibbitts.

"I was wondering if you had spoken with that young lady you mentioned?"

"Yeah. Elizabeth Custis. She lives over in Williamsburg now. Just tell me where and when you want to meet her."

For the lack of anything better, I named the dining room of the Carleton at one the next afternoon. When I arrived home, Emmie told Dorothy she could go and we sat down to dinner. But Emmie was too excited to eat.

"Christopher Farrell and Anna Corbin were married in February, 1891, at the courthouse. The witnesses were Thomas Cassidy and Wilmont Smith. His death certificate read that he died by decapitation."

"I guess you don't need an autopsy when the head is lying a few feet from the body."

"No, I suppose not," she agreed. "It was signed by a Dr. James Symes. I looked him up, and he is at Roosevelt Hospital. Robert Barclay and Eliza Handford were married just two years ago at the Chapel of the Incarnation. The witnesses were Mrs. Barclay's sister and brother-in-law, Cynthia and Edward Howell."

"How did you know Cynthia Howell was her sister?" I asked.

"I looked up the Howells' records as well. Her maiden name was also Handford. And they were married in the same church just a few years earlier. Barclay's death certificate listed the cause of death as a fracture of the skull. It was signed by a Dr. Wallace Parmalee. He's a police surgeon. How does any of that help, Harry?"

"Well, I wasn't looking for anything in particular. One thing worth noting is that the Barclays were married while the bucket shop was in operation. So she must have known about it. And not too long after, he served his four months. That's probably when Mrs. Barclay moved in with her sister. And began having an affair with Howell. Then, when Barclay got out, he moved in, too. Must have seemed a little crowded."

"Maybe his moving in was Mrs. Howell's idea? To put an end to the affair."

"If that was the idea, it didn't work," I said. "It was later that Howell was exiled to his club." Then I told Emmie my theory about there being a ring that conspired to rid the world of unwanted husbands.

"I was thinking along the same lines, Harry. That's why I went to visit Mrs. Farrell."

"What do you mean you went to visit Mrs. Farrell?"

"Well, it just seemed likely these men were killed for their insurance money, so I thought I should see what their wives were like."

"You agreed to show restraint, Emmie."

"I did, Harry. I was done at the Hall of Records well before noon. What was I supposed to do for the rest of the day?"

"Come home and pack?"

"Oh, didn't I tell you, Harry? I hired a man to do the packing and moving. He said his men could do it in just a couple days."

"What did you tell Mrs. Farrell? That you're the inquisitive wife of an insurance man and wanted to know the dark secrets of her life?"

"Don't be a gink, Harry. I told her I was an agent from the Widows Aid Society."

"Is there a Widows Aid Society?"

"How on earth would I know that? Well, I told her we stop by and just make sure the widows are provided for. She said she had nothing. The neighborhood merchants were beginning to deny her further credit, and the landlord said she'd need to find a new place if she couldn't pay the rent. I asked if she hadn't received any insurance benefits. She said she probably would never get them. Why, I asked. Bad luck was all she would say. And she didn't have any kind words for the late Mr. Farrell. Then she started crying about her state, and I gave her five dollars."

"That was very generous, Emmie."

"Well, as you'll see, not so very," she said. "I found it rather perplexing. From the way she spoke of her husband, it seemed likely the idea of killing him for his insurance would have had more than a little appeal to her. But she seemed resigned to never seeing the money. What do you make of all that, Harry?"

"I'm not sure. Maybe she just realizes the company is suspicious. But if there is a ring she conspired with, maybe she expects that they'll take most of the $5,000 as a payment. They might have had a lot of mouths to feed. If you assume Farrell wasn't aware the policy was written, they'd need a willing agent to write the policy and a doctor to write up a medical report for a visit that never took place. Then there's whoever did the actual killing. And finally, the biggest piece of it would go to the ring's leader. There might not be much left for the poor widow."

"But then what would be her motive? She would have deliberately driven herself into the poorhouse. She would have needed to really despise her husband."

"Perhaps he had a habit of humming the same tune, day after day."

"Perhaps," Emmie smiled. "Next I went by the Howells'. I asked the girl for Mrs. Barclay, but she was out. So I asked to speak with her sister and she came to the door. I explained who I was, or who I was pretending to be, at any rate. And she went away and came back with ten dollars. I told her that she had misunderstood. That I came by to see if her sister needed anything. She said no, definitely not. She thanked me for my concern and then graciously, but purposefully, sent me on my way."

"But you kept the ten dollars?"

"Well, I thought I needed to, to maintain my subterfuge."

"Sounds like a nice racket, Emmie."

"Yes, I thought so, too," she agreed. "Didn't you say Barclay was insured for much more than Farrell?"

"Yes, fifteen thousand."

"So there would be substantially more money to achieve the same objective. I mean, there would still be the one agent, the one doctor, the one killer, and the one ring leader. There would have been much more left over for Mrs. Barclay."

"Yes," I said. "And there was a second policy, for two thousand dollars—probably written when they were married."

"But why wouldn't Mrs. Farrell just have had a policy made out for some higher amount also? Assuming the price of the killing was the same, if she had had a policy for fifteen thousand, she'd now have at least ten thousand dollars."

"Huber would have wanted to have the policies written for as little as possible. Five thousand was a lot for a policy on someone like Farrell. Not so much for a successful salesman maybe, but Farrell wasn't all that successful, at least from appearances. Barclay was a stock broker. A fifteen-thousand-dollar policy on a stock broker isn't extraordinary. It could also be the ring charged more for people of a higher social position."

"There is one other question," Emmie said.

"What's that?"

"I didn't meet Mrs. Barclay, but assuming she isn't terribly unlike her sister, I find it rather hard to fathom how her social circles overlapped with Mrs. Farrell's. How would this ring publicize its services in a way which would be known to both the ladies in question? Or even publicize their services at all?"

I had a theory on this point, but I was damned if I was going to voice it to Emmie. So I just agreed it was puzzling.

The next morning, I asked Emmie to look into Barclay's employment at Haight & Jensen.

"Howell works there, and presumably that's how Barclay got the job," I said. "But I think there must be something else to it. One idea someone offered me is that Haight & Jensen wanted to develop their list of women clients."

"How should I go about it, Harry?"

"Why ask me? You're the master of disguise. Use your imagination." Of course I regretted saying those words as soon as they left my lips. Emmie didn't need to be encouraged to deploy her all-too-fertile imagination, and to do so was surely courting trouble. I had only wanted to keep her engaged on the Manhattan side of the river.

I began my day by visiting Perkins at Sovereign Mutual. I told him about Huber's gambling and the possibility that that had something to do with his suicide. He was flipping the letter opener and the pace seemed to quicken as I spoke. When I told him that I hadn't been able to link Huber to the other two men, the pace slowed down again. I didn't mention my theory about a ring of conspirators. I didn't think his fingers were up to it. I simply told him I wanted to go through the procedures involved in writing and recording the policies. He left the room for a minute and I took the opportunity to hide the letter opener beneath his blotter. He returned with a young fellow named Jenks whom he assigned to walk me through the various steps.

And he did, in painful detail. I wasted most of the morning over there, but I did learn the answer to the most important question I had—how the doctor was chosen. Arrangements with the doctor could be made either by the agent or by Sovereign. In small towns, it was usually the agent who took care of it. But in New York, doctors were usually, but not always, assigned from the head office, after the application had been received. An agent could always do so, if he chose a doctor from the list Sovereign maintained. In other words, to make sure *their* doctor got the assignment, the ring merely had to make sure Huber did the assigning. In the cases of Barclay and Farrell, the files indicated he had sent the forms to Dibble. I left there for Roosevelt Street and the ferry—and saw no sign of Emmie.

8

I sat down in the Carleton's dining room at about five minutes to one. I had taken a table toward the back of the dining room, from which I could see the lobby. I wanted to see how familiar Miss Custis was with the Carleton. Tibbitts had spoken enthusiastically about her, and I had no trouble spotting her. She was a fairly tall, attractive blonde. And from the way she looked around when she entered the lobby, I'd say it was her first visit here.

I rose and she came over and we introduced ourselves. She asked me to exchange seats with her, as looking into the sunlight bothered her. I happily did so, but from the way she kept peering over my shoulder, it seemed unlikely it was the sunlight that concerned her. The conversation was bound to be difficult, so I tried to make it less so by making use of euphemism.

"I was wondering, Miss Custis, were your duties while working with Mr. Barclay's endeavor of the same nature as when you were involved in your more recent... adventure?"

"You put it so well, Mr. Reese," she smiled. "My involvement with Mr. Barclay's endeavor was of a limited nature. I only very rarely visited the parlor itself. You see, I have always had a sort of gift for broadening my social circle. I knew Edith Stauton, whose father had partnered with Mr. Barclay. It was through my friendship with the Stautons that I met Mr. Barclay. He appreciated certain talents of mine, and he made a proposal. It seemed rather an innocent thing. I was merely to speak eloquent-ly of the pleasures and profits I enjoyed during my visits to his parlor."

"Was the future Mrs. Barclay among those with whom you spoke eloquently?"

"Yes, I'm afraid that's so, Mr. Reese." She gave a lit-tle frown of self-reproach. "It really is the one action I feel regret over. You see, any money these women lost would not be sorely missed. They would have frittered it away regardless. But with Miss Handford I was doubly deceived."

"You were deceived?" I asked.

"Oh, most decidedly. You see, her resources were as limited as mine. Her father had died and hadn't made sufficient provision for her. Her sister, Mrs. Howell, was trying desperately to find her a suitable match before her misfortune became known."

"And her second deception?"

"Her profound simple-mindedness. Have you met her, Mr. Reese?"

"Only briefly, but enough to have noted Mrs. Bar-clay's limited faculties."

"You're making me feel guilty, Mr. Reese." There was another faux frown of a somewhat different nature. "But certainly her sister, who seems to have sole claim on the family's cerebral legacy, should have found some way to prevent the disaster. Instead, she and her husband seemed to encourage it!"

"Any idea why?" I asked.

"I assumed they wanted her out of the house."

"Apparently, that didn't work out. I would have thought Mrs. Barclay might have been a suitable client for your more recent endeavor."

"Oh, I suggested it, to Mrs. Howell. But she de-murred."

"Well, if her sister was having an affair with her husband, perhaps she didn't want her freed."

"Eliza was having an affair with Howell?"

"Yes. At the time of Barclay's death, he was staying at his club in penance."

"That's the first I've heard of that," she said.

"In this more recent endeavor, I understand you had a somewhat greater role."

"Yes. I performed that same function, in helping to locate likely clients. But I also aided the investigation itself."

"By making the acquaintance of the husbands?"

"Yes, usually just that." She gave me a new look, which I took to mean it would be tactless to go further in the matter.

"Was there a common link between the two affairs?"

"Oh, yes, Mr. Reese."

"Zeimer?"

"No, certainly not Zeimer." Then she jumped up from her chair and looked over me. "Emmie!"

I turned and saw Emmie marching across the room.

"Oh, Harry. How could you?" There weren't many patrons in the Carleton's dining room that afternoon, but they were of the cultured sort who always know when something meaty is about to occur. Two dozen eyes were fixed firmly on our little triad.

Miss Custis looked at me quizzically and then told my wife, "Emmie, dear, it's not what you think."

"Elizabeth, please don't insult me by pretending you're sincerely interested in Harry."

Then Emmie turned to me, "If you needed a woman,

Harry, it should have been me. I am your wife, after all."

Though the crowd clearly wanted more, I thought it best to take our little drama out of doors. I convinced the two of them to accompany me on the ferry back to Roosevelt Street. My investigation necessitated that I remain inconspicuous and I wanted to leave the neighborhood as quickly as possible. And now I thought it a good idea to have a conference with Keegan. Public displays of this sort aren't looked upon by Wall Street interests with the same enthusiasm as the Carleton's guests had shown. If there was to be any chance he'd hear about it, I wanted it to come from me.

On the boat ride, I learned that Miss Custis and Emmie had gone to college together.

"But how did you know we were meeting there, Emmie?" her friend asked.

"I didn't, but I saw Harry get off the ferry and go into the Carleton. Then a little while later, you followed."

"I thought I saw you across the street there. But I had no idea you were married to him."

"I thought you agreed, Emmie, no more following me," I said.

"You said not to follow you on the ferries. And I didn't. But once I learned your habits, it was a simple matter to await the ferry on the other side."

They spent the rest of the ride chatting about old times and old friends. I'm sure every man learns certain things about his wife he would rather not know. But I felt I was getting an unfair share. Not even a week ago, it was revealed that my wife was acquainted with the dean of Brooklyn's sporting set. And now I was discovering she was chums with a woman who made a habit of joining criminal conspiracies. When we arrived at the Bureau, I left the two women in my office with Little and Cranston while I went to talk with Keegan. I began by telling him about the evolving direction of my investigation.

"It seemed inevitable it would head in this direction," he said. "The idea that the deaths and circumstances were linked by nothing but coincidence was rather fanciful. The thing now is to make sure the conspiracy died with Huber. Beyond that, it may be best to let sleeping dogs lie."

"Well, the only way to be sure it's over is to determine who his co-conspirators were. And if there *have* been two murders, I think it's unlikely you can keep this a private matter."

"You may be right. But keep your conjectures to yourself until we're ready to brief Redfield. He didn't hire us to run his company down. Until then, discretion is essential."

"That brings me to the events of this afternoon." I then told him about Miss Custis and Emmie's intrusion.

"Reese, how did you let that happen?"

"By marrying Emmie, I suppose." I reminded him of an episode at our wedding supper, when Emmie arranged to have a fellow pick Keegan's pocket in an effort to establish his involvement in a murder.

"Perhaps I can instill in her the seriousness of the matter," he said.

"I'd be glad to have you try. She's waiting now." I went to get Emmie from my office. When I opened the door, the four of them looked at me in the way people look at you when you've surprised them having fun at your expense.

"Here's Harrison now," Miss Custis said.

When you've been saddled with a name like Harrison, you begin to judge people according to their propensity to remind you of it.

"Yes," I said. "Emmie, would you mind coming with me?"

"I won't let Emmie face this alone," Miss Custis announced. They both rose.

"All right, fine," I said. I led them into Keegan's office. "This is Miss Custis, whom we were speaking of."

"Miss Strout, you mean," Emmie interjected.

"No, dear. Custis," her friend corrected.

"Then you've married?"

"Certainly not, Emmie. It just seemed a change was in order."

"Yes, well," Keegan said. "Please sit down everyone." Then he looked over at my wife. "Emmie, you need to appreciate the situation we're in. It's very important that Harry be able to pursue this matter quietly."

"Well, I apologize for my outburst in the restaurant, Mr. Keegan," she said. "But surely, if someone is going to arrange to have Harry murdered, it should be me."

"Have me murdered?"

"Yes, isn't that what you were arranging with Elizabeth?"

Miss Custis née Strout was vainly trying to cover the fact that she was laughing. "Oh, Emmie." Then she laughed some more.

Keegan was likewise amused, but at least more successful at maintaining his composure. "But Emmie," he said, "you can't do this sort of thing again, for whatever reason."

"You know," Miss Custis said, "there was nothing about Emmie's remarks that would compromise whatever Harrison was up to. All she said was that if he needed a woman, he should have come to her, his wife. The others there certainly interpreted it as a scene of domestic intrigue, and nothing more. If I know anything about men, having a woman confront him over another woman in so public a way will make Harrison the envy of Carleton House."

She had a point, of course, but Emmie didn't need anyone helping her feel justified. We said good-bye to Keegan and then the three of us headed out of the building.

"I'm afraid I need to go now," Miss Custis told us. "Was there anything else you wanted to ask me, Harrison?"

"Yes, two things, really. When Emmie interrupted us, we were talking about the two...."

"Endeavors?"

"Yes, thank you. I had asked you if there was a link between the two, and you said there was."

"I was the link between the two."

"But no one else?"

"No. You see, I was the one who crafted the second endeavor. And your other question?"

"Would you please stop calling me Harrison?"

"Of course," she smiled. "Now I must go." But before she could leave, Emmie invited her to dinner that evening. She accepted, took the directions, and was off. Then I walked Emmie down to the ferry.

"Emmie, we need to talk."

"All right, Harry. What about?"

"Miss Custis."

"Call her Elizabeth, Harry."

"Well, do you know what Elizabeth has been involved with over the last two years?"

"My last letter from her led me to believe she was a sort of private detective. But that was some time ago. My reply was returned as undeliverable. You see, that's what I assumed you were meeting her for. To hire her to pose as your wife and then to arrange your murder through the racket."

I gave her the facts as I knew them—about the two schemes, what Tibbitts had told me, etc.

"I must admit," she said, "I'm surprised, Harry. Elizabeth was always mischievous, even somewhat grasping. But she really has taken it too far, hasn't she?"

"Yes. She's somehow kept herself out of jail so far. But she's put herself in a very vulnerable position."

"What do you mean by that?"

"Believe me, you would not want a police detective to know your secrets. The point is, we can't really trust her discretion."

"Oh, don't worry. I learned that about Elizabeth a long time ago. But don't think her all bad, Harry. She was a very good friend at times."

"By the way, what did you learn at Haight & Jensen?"

"I learned that they are only interested in people with at least ten thousand dollars to invest. I was shocked, Harry. After that the man just led me out. But he was very nice about it."

"Well, that was something, Emmie. It means they're legitimate."

"And they do have a have a room set aside for ladies, so there is something to that part of the story."

When she got on a ferry to Brooklyn, I walked back to the office. There was, of course, one other question I would have liked to ask Miss Custis: had the divorce ring evolved into something more deadly? Even if it had, she would have certainly denied it. But I might have learned something from the way she denied it. Emmie's presence made it a little too awkward. When I went into our office, Little and Cranston both started snickering.

"Sorry, Harry," Cranston said. "Oh, a fellow from Newcome's just telephoned."

He handed me a slip and I phoned Ratigan.

"Outside of his name, there's nothing suspicious about Dr. Dibble," he said. "He's considered a good doctor, and has a tolerably successful practice. No one has seen him drunk, or gambling. And he doesn't sleep with the nurses."

"So no money problems?"

"He's not rolling in it, but no one's pounding on the door either."

"What about his wife?"

"Died a few years ago. No children."

I thanked him and hung up. Then I went downstairs to take a walk. I could imagine a scenario where the doctor wouldn't need to be in on the racket. All they needed to do was have someone else at Farrell's and Barclay's who could pose as them. The reason I had suspected Dibble was that I assumed there had been a reason Huber had written both policies with Sovereign. But if it wasn't to use a particular doctor, maybe it was to ensure that whoever processed the claim would be a friend.

I went up to Sovereign Mutual and made my way to the Claims Department. Osborne wasn't in so I spoke with his second in command. He explained the claims were assigned to different clerks based on the surname on the policy. Farrell's and Barclay's would have gone to two different men. One fellow was out of town, but I spoke with a man named Jameson, who would have been given Farrell's claim. He had flagged it as per instructions from Perkins to flag anything written by Huber. If the ring wanted to ensure that a particular man processed the claim, say Jameson, for example, they'd need to restrict their client list to those with names beginning with D, E, or F. I presumed it was safe to eliminate that possibility. Still, I was sure there was some reason they had used Sovereign.

When I arrived home, I found Dorothy cleaning frantically while Emmie prepared dinner. I was promptly sent out for supplies. Emmie had never put so much care into preparations for a guest. At twenty minutes past the appointed hour, Miss Custis made her entrance.

During dinner, I learned that Elizabeth had maintained a stable of ponies in college. In the argot of students, this meant not that she was an equestrienne who preferred diminutive mounts, but that she supplied her fellows with translations of the classic Greek and Latin texts. Year after year, the colleges taught Homer, Virgil, etc. by having their students translate the same works. A member of the class who could readily provide his, or her, fellows with the prepared translations was both popular and prosperous.

"Of course, you never resorted to ponies, did you, Emmie?" I asked.

"Oh, I couldn't afford Elizabeth's prices."

"I wasn't as mercenary as that, was I, dear?"

"You most certainly were. Once, I desperately needed a translation of a passage from Livy. She made me copy several chapters of some silly book as payment."

"What silly book was that, Emmie?" Elizabeth asked.

"Oh, I believe it was *A House-Boat on the Styx*."

"The farce? Wasn't it written in English, and just a few years ago?" I asked.

"Yes, that's just it," Emmie said. "There was nothing difficult in copying it out, it was merely laborious."

"But what use was it?" I asked.

"When the new freshmen arrived," Emmie explained, "Elizabeth would quickly ascertain which were the wealthiest. These she befriended quite aggressively, and shamelessly. She would explain to them the rigors of the classics course and then suggest she could procure the ponies. For a price, of course. If the girl were particularly guileless, Elizabeth would include all sorts of extraneous material."

"The ideal candidate was a girl from the West," Elizabeth confirmed. "Say, the daughter of a rich miner. She was desperate to make a hit at school, and had nearly unlimited funds. I could sell her anything."

"You have a truly commercial spirit, Elizabeth," I said.

"It was born of necessity. I had no wealthy father to pay my way," she said. "And besides, you know what Emerson said about virtue."

"Well, it slips my mind just now," I admitted.

"The only reward of virtue is virtue," she recited. "And, well, that's hardly enough, is it?"

While I wouldn't want to be on the other end of any financial arrangements with dear Elizabeth, there was no disputing she was a most entertaining dinner guest. When the table had been cleared, Emmie sent Dorothy home and we sat down to coffee. Then Emmie brought out her clippings. These were short pieces she had written to be placed in various British newspapers. They were loosely based on real events, but Emmie had allowed her imagination free rein. The results were very amusing—and probably hewed to the facts as well as the average newspaper story.

"That's me, Emmie!" Elizabeth was pointing to one of Emmie's stories.

"I thought that might be the case," Emmie said.

I had forgotten that one of Emmie's columns concerned the Zeimer divorce mill. Emmie had written her story from the viewpoint of a young woman involved in the ring. It was based on the testimony recounted in the newspaper, and Emmie had had no idea the woman was her friend.

This led to Emmie asking all sorts of questions about Elizabeth's previous endeavors. We learned many interesting details about her life after college. I don't think I've ever heard a more unflattering self-portrait. Emmie's description of her friend as "somewhat grasping" was indeed accurate—provided you left out the qualifier. When the subject of ladies-only poolrooms came up again, it caught my attention.

"I can understand your using gambling parlors to meet prospective clients for the bucket shop, but why would it be a likely source for women wanting a divorce?" I asked.

"Could we please avoid the term bucket shop?" Elizabeth asked.

"Endeavor number one, then."

"Thank you," she smiled. "As you say, with endeavor number one the connection is simple, so naturally I visited several of them regularly. By the conclusion of that episode, I was familiar with their workings and well-acquainted with the proprietors—some of whom shared confidences with me. From this, I learned that there were women who had amassed sizeable debts and then had their financing cut off by miserly men—husbands, fathers, trustees, and so on."

"So," Emmie said, "if the miser were a husband, and she could obtain a divorce on favorable terms, she could pay the proprietor and gamble happily ever after."

"Yes, but the crux of it was that it must be on favorable terms," Elizabeth explained.

"And that's where the second part of your duties came in?" I asked.

"Yes, much as Emmie depicted in her story."

The evening went quite late. When I began to doze, Elizabeth tactfully said she needed to leave and I went out and hired a cab for her.

9

Once we were alone, it didn't take long for Emmie and me to discover we had been thinking very similar thoughts.

"For a woman deep in debt," she said, "an insurance policy would work as well as a divorce, wouldn't it?"

"A little more dangerous, but the payback would be surer."

"Of course, it doesn't mean Elizabeth is involved in murder. It just means someone else could have been doing the same sort of thing."

"It would explain the link between Farrell and Barclay," I said, "that their wives both gambled."

"You know, Harry, I almost came down to New York to live with Elizabeth after we left school."

"Honestly?"

"Yes, but Mother wouldn't let me."

"I take it she knew Elizabeth."

"Yes, it was partly that, and partly just the idea of me coming to New York. But if I had come to stay with her, you and I might never have met."

"That's true. I only rarely visit Blackwell's Island."

"Why Blackwell's Island? Elizabeth hasn't gone to jail."

"Are you sure you'd have managed the court system with the same adroitness?"

"No, I'm afraid you're right."

The next morning at breakfast, Emmie asked about my plans.

"I thought I'd call on the widows Farrell and Barclay. If we're right, they'd be the only people we can be sure have a direct knowledge of the scheme."

Emmie was determined to accompany me, so the two of us took a car to Park Row and then the L up to the Howells'. We agreed that I would go to the apartment, as Emmie's previous visit would give her away. The girl at the door said no one was in, but if I liked I could leave a card. I could get nothing else out of her, so we went down and chatted with the doorman. He told us Mrs. Barclay was indeed out, as was Mrs. Howell, and that they wouldn't be back soon. Then he made a point of acting distracted by a speck of dust on his uniform. I handed him a dollar.

"How do you know they won't be coming back soon?"

"Well, they left with luggage," he said, and then found another speck of dust that needed attention. I handed him two more dollars.

"They left for Europe, on a German boat, from Brooklyn. First thing this morning."

We thanked him and headed over to Mrs. Farrell's.

"I suppose there's nothing odd about a recent widow being taken to Europe by her sister," Emmie said.

"No, but it might be interesting to find out when they arranged the trip."

"How would we find that out?"

"I'll leave that to Ratigan."

We went up to Mrs. Farrell's apartment and this time Emmie went to the door. There was no answer.

"You don't suppose she's gone away, too, Harry?"

"She may have just passed out. That five dollars you gave her might have fueled her for days."

Emmie suggested we locate the janitor. We found him in the basement and before I could say a word, Emmie explained our situation.

"I'm Grace Corbin, Anna Farrell's sister, and this is my fiancé, Clyde Pratt. I'm terribly worried about her. There's no answer at her door, but she said she'd be in all day."

"You should be worried, miss. Your sister's in a bad way. Someone needs to look after that woman. She hasn't paid her rent. The landlord's ready to put her things on the street."

"Well, we've just come down from Boston. I don't suppose you could let us into the apartment?"

"I'm not sure I should, miss."

Then Emmie instructed me to give the man a few dollars toward Mrs. Farrell's back rent. Convinced now of our virtuous character, he led us up to the apartment and unlocked the door. The place was even more of a mess than on my last visit. But there was no sign of Anna Farrell.

"If you don't mind," Emmie said, "perhaps we could wait here for her? That way I could clean up some."

"All right," he said. "It sure needs it, don't it, miss?" Then he went off.

"Clyde Pratt?"

"I'm sorry, Harry. It was all I could think of. I knew a Clyde Pratt back home."

"Well, let's see what secrets Mrs. Farrell is hiding."

Emmie took the bedroom and I started in the parlor. There were several notices from creditors lying about, along with an assortment of slips from policy shops. In a drawer I found a letter from Sovereign Mutual informing her there'd be a delay in the payment of her claim. But there was no trace of the original policy itself. However, I did come across some correspondence from the morgue. They were asking her to claim her husband's body. From the sound of the final letter, I concluded she had allowed him to be sent to Hart's Island. In the kitchen, there were two empty liquor bottles, and half a dozen from a patent medicine of the highly flammable kind. There was no food in the house at all.

In the bedroom, Emmie was emptying the bureaus, and I told her what I had found.

"I think she's left, Harry."

"Why?"

"Oh, just from the things that aren't here. Like the kimono she was wearing when I came by."

"Anything that might indicate where she might have gone?"

"No, but I haven't come across any papers at all."

"Well, keep an eye out for a copy of the policy."

In the bottom of a wardrobe Emmie found a cigar box with some letters from a Sarah Edelmann. She read them aloud while I continued the search. From the contents, it was apparent she was Anna's sister. In one, Sarah informed her that their father was dying and asked Anna to return home. It was clear there had been some estrangement. Another provided a new address for Sarah, in a suburb of Providence. I took this one and pocketed it. There were also some old cabinet photographs and a hymnal she'd been given as a prize as a child. But we found nothing else. Emmie said she was meeting a friend for lunch and needed to be off.

"What will you be doing this afternoon?" I asked.

"Furniture shopping for the new place. What will you be doing?"

"I need to check in with Keegan."

I stopped at a lunch room and then went down to the Bureau. Keegan was in, so I told him about the absence of the widows.

"I'd say it's a good sign," he said.

"How so?"

"Well, it means the ring knows they're in danger. They must have warned the women off. I doubt they'll be active now."

"Yes, that's true," I agreed. "But it will make it doubly hard to uncover it."

"If it dies quietly, maybe we should just let it die."

The thought of giving up my career as a gambler kind of unsettled me. "I'm sure there must be someone at Sovereign involved. Why else would Huber send both policies there? They wouldn't want to leave him in place, would they?"

"No, of course not. Do you have someone in mind?"

"Well, I was thinking the doctor, but that drew a blank. I tried the Claims Department, but the Farrell and Barclay claims would have been processed by different men."

Then it dawned on me—any suspicious claim would be sent to one man: Osborne, the manager. I left Keegan and telephoned Ratigan. I gave him three assignments. First, to find out if Osborne had anything to hide. Particularly a gambling habit. Second, to find when Mrs. Barclay and her sister booked passage. And third, to see if he could locate Anna Farrell in New York.

"You won't need to check the Astor for her," I said. "She might be hitting the pipe."

"Are you sure it was that? Morphine's the drug of choice now. You can get it at any drugstore."

"I wouldn't really know the difference. It just seemed something more than drink." Then I described her and her symptoms.

He said he wouldn't have a report on Osborne until at least Tuesday, but I could phone at the end of the day and he might have the information on Mrs. Barclay, and perhaps something on Anna Farrell.

Now I had other work to do. This was the last day of the races at Bennings and I had a good tip on the Spring Handicap. I went up to the Roosevelt Street ferry and once in Williamsburg took the Metropolitan Avenue car out to the Tammany Club. The place was packed. I managed to bring up William Huber several times and now mentioned the rumor about him being in deep to the poolrooms. But it seemed the more a fellow was acquainted with Huber, the less credence he gave the rumor.

Nevertheless, the afternoon wasn't entirely unproductive. My tip paid off—Moor won the Handicap at six to one. I left the cashier with three hundred dollars. Then I went home and phoned Ratigan. Mrs. Howell had booked passage for two on Friday morning at the Thomas Cook office. They sailed on the *Hohenzollern,* which left at eleven that morning for Gibraltar.

"I didn't know you could book steamships at the last moment that way," I said.

"You certainly couldn't count on it, but it's not so odd."

"How long will they be away?"

"They had no fixed itinerary, and no return passage."

"How about Anna Farrell?"

"Nothing. Which means she isn't in any hospital, police custody, or the morgue—under her name or as unidentified. The neighbors think she's left, but no one actually spoke with her or saw her leave. Tonight we'll check the flop houses, and the pipe joints—but they're mostly for tourists now. I can have someone telephone you in the morning."

Emmie came in soon afterwards and I told her about my afternoon.

"I almost wish I spent the day with you," she said.

"No luck with the furniture?"

"Oh, you didn't believe that, did you, Harry?"

"I suppose if I did, it was my own fault."

"It was Elizabeth I had to meet for lunch. She gave me a tour of the ladies-only poolrooms in Manhattan."

"Did you learn anything?"

"A little. The women seem to just bet blindly, or on the least rumor. Some of them went through rather large sums. And some regular visitors were extended credit."

"Where were they?"

"The ones we visited today were all in the Tenderloin. We went to three different ones. I have the details in my notebook. Most of the women were better-off, though there were all types. I could see Mrs. Farrell, and Mrs. Barclay, visiting any of them. I wasn't prepared to ask directly if either of them had been there. And Elizabeth agreed it would be unwise. She said she knew of a couple others, further uptown. But I'm not sure there's much more to learn. And I lost on every race, Harry."

"That's OK, Emmie. The family did well today."

"What do you mean?"

"I made three hundred dollars on Moor in the Handicap."

"What made you bet on him?"

"One of my new friends gave me a tip."

"You bet on a tip? That's what I did in Glens Falls, Harry."

"Well, this fellow told me the race was fixed."

"All tips seem to include that assurance. It makes them more credible."

"Emmie, you seem to be souring on the turf."

"I don't like the lack of control. You win by pure chance."

"I find this a great relief." If you imagine any comfort I took from Emmie's revelation was destined be brief, you imagine correctly.

"Harry, where do you think Anna Farrell has gone?"

"I think she's left town. Somehow the ring must have decided things were getting too hot. So someone went to see her and Mrs. Barclay and advised them to leave town. Mrs. Barclay took the comfortable way, but it may be Mrs. Farrell's travel budget consisted of your five dollars."

"So she couldn't go too far."

"No. And when she got there, she'd need to be sure she was welcome."

"Her sister's?"

"That's what I'm guessing. She'll be scared now. And if some detective came poking around, he might just spook her. And then we wouldn't find out anything."

"So we're going to Rhode Island?"

"Yes, if you want to come along."

The next morning—that was Sunday the 14th—an operative from Newcome's telephoned. There was still no sign of Anna Farrell. I asked him to keep looking. Then we went to Grand Central for the ten o'clock train to Providence. After lunch, Emmie found a couple of women to play bridge-whist with us. We started at five cents a point. Then, after Emmie had deliberately let them win the first hand, they agreed to raise the stakes to ten cents a point. We won handily. It was only when we were well into the game I realized Emmie was cheating. Apparently, the only thing Emmie objected to with games of chance was the leaving them to chance.

We arrived in Providence just after three and then took the interurban to Seekonk. All we had was Sarah Edelmann's name and a street, but it wasn't too difficult to find her home. There were two children playing out front in the mud and Emmie took it upon herself to inquire of them.

"I was wondering, is your Aunt Anna in?"

A little boy, maybe seven years old, looked up. "Aunt Anna's dead."

The boy's pronouncement caught Emmie off guard. She stared at him open-mouthed.

"Is your mother at home?" I asked.

"Yeah, she's inside." And he pointed to the house.

I led Emmie up to the porch and knocked. A slight, middle-aged woman came out the door.

"Mrs. Edelmann?"

"Yes, but we don't need anything."

"We aren't selling, we're looking for your sister, Anna Farrell."

"I've no idea where she is, mister. I haven't seen her in six, seven years."

"Your little boy told us she's dead."

"Dead to us. I just told him that because he saw the photographs of her. I didn't want to tell him his aunt wanted nothing to do with us."

"She left home on bad terms?"

"Oh, she did everything on bad terms. She was born bitter."

"So you haven't been in communication with her?"

"I stopped writing her years ago. She never replied, so what was the use? Why are you looking for her now?"

"We think she may be in danger," Emmie said. "And perhaps she'd come here as a safe haven."

"I don't know if I'd let her in if she did come now. This danger, did she bring it on herself?"

"Yes, probably so. Do you know of anywhere else she'd go?" I asked. "If she thought she needed to leave New York?"

"No, there was just the two of us. Our parents are dead."

We thanked her and headed back to Providence.

10

We just made the 6:10 express back to New York and went immediately to the dining car.

"What now, Harry?"

"I don't know. I think Keegan and the Sovereign people would just as soon drop the matter. And I'm sure the police would, too."

"Well, we can't let that happen."

"You can't expect them to keep it open simply because you find it diverting, Emmie."

"It would mean back to the tract on burglary insurance for you, Harry."

"There are aspects of that you'd find very educational, Emmie. Particularly the chapter on Madame B_____."

"Who is Madame B_____?"

"She's suspected of being one of the biggest jewel thieves in Europe."

"What's her real name?"

"Oh, I can't tell you that. We've been sworn to secrecy. You see, she's never been convicted. And she successfully sued a writer in London for libel when he intimated what everyone seems to believe is true."

"She does sound fascinating. You must tell me the rest of that story sometime. But we have our own case to solve."

"What do you suggest?"

"I think we've been too cautious."

"We're dealing with ruthless people, Emmie. If we're right, Farrell and Barclay were murdered, and William

Huber driven to suicide. Besides, you underappreciate caution."

"I'm not suggesting anything dangerous. But we have a hand and we need to play it."

We were now heading through the parlor car and Emmie soon found her mark. A middle-aged fellow who had a prosperous air about him. He was speaking to another fellow. As we passed, Emmie loudly lamented not having anyone to play cards with.

"If you'll excuse me, ma'am," the mark said, "I'd love a game. And perhaps Mr. ...?"

"Peterson's the name," the other fellow piped up. "Sure, I'll play."

It wasn't bridge-whist this time, but fifty-cent-ante poker. Peterson lasted three hands, and when he parted with us, the limit went to a dollar. It didn't take long before I realized that if there *was* a mark in the game, I was it. I politely bowed out and left the family honor in Emmie's hands. Her first setback arrived when her companion insisted on buying a new deck from the porter. Then he kept suggesting different variations of the game, most of which Emmie was unfamiliar with. I wandered off and found a newspaper and didn't see Emmie again until we were twenty minutes out of New York.

"What a delightful man, Harry."

"I assume that means you did well, Emmie."

"Unfortunately, not monetarily. Remember that three hundred dollars you won?"

"Yes, it's here, safely in my wallet. And I'm not going to stake you, Emmie."

"Oh, the game's over, Harry."

"Good. Then you won't need it."

"That's just it, Harry. You see, I've already lost it."

"How did you lose the three hundred dollars in my pocket?"

"Well, Mr. Mattocks agreed that I should refrain from bothering you until the game was over."

"How considerate of you both." I took out my wallet and handed her the three hundred dollars. She went back to settle her debt and returned smiling.

"Losing my big winnings seems to have elevated your mood, Emmie."

"Oh, it's not that. I am sorry, Harry. No, it's just that Mr. Mattocks taught me a great deal."

"I should hope so, since the lesson cost a hundred dollars an hour."

It was late when we arrived back at the apartment. The sound of snoring drew us to the spare room. We found Dorothy there, entwined with a young fellow.

"Let's not wake them, Harry." Emmie seemed touched that our maid had chosen our apartment as a place of assignation.

"No, no," I agreed. "That would be inhospitable."

They must have left during the night, because the next morning Dorothy made a show of her arrival by slamming the door. Emmie wanted to leave our little adventuress's indiscretion unmentioned, but I couldn't help myself.

"Dorothy, I have but one question. Are his intentions honorable?"

This was not a girl who embarrassed easily, but we witnessed the most vivid blush I'd ever seen.

"I'm so sorry, Mr. Reese." She was immediately reduced to tears. The weight of eighteen years of Catholic training in guilt fell on her slender shoulders all at once.

"Harry, don't be a gink," Emmie admonished. Then she led the girl into the kitchen.

It seemed a good time to make my exit, so I grabbed my coat and hat and headed to the Bureau. When Keegan came in I updated him.

"I'm still waiting for the report on Osborne, but I've no real reason to think anything will come of it."

"Well, if that report doesn't turn up anything, consider yourself off the case. Our job will have been completed."

I went back to the office, where Little and Cranston were putting the finishing touches on our first draft. By the end of the day, it was complete. We all agreed we had rolled that log about as long as was possible. We still needed to work in Keegan's introduction, and there would be a little more editing, but we would be done by the end of the month.

I packed up the chapter on Madame B_____ to show Emmie and was about to leave when the phone rang. It was her, suggesting we dine at the Carleton.

"What are you up to, Emmie?"

"Why must I be up to something, Harry?"

Why indeed. At the Carleton, I found Emmie and Elizabeth seated together. When I came in, they each gave me a peck on the cheek. The staff, and those clients who had witnessed our little drama of the previous Friday, were pleasurably amused.

The conversation consisted of further accounts of their years at college. These reunions are generally pretty dull for those who weren't a party—recollections of events you know nothing about, opaque anecdotes about people you've never met, etc. But stories involving Elizabeth were anything but dull.

"Does Emmie still celebrate the Feast of St. Elphege?" Elizabeth asked.

"Emmie, I'm afraid, allows most of the feast days to pass unnoticed," I said. "Had she a special fondness for St. Elphege?"

"Elizabeth's playing horse," Emmie explained. "We had an elocution class together and one day I needed to go to the doctor. I asked Elizabeth to explain my absence to our teacher. The next class, Miss Peck asked me, 'Miss McGinnis, can you tell us about St. Elphege?' 'St. Elphege?' I asked. 'Yes, Miss Strout explained you were away last class for reasons of faith, to observe the Feast of St. Elphege.' This was the first I had heard of the man, and I knew nothing about him but his rather silly name. 'Yes, of course,' I said, 'St. Elphege is the patron saint of children with awkward names, Miss Peck.'"

"And that satisfied her?" I asked.

"Well, Papists were about as common as Hindus at Smith," Elizabeth said. "But one of the few things known about them was that they had several hundred saints. I always felt Emmie made poor use of her exotic status."

When we rose from the table to leave, Emmie spoke in a voice louder than necessary.

"By the way, Harry, I've asked Elizabeth to come stay with us. That should solve our little problem."

She ignored my quizzical look, took Elizabeth's arm, and led her out to the street. As I was paying the waiter, the fellow I knew to be the manager approached.

"Mr. Reese, I'm not one to pass judgment on my fellows, but, well, you just make too much of a display of your domestic habits. I think it might be better if you, and your young ladies, patronized another dining room."

I found the two of them waiting by the car stand.

"Well, Emmie, you got us thrown out of there. What was that about?"

"Elizabeth is staying in this dreadful place. I told her she could stay with us until she can settle someplace else."

"All right. But why the announcement?"

"I decided you needed a more public alter ego, if we're to get anywhere. And now—well, you're likely to be a topic of conversation."

I was back in Emmie-land. Elizabeth was trying to cover her laughter with her handkerchief. But she couldn't help herself, and soon tears were streaming down her face. She led us down to the house on Lynch Street where she had been lodging. As it turned out, the two of them had already begun the move that afternoon. We picked up the last of Elizabeth's luggage and hired a cab for home. Then the two of them spent the evening reading the account of Madame B_____ aloud to each other. They both agreed our book showed literary promise. Later, when Elizabeth had gone to our spare room and we were alone, I interrogated Emmie.

"Emmie, why in the world would you invite Elizabeth to stay with us? You agreed she couldn't be trusted."

"That's why, Harry. This way we can keep an eye on her."

"And she can keep an eye on us."

"Besides, that house she was staying in was really too squalid."

"Yes, altogether too squalid. I wonder how long she'd been staying there?"

"Why do you ask that?"

"It doesn't seem like the kind of place someone like Elizabeth would choose for herself."

"Well, it did seem obvious she hadn't been there long. Maybe it was just all she could afford?"

"I'll bet she didn't move there until last week, when she knew she'd be meeting me."

"Why?"

"Because she was told to."

"Why was she told to?"

"I'm not sure," I said. "By the way, did you give her fresh sheets?"

I startled Emmie with that. She had an uneasy look on her face. "I'm sure Dorothy took care of that."

"Oh, yes," I said. "One can always count on Dorothy."

The next morning, Emmie told me that she had found Elizabeth a situation.

"What sort of situation?"

"A job. In the afternoons. It involves Mr. Larabee."

"The butcher?"

"No, I mean Mr. Demming."

"Oh, that Mr. Larabee," I smiled. "I probably don't want to know the details, do I?"

"No, dear."

Elizabeth had yet to emerge, so we breakfasted alone.

"I have something else I asked Elizabeth to work on, Harry. But I'd like to make sure there's anything to it before I tell you about it. It will be a surprise."

"How delightful. I only hope it's a surprise and not a shock, Emmie."

I went back to the newspaper and an item on page two caught my eye, "Suicide of Mrs. Marquisee."

A body found in the canal off Newton Creek on Sunday morning has been identified as Clara Marquisee of 36 Troutman Street. Mrs. Marquisee had

*resided for many years in the Eastern District with
her husband Jacob, a well-known builder. An autopsy determined she had taken a fatal dose of Paris green before jumping off the Montrose Avenue
Bridge.*

*Sergeant Corwin of the Stagg Street station
has investigated all possibilities and feels certain
the death was a suicide. Mrs. Marquisee reportedly
had been in low spirits lately, though none of those
questioned seemed to know the specific cause....*

"Read this, Emmie." I handed her the paper. She
read the piece, gave me a weary smile, and handed it
back. Early in our relationship, she had shown a certain
partiality for bodies in canals and the subject had become
a sort of motif of our marriage. But after living in the city
for several months, she lost her enthusiasm for the
subject. Bodies were fished out of New York's waterways
with an almost suspicious regularity.

"I haven't told you the special relevance of this account, Emmie."

"What do you mean, Harry?"

"Well, when I went through William Huber's files,
there was a copy of a policy in the name of Marquisee."

"Clara Marquisee?"

"That I can't say. It was the surname I found memorable. But it's not the only coincidence. Sergeant Corwin
was the one who investigated William's death."

"What are you going to do?"

"Go visit Sergeant Corwin. And then see if I can get
into Huber's files again."

"Will you wait for me to get ready?"

I hesitated, but having told her where I was going

there was little point in evasion. "All right, Emmie." Perhaps by keeping Emmie near, I could prevent her from hatching any more schemes I'd prefer not knowing the details about. I tore the story from the newspaper and put it in my pocket. I thought briefly about calling Newcome's for the report on Osborne, but decided not to. If it was negative, Keegan had told me I was off the case.

We took a car over to Williamsburg and when we neared Broadway, I suggested she let me visit Corwin alone. "He's not a particularly chummy fellow. And I don't think he'd look favorably on my bringing my wife with me."

"All right, Harry. But it's raining still. Why don't I do a little shopping at Batterman's. I'll meet you in the restaurant there, then we can go next door to Huber's office."

As I rode the car up to Stagg Street, it occurred to me that I had never told Emmie exactly where Huber's office was. At the precinct house I asked for Corwin.

"He's out—come back in an hour."

"Perhaps I should just wait?"

"Come back in an hour."

I decided to come back in an hour. I walked down to Montrose Avenue and then to the bridge over the canal. This was a route used by the Long Island Railroad. Their tracks took up most of the street and nearly all the bridge. It was a typical industrial canal, stagnant and filled with things you'd rather not know about. The bridge was barely high enough to let a barge pass under it and there'd be little chance a jump off it would kill a person. Which presumably explained the Paris green.

I pulled the article out. The Marquisees lived just a few blocks away, on Troutman Street. I found the house and rang the bell. No one answered. I tried knocking loudly and eventually roused a neighbor.

"There's no one home there," she yelled from her door.

"You wouldn't know when they might be returning?"

"Oh, they won't be returning." She motioned me over to her house and we stood on the stoop. "It's not something I want to shout about. You see, just last week, Clara—Mrs. Marquisee—she killed herself."

"She killed herself?"

"Yes, they found her in the canal, by the bridge there. She'd taken Paris green, they say. Poor Clara."

"Why do you think she killed herself?"

"I don't know—she had a nice home."

"And Mr. Marquisee?"

"He's been staying with his daughter. Just over on St. Nicholas."

"Do you know the address?"

"No, but her name's Renton now."

I went back to the precinct house and the man at the desk took me back to Corwin. He recognized me.

"Is this about Huber?" he mumbled through a tired cigar.

"No, Clara Marquisee."

"You have a thing about suicides?"

"Not as a rule. But there's something that ties these together."

"What?"

"I've been looking into Huber's death because there's been a couple other deaths that seem to have some connection to his." I then told him a sort of abridged version of the case.

"That doesn't mean Huber didn't kill himself. And

what does it have to do with Clara Marquisee?"

"I feel certain I saw a policy on a Marquisee in Huber's files."

"Well, let's go see."

I was pleasantly surprised at his agreeability. We walked down to Graham and Broadway and up to the Hubers' office. I couldn't very well ask for time to go fetch my wife, but I soon learned that wouldn't be necessary.

"Sergeant, arrest this woman." Huber *père* had Emmie in his grip.

"Who's she?" Corwin asked.

"My wife."

Corwin looked back over his shoulder at me. It wasn't a look that gave me comfort.

"Hello, Harry."

"Hello, Emmie." I went over and removed Huber's hand.

Corwin told him why we were there. Then he turned to me, "Go find the file and we'll leave Mr. Huber alone."

I went into William's office and found where the Marquisee file should have been. Nothing. I quickly flipped through the entire drawer. Then I walked out to the others.

"Emmie, did you find it?"

"No, I'm afraid this is as far as I got."

Neither Corwin nor Huber was looking amused. Huber insisted Corwin arrest Emmie, so he put the handcuffs on and led her outside.

As soon as the three of us got to the street, he freed Emmie.

"There's nothing I can arrest you for, but if I see either of you again I'll find something."

We thanked him and walked over to Broadway and caught the Myrtle Avenue L.

"I'm sorry, Harry."

"How did you know where Huber's office was?"

"From reading your notebook."

"And how did you think you'd get into William's office?"

"Well, I told the girl at the desk there that I had come from Sovereign Mutual to pick up some files from William's office."

"And she didn't find that convincing?"

"She said she thought the young lady who came yesterday was from Sovereign Mutual. And then Mr. Huber came out of his office. Harry, that man has a rather severe temper."

"Yes, I noted that on my previous visit. I guess he doesn't want anyone digging up dirt on his son. Apparently, he was very fond of William. I could say you should have waited for me, Emmie. But I won't."

"Thank you, Harry. Where are we going now?"

"Well, I'm going to Sovereign to look for their copy of the Marquisee policy. Maybe you should go home and see if you can stay out of jail."

"Let me go with you, Harry."

"All right, Emmie. But you'll have to wait downstairs."

At Sovereign, I left Emmie in the lobby and went up to find Jenks, the fellow who had given me the tour. I assumed that Keegan's eagerness to close the case was shared by the people at Sovereign and I wanted to do this as quietly as possible. As I hoped, Jenks didn't ask any questions but led me to a file where index cards for each policy were kept. There were separate sections for active and inactive policies. There were no Marquisees in either. Then we went to another room, where the policies themselves were filed. Again, no Marquisees. I thanked him and went down to Emmie.

"Nothing, I'm afraid," I told her.

"What does that mean, Harry?"

"Maybe my memory is faulty."

"But it is such an odd name. What now?"

"Now? I go back to my editorial duties and you go home and see to our houseguest."

"Yes, I suppose so."

11

When I arrived at the Bureau, I phoned Ratigan. He told me they'd found nothing on Osborne. He had a wife and two kids over in Brooklyn. He didn't gamble, and drank rarely. He owned a brownstone in Park Slope and had a healthy bank account.

"Have you seen anything of Anna Farrell?" I asked.

"No, and I doubt we will at this point."

I told him to wrap things up and send in an invoice and then went in and told Keegan and he said that would be the end of it. I left and found Little and Cranston heading off to lunch, so I joined them. On our way back to the office, the sun came out and it was turning into one of those perfect spring days. None of us could bear the thought of spending it inside. So Little went up and made it known we needed to visit a law library to check citations, and then we went off to Aqueduct.

It was just the second day of racing in New York, and there was a big crowd. We found a cramped spot in the stands and when we had made our pick, I was elected to go off and negotiate the betting ring. This was more difficult than you might think. The action in the ring resembled that on the floor of the New York Stock Exchange on the day of a market crash. I saw Demming near the periphery, but when our eyes met he shook his head and so I said nothing.

Eventually, I found a bookmaker whose attention I was able to win and made our bets. Then on my way out I saw Elizabeth, trying to hold her place on the far side of the seething throng. I thought of approaching her, but figured she too would rather not be seen. She wasn't the only woman at the track that day, but she was the only one brave enough to enter the betting ring.

We had a gay time, until just before the fifth race. Little reported he had seen Keegan in the betting ring. An orderly retreat was called for and we made our way out of the park. I left them on the L at Vanderbilt and walked down to the apartment. Emmie was there typing.

"A new story, Emmie?"

"Oh, no. I was making a copy of your chapter on Madame B_____."

"I saw Elizabeth this afternoon. Would you care to guess where? Demming was there as well."

"You went to the races without me, Harry?"

"It was a stag event. Little, Cranston, and I were doing legal research."

"Still, Harry."

"It barely evens the score, Emmie."

"Well, you can make it up to me this evening."

"What do you have in mind?"

"A trip to the Eastern District night spots. And if you don't agree to come along, I'll go myself."

I decided to go along. I wasn't sure if she really would go off on her own, but that's how the smart money would bet. Besides, after the letdown of losing the Huber case, I was feeling in need of a diversion myself. Elizabeth showed up just before dinner, looking like a Napoleonic camp follower on the long retreat from Moscow. After bathing, she returned to us seemingly refreshed.

"I don't think I'm cut out for this work, Emmie. My bottom is fairly black-and-blue and some yap's elbow seems to have loosened one of my teeth."

"I'm sorry, Elizabeth," Emmie said. "But do remember that every vocation has some downside."

"Perhaps. But I would prefer to find one where the downsides are of a more spiritual nature."

"I imagine you won't feel up to looking into that other matter this evening," Emmie said. "It might not make any difference now anyway."

"Oh, I intend to look into that matter, as you phrase it. For my own reasons if not yours."

Not long after, Elizabeth went off on her other matter and I took Emmie on her tour of the Eastern District's vice dens. She had a list of the places she wanted to visit, gathered from various newspaper accounts. It began on a disappointing note. We'd gone up to Grand Street, near one of the ferry landings in Williamsburg. Just as we entered Palace Hall, the bartender stopped us. He motioned me over to him.

"Got a lady friend with you?" he asked.

"Yes, my wife."

"Sorry, sir, but we're all full."

"All full?"

"Well, you know how it is." He gave me a wink.

I took Emmie back outside and recounted the conversation.

"I don't understand, Harry. It wasn't full by any means."

"No, but the ratio of women to men was a little high. Apparently, the local talent doesn't like competition."

"Do you mean all those women in there are... chippies?"

"Let's say most, and perhaps just chippie-esque."

"What does that mean?"

"Well, some may not be strictly professionals, but

they have reached a sort of accommodation with the proprietor. I'm sorry, Emmie."

"That's all right, Harry. It's all grist for the mill." She was putting an account of the event in the notebook she carried with her.

Our next stop was the Bon Ton Music Hall. This time, we made our way past the barroom and into the concert hall itself. By the liberal use of papier-mâché, they had made the place up as a sort of grotto. A near complete lack of lighting accentuated the effect. A small band was playing a two-step, badly. But the crowd was lively, and friendly. Particularly the young women. When Emmie had seen enough, I suggested we move on to the Hotel Le Roy. But along the way we were diverted by the Penny Pleasure Palace. I put up two cents and that allowed us a minute or so before the tableau vivant "Susannah in the Bath." Though a little too sleepy to put much into it, Susannah was indeed fetching. And in the dim light, her pink tights were easily overlooked.

At the Le Roy, the same colored fellow was on the piano. A while later he was joined by another fellow on the banjo, then another on the accordion. We'd arrived just in time for a cake walk and the contestants each took the floor in their turn. There were a number of noble efforts, but most were nothing more than poor rooster imitations and were quickly heckled off the floor. One fellow put a little too much into it and fell backwards, repeatedly, until finally rendering himself unconscious. Then two of the house girls gave their rendition. It quickly degenerated into a sloppy can-can, but there was no denying they had a keen sense of what would please their audience. Finally a very elaborately dressed colored fellow came on the floor. He was obviously the featured act, maybe a professional. By popular vote, he won the cake. Then we made our way out. We were next door to the Frauenverein now, but I saw no reason to mention it to Emmie. Of course, that would hardly have been necessary.

"Now it's my turn to escort you, Harry."

She half dragged me through the entrance and then into the room of the perpetual whist game. She greeted two of the women with a familiarity I found troubling, but not at all surprising, and then led me upstairs.

"I should have known you'd be a member," I said.

"You've been here before, haven't you, Harry?"

"Yes, once."

"And you didn't tell me about it."

"You never told me about it, Emmie."

"Yes, but that's understandable. I saved you anxiety."

"How thoughtful."

We went up to the mezzanine, where I began to explain the mechanics of the roulette wheel, but Emmie knew all about it. Then we went back down and I spotted Sally Koestler sitting with Charlie Sennett, the fellow Demming had objected to. We went over and I introduced Emmie, and Sally asked us to join them.

"How's business?" she asked.

"Well, as far as William Huber's concerned, going nowhere."

"Dead end?" Sennett asked.

"It seems that way. Did you know him?"

"I crossed paths with him, but I wouldn't say I knew him. Not like Sally did. Sad story."

"Yes." It seemed unlikely Sennett allowed it to cause him much distress.

It was then that things took a turn toward the fantastic. More precisely, Emmie-land. Elizabeth entered the room with an escort. An attractive, blond fellow of about thirty-five. Spotting our party, she led him over and introduced him to us as Edward Howell. While he went off for drinks, I introduced Elizabeth to Sally and Sennett. Given Emmie's involvement in this "other matter," it seemed a safe bet this was indeed Mrs. Barclay's brother-in-law. Howell returned and the conversation somehow veered towards women's fashion, a subject both Howell and Sennett seemed to know as well as the ladies. Then the little band started up and Sally voiced a need to dance. Howell hopped up and took her out on the floor.

Then Emmie whispered in my ear, "I think we should go now, Harry."

"Yes," I whispered back. "Elizabeth seems to have the 'other matter' well in hand."

We said our good-byes and walked over to Marcy Avenue and caught a car.

"What did you expect to gain by having Elizabeth seduce Edward Howell?"

"I wasn't sure, really. But I wasn't going to just give up on the case. And with his wife away, there seemed to be an opportunity."

"Well, at least you didn't take on the task yourself."

"Oh, I'd never make a convincing seductress."

"You led me astray."

"I don't think I did, Harry. But thank you for saying so."

"You're welcome, Emmie."

"On the other hand, your friend Sally seems quite the peach."

"Why do say that?"

"The shameless way she jollied all the men."

"She didn't jolly me."

"She tried, you just didn't notice."

"I need to work on my powers of observation."

The next morning, the two of us breakfasted alone again.

"I'll be across the river this morning, Harry. Perhaps we can meet for lunch?"

"What will you be doing across the river, Emmie?"

"Oh, nothing interesting, I'm afraid. I was going to look at some curtain fabric. Remember, we've just two weeks to our move."

We agreed on a rendezvous and I went off to the Bureau. I hadn't been there five minutes when a phone call came for me. It was Ratigan.

"I know you said to wrap things up, but I thought you might want to hear the latest news on Osborne. He's at the morgue."

"You're kidding."

"No, he's there all right. One of our fellows was over there taking the morning roll call and recognized the name. The description fits."

"How'd he die?"

"Found in the East River, apparently drowned. That's all we know."

I thanked him and called Tibbitts and was told he was at the morgue. Keegan wasn't in, but I assumed this reopened the case and so I left for the morgue. It was next to Bellevue, right on the river. I asked for Tibbitts and in a short while he came out.

"Things are getting interesting," he said.

"Have you learned anything?"

"The doctor's just looking at him now. Come on."

He led me to a white room where Osborne was lying beneath a bright light. The doctor and his assistant flipped him from side to side, on his stomach and then back around, the doctor scanning everywhere we could see and peering in the places we couldn't. Then the assistant rolled the body away while the doctor went to a sink to wash.

"What's the verdict?" Tibbitts asked.

"There are no obvious wounds. No cuts, no abrasions."

"Suicide?"

"I don't see how. He didn't drown. I'm guessing heart failure. There'll be an autopsy. Perhaps this afternoon."

"Well, can you make it as soon as possible? There's a lot of heat on this case."

"All right, but it won't be completed before noon. I can telephone with the results."

"No, I won't be in the office. I'll come back here."

Tibbitts and I walked out to the street.

"I think I have a witness," he said.

"Of what?"

"About five o'clock yesterday afternoon, a guy on the 10th Street ferry saw someone drop off the tail of another ferry. He told a crewman, and they signaled the other boat. But by that time, no body could be located. The ferry people thought that maybe the witness was seeing things, but they reported it just the same. Osborne was found down by Pier 60. That kind of fits in, too. That's where the current would take him. This witness is way up the West Side. Do you want to go with me?"

"No, I need to go over to Sovereign. They may be in a panic."

"That's why I want to go in the opposite direction," he smiled.

"Did you talk to someone there?"

"No. One of our fellows saw Osborne worked for Sovereign from something in his wallet. He knew I'd been working this case, so he called me. But they know about it now."

When I got to Sovereign, I went up to see Perkins.

"No one's told me a thing about it," he said. But I noticed the flipping of the letter opener had quickened.

"Isn't that odd?"

"Not really. I'm the Superintendent of Agencies. They must have told Redfield or someone else upstairs."

He seemed to have become determinedly uninterested in the case. A case he had raised the alarm on. He suggested he could take me upstairs, but said it with a notable lack of enthusiasm. I declined and left him. There wasn't any panic evident in the Claims Department. I went into Osborne's office and closed the door.

He had his own files, where he kept copies of any claim he had questioned. Some were ultimately paid, others weren't. There were two cabinets of them and it would take days to go through them, so I concentrated on the desk. He had a calendar, but the only appointments he seemed to have were meetings with others in the building. And there was nothing listed for the previous afternoon. I went through the desk a little more carefully, even pulling out drawers. Then, under the blotter, I spotted two cards, like the ones they used to track policies. I was just reaching for them when the door flew open. I dropped the blotter and rose from the desk to greet a fellow who had the look of a cop out of uniform.

"Who are you?" he asked.

"My name's Reese. I'm with the Gotham Insurance Bureau. Investigating a matter at Mr. Redfield's behest."

"Why don't I know about it?"

"I couldn't say. Who exactly are you?"

"Arkin. I'm head of security."

"Did you know Osborne was found dead this morning?"

"No—how do you know it?"

"I happened to be visiting the morgue."

He took me to a room on the first floor and left me with an underling. Then he went into an inner office and made three phone calls. He strolled out with a superior grin on his face.

"They say your services are no longer needed. And they already told your boss as much."

"He must have neglected to mention it. Thank you for clarifying the matter."

It was getting near noon, so I made my way back up to the morgue. Tibbitts came in right after me and led me back to a room where the autopsies were performed. The doctor was just finishing.

"I was right," he said. "He had an enlarged heart. He could have died at any time. He must have been aware of it."

"It couldn't be anything else?" I asked.

"There may have been something that aggravated the condition and caused the heart to fail at that particular time. But cause of death is certainly heart failure."

"What sort of things would aggravate it?" Tibbitts asked. "Alcohol?"

"Perhaps. But it could be anything—physical exertion, mental stress, some patent medicine. Or it may have just been his time."

We left him and I asked Tibbitts if he'd learned anything from his witness.

"Nothing new," he said, then read from his notebook: "He was in the bow of a boat headed from Greenpoint to 10th Street. A boat going from 23rd Street to Williamsburg crossed in front of them and he saw a guy on the rail near the stern of the boat, reading a newspaper. The guy dropped the paper and slumped over the rail. He thought the guy was throwing up, but then he just fell forward and into the river. He figured someone on the other boat must have seen it. But when the other boat didn't stop, he went up and told the crew of the boat he was on. It was probably ten minutes before they got to the spot and the current must have taken him down." Then he looked up. "Kind of sounds like a guy with a bad heart, whose time had come."

"But I wonder if someone made the appointment for him. No one can still believe this is all happening by chance. Have you spoken to Osborne's family?"

"A fellow from Brooklyn brought his housemaid over to identify the body."

"Not his wife?"

"She's out of town, visiting her sick mother or something. They wired her the news."

"Had the maid reported him missing?"

"No." He glanced at his notebook. "She said she was planning on doing it this morning, but then the locals showed up at the door and told her he was dead. She last saw him yesterday morning."

"Did she mention his heart?"

"Yeah, she said something about it. How'd it go with Lady Custis? Is she cooperating?"

"Oh, yes. Definitely an interesting girl."

"And dangerous," he smiled.

He went off to file his report and I went down to meet Emmie. I was twenty minutes late and she was at a table reading.

"You're late, Harry. The waiter has stopped being friendly."

"When I tell you why I'm late, Emmie, all will be forgiven."

And of course it was.

12

When I arrived back at the Bureau, Keegan was in his office. He already knew about Osborne's death, but I told him what the doctor had to say. And about my reception at Sovereign.

"There's little chance this death is a coincidence," he said.

"Yes, and here's another for you. A woman named Marquisee killed herself last week. She lived in the Eastern District and her husband is a builder. Since Huber's father is a real estate lawyer, they almost certainly knew each other. I was sure I saw a policy in that name when I looked through Huber's files. But I found no trace of it at Sovereign this morning."

"Do you have the copy from his office?"

"When I went back to get it, it was gone. The girl in the office said someone from Sovereign came and picked up some files the day before. I thought perhaps I'd just misremembered."

"But now you think Osborne was involved and he took the files?"

"No, it was a young woman who took the files. But Osborne may have sent her. The doctor said mental stress might have been the catalyst for his heart failing. Being a party to an unraveling conspiracy certainly would have caused a fellow like that a lot of stress."

"Yes, it seems the likely explanation."

"Why is Redfield trying to shut down the investigation?" I asked.

"He's starting to panic. He's deluded himself into thinking he can keep a lid on this and it will blow over."

"But he brought it to us. What changed his mind?"

"Their shares are crashing. Didn't you know?"

"No, it's not something I follow. Doesn't that mean it's already public?"

"Think of how many people know about this. Several people at Sovereign, the police, people here, Demming, people at Newcome's, and anyone else you consulted. If just a few of them acted on it, it would be enough to start rumors on the Street."

"Acted on it how?" I asked.

"By shorting Sovereign's shares, of course."

"What's shorting exactly? Selling the shares?"

"Yes, selling shares you don't own. You then have a negative position. If the price of the share goes down, your position increases in value."

"I see. So the people who've shorted the shares want them to fall further?"

"Yes, that's obvious," Keegan said. "However, the people to whom Sovereign sells insurance still know nothing about it. There's no way to keep this from eventually becoming public, but they should be able to gain some control over how that happens."

"So am I back on the case?"

"Yes, but don't contact anyone at Sovereign directly."

"Then who are we working for?"

"I'm going to confide in you, Harry. Redfield is cracking up over this. There are those on Sovereign's board who want to replace him before anything becomes public. But they aren't ready to execute their plan yet. That information doesn't leave this room. Understood?"

"All right. So once they do take control, we can expect their cooperation?"

"Most assuredly. I've been in contact with most of them."

"The police detective working on this is pretty suspicious himself. I don't see how Redfield can call him off."

"He'll try," he said. "What we need is a complete explanation of what the scheme entailed and who's behind it. Names, dates, everything. That way, when we make it public there can be no second-guessing."

"I have to admit, I'm pretty far from anything like that."

"Yes, I know. But move as quickly as you can. And try to share as little information as possible with the police—they have their own allegiances."

There was a note from Emmie on my desk. She'd stopped by while I was with Keegan to let me know she wouldn't be home until late that evening. Then I telephoned Ratigan and asked to meet with him at his office. When I arrived, he greeted me with a smile.

"So the investigation is on again?"

"Yes, but before we get to anything else, I'd like you to find out what Osborne was doing the day he died. He was on the ferry between 23rd Street and Broadway in Williamsburg. But he worked downtown. And it certainly wouldn't be his usual route home."

Ratigan assigned a couple operatives to that and then I spent most of the afternoon giving him all the details I'd accumulated on the case. We agreed his people would look again at Huber, Barclay, and Farrell, as well as the wives. And now Jacob Marquisee—the only living link still in town.

"I'll try to talk to Marquisee directly," I said. "But

see if you can link him to any of the Hubers. And also find out if Mrs. Marquisee was a gambler."

I took the ferry across to Williamsburg, but it was too early to expect Marquisee to be home from work. And as I passed the Carleton, I felt an intense thirst. I went into the saloon via a side entrance. The bartender greeted me with a smile.

"I'm not sure I should serve you, Mr. Reese."

I made as if to leave, but he motioned me back. "Just having fun."

Emmie was right, her little theatre had increased my notoriety. The gang was even more convivial than before, and I made several new friends. Eventually, I managed to make Clara Marquisee's suicide the topic of conversation.

The bartender offered the requisite banality, "Very sad."

"Marquisee took it hard, I heard," another fellow added.

"Do you know him?" I asked.

"We used to live just around the corner."

"Does he know why his wife killed herself?"

"Oh, I don't know him well enough to ask him that. Of course, the women talk," he said. But then he left it at that.

"What do they say?"

"You know women."

That brought a big round of laughter. The times in my life when I was the envy of my male comrades were few indeed and I was enjoying my status as the local Don Juan.

"Does your wife have a theory?" I asked the Marquisees' former neighbor.

"Well, I don't want to speak ill of the dead, of

course. But she says Mrs. Marquisee would visit the race track. And perhaps she didn't always win."

"But the track just opened," another fellow observed.

"I'm just telling the man what my wife said."

Before things became unfriendly, the bartender brought the conversation back to a more mutually congenial subject: me. It was decided that if I were to choose to live more conventionally, I should bring the surplus girl around and they would hold an auction. One of the fellows made up a sort of contract to that effect and we gave it to the bartender for safekeeping.

I then took a car over to Ridgewood, where Marquisee's daughter lived. I found the Rentons' home on St. Nicholas Avenue. It was a new house, but modest, perhaps a gift from her father. A girl answered my knock and told me Mr. Marquisee hadn't arrived home yet. As I turned to leave, an older fellow was heading up the steps. It turned out to be Marquisee. I introduced myself and explained I was looking into Huber's death. He didn't ask me in.

"I don't know anything about Huber's death."

"But you did know him?"

"Of course. I've dealt with his father for years. All I can tell you is he seemed like a nice boy. I sent some business his way. No complaints."

"You mean fire policies?"

"That's right. People buy a new house, and one of the first things they want to do is to make sure they don't lose it."

"What about life insurance?"

"I imagine some bought that, too. I wouldn't know."

"How about on yourself?"

"Me? What for?"

"Well, for your wife if something were to happen to you."

"I own twenty-odd houses I rent out, and a building on Broadway. That's my insurance."

"So you never saw William Huber about a life insurance policy?"

"No, who said I did?"

"No one. I just saw a name similar to yours. There wouldn't have been a policy on Mrs. Marquisee for some reason?"

"What for? And what would it have meant if there was? That she killed herself for insurance money?"

"No, no. Of course not. But there is the coincidence of your wife's death not long after Huber's. And both dying by their own hand."

"This is just nonsense. I don't have time for this." He went inside and closed the door.

I headed for home. Elizabeth was the first of my harem to return. She didn't look quite as bedraggled as on the previous day.

"I went prepared for battle," she told me. "Three petticoats and Emmie's parasol. It has a lovely sharp point. Today, I gave as well as I received. In fact, I may have blinded one fellow."

"What exactly is the task you perform?"

"It's rather opaque. I wait for a man to give me a sign, and when he does I bet the money I'd been given previously in the way he indicates. Emmie tried to explain it. It involves mathematics of some kind. But the essence is that Mr. Larabee is getting the better of some bookmaker who is too clever for his own good."

"And he shares his gains with you?"

"Well, I certainly wasn't doing it for love. But I'm

afraid I've retired from the work. I hope Emmie won't be cross."

"Why would she be cross?"

"She's taken a proprietary interest in my rehabilitation. Though I can't imagine why she assumes I want rehabilitating."

"Toiling among touts at the race track seems an unusual path to redemption."

"I've concluded that Emmie's nature is a result of her trying to conform a thirst for the exotic with a righteous zeal. It leads her to see her silliest notions as moral imperatives."

While she was bathing, Emmie came in looking in a very similar condition. One of her shoes was broken and the sleeve of her jacket was soiled.

"What happened to you?" I inquired.

"Oh, it's always such a pushing match over at the bridge."

"It looks like you lost your bout. Where were you all day?"

"I told you, Harry, shopping for curtain fabric." She then emptied a bag of small squares of fabric. "Take your pick."

I'd seen the bag at lunch, so she must have really gone shopping in the morning. Where she had been in the afternoon was anyone's guess.

"I should tell you, Emmie, I'm back on the case. But Keegan made clear that we need to keep things quiet. No public displays. And no contriving your own schemes."

"All right, Harry."

We spent a quiet evening at home. I knew Emmie was up to something, but I wasn't sure what. The next morning we all breakfasted together.

"Elizabeth is going to come with me to look at furniture today," Emmie said.

"Just don't drain the bank account," I said.

"Oh, there's little chance of that."

She didn't even mention the case, which merely confirmed she wouldn't be spending the day furniture shopping. I went directly over to Newcome's. Ratigan had a little stack of slips in front of him and read them off.

"Mrs. Osborne was at her parents' in Cincinnati. She left yesterday and will arrive here around three. Her brother's with her." Then he looked up. "Did you know her brother worked at Sovereign, too?"

"No. Maybe Osborne got him the job. What's his name?"

"Eugene Donigan."

"Why were they both at their parents'?"

"According to the maid, their mother was ill."

"Can we check that?" I asked.

"Sure. You think he sent his wife out of town?"

"Well, if the thing was blowing up, he might have wanted to shield her."

He made a note and moved on to the next page. "Mrs. Barclay and her sister seem to be planning an extended stay in Europe. Edward Howell was born pretty well set."

"Wealthy?"

"Not by John D standards. But he came from old money."

"Why's he working at Haight & Jensen then?"

"I was using the past tense. The family lost most of it over the years. It's not clear how." He went to the next page. "Still nothing on Anna Farrell. All we can say for sure is that she isn't dead or in a hospital. But people can just disappear and still be in New York." Then the next page. "Nothing new on her husband." Another. "Some interesting stuff from Barclay's past. He was a writer for a green goods operation about ten years ago, before he worked his way up in bucket shops. He seems more like the type to have been involved in a scheme like this than one of its victims."

Then a girl came into the office. She handed Ratigan a sheet of paper and left. He read it and looked up with a smile.

"Here you go. A list of Osborne's effects."

He handed it to me. It listed and described every item found on Osborne when he was brought in. The only interesting item was a page torn from a notebook in his pocket. The operative had made a copy of it, indicating some parts were illegible due to the soaking in the river. There were what looked like two addresses. The first belonged to the Marquisees. It just had the number, then "Troutman, ED." The second was a three-digit number beginning with 4, then "1st A." A notation indicated the second two digits were illegible. At the bottom of the page were the words "Rush (Green)."

"400-something First Avenue?" I asked.

"That's my bet. That would run from around 25th Street to about 30th Street. If I were going from there to the Eastern District, I'd take the 23rd Street ferry."

"What about the 'Rush Green'?" I asked.

"No idea, except maybe he felt the need to do what he had to do quickly."

"So he was on his way to the Marquisees'. To do what?"

"Can't say. But I did have a fellow look into them." He pulled another sheet out from the stack. "Marquisee does well, builds houses mostly for working men. Not much on Mrs. Marquisee. Some rumor in the neighborhood they'd been having loud quarrels. Our man walked up to the bridge she jumped off. He says that canal is a kind of cesspool. Then he wrote a question, 'Why here? Paris green would do the job.'"

"He's right about the canal. And the bridge isn't ten feet above the water. The only reason I could come up with is that she didn't want her husband to find her. Not that that really explains it. I heard a rumor she visited the track, but that was third- or fourth-hand gossip."

"I'll check on it. That might account for their bickering. Any idea what's on First Avenue?" he asked.

"No, but maybe another policyholder," I suggested. "I guess we need something else to go on before it would be worth looking there."

"Yeah, that would be a lot of people. Anything else for the present?"

"Well, remember I told you about seeing some index cards under the blotter in Osborne's office?"

"I do, but forget it. Most of our clients are corporations. Having one of our operatives caught trying to pilfer something in a major insurer would be very bad for business."

"Just thought I'd ask."

I went down to the Bureau, where there was a phone message from Tibbitts. I tried him, but he was out. I didn't want to go out without finding out what he had, so I spent the rest of the morning trying to come up with viable explanations for all that had happened so far. The insurance scheme still seemed the best one. I even managed to work in Mrs. Marquisee's suicide. Perhaps she had debts and they came to her with the scheme of writing a policy in her husband's name. Only they told her they'd be filing a false claim. It would be fraud, but nothing more. Then when she heard about Huber's suicide, she realized she had put her husband in danger and thought she'd put an end to it by killing herself. Now there would be no motivation for killing her husband. Just after noon, Tibbitts came into the office.

"I was downtown, so I thought I'd drop by. I may have something that interests you. But let's go eat."

He led me back to the Black Hole of Thames Street.

"We found this on Osborne." He handed me the torn page from a notebook that was among Osborne's effects. He had come to the same conclusions Ratigan and I had.

"You know about Mrs. Marquisee?" I asked.

"I do now. I called the Hamburg Avenue station over there and the fellow recognized the address. You already knew about her?"

"From the newspaper. I thought there might be a connection, but couldn't find anything until this showed up. What do you make of the other address?"

"I was thinking about that last night. If Osborne died because something aggravated his heart problem, I figure it has to be drink. He wasn't the type to be hitting the pipe, or anything like that. So this morning I walked that stretch of First Avenue and stopped in the saloons. I described Osborne and said he might have been meeting someone else there Tuesday afternoon. I found the place."

"That was a lot of saloons to visit," I said. "Did you get a description of whoever Osborne was meeting there?"

"A vague one. He said an older fellow. But another guy was working with him at the time and this other is the one who served them. That guy should be coming in about now. When we finish, we can go see what he has to say."

This place was just below 26th Street. We went up to the bar and spoke with the fellow who seemed to be the proprietor. Then he called over the other fellow. He confirmed he had seen Osborne, even describing the color of his suit.

"What about the other man?" Tibbitts asked.

"He was older. Wore a funny hat."

"Funny how?" Tibbitts asked.

"It was like this gentleman's," he said, pointing to my derby. "But too tall. When he took it off, his grey hair kind of shot every which way."

"How tall?"

"Oh, five foot four, or five, maybe. Kind of heavy."

"What time was this?" I asked.

"About half past three, maybe four."

"How long did they stay?"

"Not long. One round."

We thanked him and left.

"Sound like anyone you know?" Tibbitts asked.

"Maybe," I said.

"Can't be many people look like that."

I left him and went back to the Bureau. There was a message from Emmie saying she'd be late again that evening. I had, of course, recognized the description the bartender gave us. It was Demming. There was only one problem with that: I'd seen Demming out at Aqueduct that afternoon. He was nowhere near First Avenue. I left the Bureau and went back up to the saloon on First Avenue. The man who gave us the detailed description wasn't there. The other fellow told me he'd left for the day. He seemed to work a very short shift.

13

I arrived home at seven and at about half past, Elizabeth came in.

"You know, Harry, your wife is quite insane. If I'm to suffer any more of her rehabilitation, I'm very likely to end up in the hospital, or in jail."

She then went to bathe and I returned to the newspaper. It was well after eight when Emmie came in. She was dressed in the outfit she wore to clean, and looked as if she'd been doing exactly that.

"Another rough day shopping, dear?" I asked.

"Yes, but I got what I wanted," she smiled. Then she went in to bathe as Elizabeth emerged.

"I don't suppose you could divulge the nature of today's adventure?" I asked.

"I've been sworn to secrecy. Besides, I must fly."

"Important appointment?"

"Yes, with Edward Howell. Good-bye, Harry."

When Emmie came out, we finally ate the meal Dorothy had left two hours before. It was a testament to Dorothy's cooking that it tasted no worse cold than warm. Or, perhaps more correctly, it was no better warm than cold. After we had eaten, Emmie presented me with two large index cards.

"From Osborne's desk?" I asked.

"Yes, Harry. But I'll say no more on the subject just now."

"I don't want to preach, Emmie. But you had agreed you wouldn't initiate any schemes."

"But I didn't, Harry. Going through Osborne's desk was your scheme. I merely completed the task. You really should be thanking me."

I reluctantly conceded her point. She had given me two five-by-seven-inch policy cards. These were designed to make it easy to look up information without having to pull the original policy documents. On the back of each card, someone would note when each payment had been made. The first was for a fellow named Richard Warner, whose policy had been written on March 5th. He was a machinist, and lived on First Avenue in Manhattan. It was for $2,000 and the agent's name was Horrigan. The second card was for Jacob Marquisee, and dated March 1st. It was for $8,000 and the agent's name was Gunther.

"This ties in with what I learned this morning, Emmie." I then told her about the piece of paper in Osborne's pocket.

"So, Osborne went to Warner's home and then was going to Marquisee's," Emmie said. "To do what, warn them?"

"I don't know. I need to see if I can get ahold of someone at Newcome's."

I telephoned the agency and spoke with a night supervisor. He said he'd go up to Warner's himself and then phone me back.

"Did you notice anything else about the cards, Harry?"

I picked them up again. Looking closely, I could see the agent's name had been changed on each of them.

"So you did see the policy in Huber's office," Emmie said. "Who do you think removed the files? The girl there said a young lady picked them up."

"Well, Osborne could have sent someone from Sovereign to do it. She would have had no idea what it was about. But then there would be one more person who might slip up. Where was Elizabeth on Monday?"

"On Monday?"

"Well, on Tuesday the girl at Huber's office told you a young lady had picked them up the previous day."

"I was with Elizabeth from lunch on. Why do you think it was Elizabeth?"

"Because I think my introduction to Elizabeth was a set-up." Then I told her about Tibbitts' little charade of that afternoon.

"So Sergeant Tibbitts is part of the ring?"

"I don't know his connection, but he's definitely trying to hide something. And he's the one who told me about Elizabeth. If Tibbitts told her to pick up those files, she couldn't afford to refuse. And at the time she was boarding just a few blocks from Huber's office."

"Yes, I suppose you're right," she admitted. "But why did you go back to that saloon this afternoon?"

"I was suspicious from the moment Tibbitts mentioned it. There are dozens of saloons on that stretch of First Avenue. Then when we arrived there, the fellow who gave us the description didn't look like a bartender. And he was too ready to talk."

"Mr. Dooley seems to talk quite a lot."

"Mr. Dooley is a fraud."

"Well, he's very popular. Every newspaper seems to carry Mr. Dooley."

"I can't believe you're defending that travesty, Emmie. He spends all day philosophizing. No one goes into a saloon to listen to a bartender philosophize. It's the bartender's lot in life to listen to the harangues of his customers. That's what he's paid for. And that idiotic patois he's made to speak—I've been in a thousand Irish bars in a hundred towns and not once have I heard an Irish bartender carry on in that gibberish."

"Perhaps it's the philosophizing itself that attracts, and not its delivery."

"Philosophy be damned."

"I never know what will upset you, Harry."

"It's simply a matter of principle, Emmie."

"Yes, dear. But getting back to this afternoon, you felt the bartender was overly Dooley-like?"

"Well, yes," I agreed. "You see, he gave a detailed description of a man he'd allegedly seen just once, briefly, two days before. A man I saw out at Aqueduct that same afternoon. How could he describe Demming so well?"

"He was someone who was acquainted with Demming and was sent precisely to give his description. That's very good, Harry."

"Thank you, Emmie."

"But why would Detective Tibbitts conceive of a plan to implicate Mr. Demming? And how would he acquire this faux bartender so quickly?'

"I can't figure that out," I conceded. "By the way, how did you get the cards from Osborne's desk?"

"Well, yesterday I tried sneaking in at the end of the day. I made it upstairs and was just down the hall from his office, when a night watchman challenged me. I was able to evade him, but only at the cost of my shoe. This evening I had a more foolproof plan. I went in with the scrub women and had Elizabeth go in separately to distract the night watchman. It took some time to scrub my way into his office, but once I had the cards, I re-signed."

"Why did you say *more* foolproof?"

"Well, the one flaw involved that same watchman. Rather than allow himself to be diverted by Elizabeth's charms, he detained her. She had to ransom herself with a bribe. Can you reimburse her from your expense account?"

The telephone rang before I could answer. The fellow from Newcome's was on the line.

"As near as I can make out, Warner and his wife left Tuesday afternoon, sometime before five o'clock. They had bags with them. No one has seen them since."

"But no one knew why they left?"

"No. Or where they went. I got into the apartment and it looks like they left in a hurry. There was something on the stove they just left. I found some letters from Mrs. Warner's family. She's from Chicago. Should I have our office there check on them?"

"Yes, please."

I hung up and told it all to Emmie.

"At least they're both alive," she said.

The next morning Emmie and I went up to the Warners' building on First Avenue. We spoke to a number of women about the place, including one who saw them leave, Mrs. Shannon. She was a rather gossipy sort, so we asked her what she knew of Mrs. Warner.

"Oh, she was friendly enough. A little peculiar, maybe."

"In what way peculiar?" Emmie asked.

"She would say silly things, as if they were really true. Kind of like a little child would do. She told me once she was the daughter of a very rich man and that her husband had kidnapped her. Then a week later, she said she was a princess, and her husband had cast a spell on her. Just silliness, like a little child."

"Do you know if she gambled?" I asked.

"You mean the policy shops?"

"Yes, or elsewhere."

"I don't know if she did, but I don't know she didn't."

"Did you know Mr. Warner well?"

"No, he kept to himself mostly. He was friendly, but not one for chatting."

We got into the apartment, and Emmie threw out the abandoned meal. There were several photographs of the couple, so we took what looked like the most recent. We also saw the letters. Mrs. Warner was clearly close to her family. There was no evidence either of them gambled. While we were there, one of Ratigan's operatives showed up. He had a photograph of Osborne and we went with him as he showed it around the building. One woman thought she may have seen him enter the building, but whether it was Monday or Tuesday, morning or afternoon, she couldn't remember. No one knew where Richard Warner was from.

The three of us then went over to Prince Street and the machine shop where Warner was employed. I asked to speak with the foreman. A big, middle-aged fellow came over.

"I'm Henninger. What can I do for you?"

"I'm trying to locate Richard Warner."

"So am I, brother."

"He's missing?"

"More like skipped out. Right in the middle of the afternoon. Why are you looking for him?"

"Well, I think he's in some danger. Was that Tuesday afternoon?"

"Yeah. A kid comes in and asks for him. Told him something'd happened to his wife. So he leaves in a hurry. That's the last I saw of him. When he didn't come in Wednesday, I went around to his place. No one was there. Same yesterday. The neighbors said his wife wasn't sick. They just left."

"And no idea where he went?"

"No. No idea."

"Where was he from?"

"All anyone knows is that he grew up on a farm, upstate someplace. Maybe near the canal."

"The Erie Canal?"

"I assumed so. He just said canal."

Then we left him and went over to Newcome's, and Emmie and I went into Ratigan's office. It was obvious he didn't like having her there. But if he wanted to get her out, he'd have to do it himself. I told him about the possible sighting of Osborne at the Warners' building.

"If he went during the day, Warner would be at work, and Osborne had that address," I said. "So he must have gone to see Mrs. Warner. Probably to tell her to get out of town."

"So he must have warned Mrs. Barclay and Anna Farrell as well," Emmie said.

"That would make sense," Ratigan allowed.

"Any news from Chicago?" I asked.

"Not yet."

I told him what we had heard about Warner coming from a farm near a canal upstate.

"I don't suppose there's a way to find out where?"

"You'd need a small army of detectives. That would be a job for the Pinks."

"Heaven forfend!" Emmie had read my mind.

"No, we don't need a lot of loose cannons running about," I said. One was plenty.

Then Emmie and I went off and had lunch. Before parting, Emmie told me that Elizabeth had something planned for the evening. I tried not to think of the possibilities and made my way to the Bureau.

Keegan was in and I told him what we had learned, and about Tibbitts setting up the false witness.

"I could try to have him taken off of this," he said.

"Maybe it would be better not to. Now, anything he says or does is really a clue. Besides, we probably couldn't trust another cop any more than we can him."

"Yes, that's certainly true."

"I thought I'd go out to Aqueduct and ask Demming what he thought it was about."

"Yes," Keegan said enthusiastically. "Perhaps I should go with you."

There wasn't any point in his going with me, but it would have been tactless to say so.

When we arrived at the betting ring, Keegan went off to find his favorite bookmaker and I located Demming. He was busily exchanging hand signals with some other fellows about the place. As the horses went to the post for the next race, the bookmakers and their patrons rushed out to watch and I was able to get his attention. I told him about his being sighted in the First Avenue saloon. He found it very amusing.

"You see, Harry, this is their way of telling me not to put my nose where it doesn't belong."

"Who? Minden?"

"Him, or Bannon. He must have seen us together, and he may have learned all about you by now."

"They'd give you up, just for speaking with me?"

"It was meant as a shot across my bow. Don't take that part of it too seriously."

"Which part should I take seriously?"

"That they are involved in this at all. It would seem there's more to this than I realized."

I left him and went back into Manhattan to see if I could find a way of locating the Warner farm through some sort of directory. At about five I was in the Astor Library and I ran into Emmie. She'd been on the same quest.

"It's no use, Harry. Apparently there are thousands of farms in New York State, but no one has considered it worthwhile to list them for us. What's the use of the Grange?"

"I suppose they have other concerns, Emmie."

"Perhaps, but it seems rather selfish."

We went home to Brooklyn, but separated on that side of the river. I was to go to Graef's for wine, and Emmie to the fish market on Washington Avenue.

At the apartment, Elizabeth and Dorothy were making elaborate preparations. Emmie and I changed for dinner and it wasn't long afterwards that Dorothy emerged from the kitchen with a platter on which sat a head of cabbage. It had walnut eyes, a carrot nose, and pimiento lips. She placed it on the table as a centerpiece, then left us.

"What's this about, Emmie?" I asked.

"I'm not sure. What's the date?"

"The date? The 19th, why?"

Just then Elizabeth came out and had us sit down.

"We are here today to celebrate the feast of St. Elphege, the patron saint of children with awkward names. Though he is no longer a child, it is hoped our observance will bring some succor to Harrison."

"St. Elphege is depicted as a head of cabbage?" I

asked, unwisely. Elizabeth silenced me with one of her cold looks.

"St. Elphege," Elizabeth went on, "as you no doubt know, was Archbishop of Canterbury in the eleventh century, not long before the arrival of the Conqueror. Unfortunately, just as he was getting comfortable in his new quarters, the Danes took it upon themselves to invade. They carried Elphege off and treated him most cruelly, stoning him and whatnot, until one of the Danes took pity and ended his suffering by dispatching him with an axe. He is sometimes represented with an axe cleaving his skull, thusly."

Her hand emerged from under the table holding a meat cleaver. She dispatched St. Elphege with such force the platter below shattered.

"Sorry, Emmie."

"Oh, that's all right, dear," Emmie assured her.

"That was a gift from my mother," I reminded her.

"Was it?"

We then had the most appetizing meal ever prepared in that apartment. Though I was a little uneasy throughout it, as St. Elphege seemed to be looking at me accusingly. His left eye, anyway.

The next morning, Emmie and I went in to Ratigan's office to see if he had learned anything new.

"It doesn't look like the Warners went to Chicago. At least, they aren't staying with her family there. A man spoke with her parents last evening. They say they haven't heard from their daughter in several weeks, and they aren't sure exactly where Warner comes from. Upstate somewhere. But it was a farm."

With no other lead, Emmie and I returned to the Warners' building. While she was seeing if there was anyone about we hadn't spoken to yet, I got myself back into their apartment. We had searched it fairly thoroughly earlier, but there was always a chance we had missed something.

I went through the kitchen and the only interesting thing I found was a tin of rat poison. Its existence might not have been worthy of note in itself, but that it was on a shelf in the midst of canned fruit seemed curious.

I emptied every drawer, looked under every piece of furniture, and went through the pockets of each piece of clothing. If the Warners did decide to return, there would certainly be some tidying up to do. I was about to call it a day when Emmie arrived with an older fellow.

"This is Mr. Gilbo, Harry. He says he remembers seeing a photograph Mr. Warner showed him. It was of a canal."

"Do you know where he kept it, Mr. Gilbo? I've looked everywhere."

He surveyed the scene. "Yes, you certainly have."

"I assure you, we wouldn't have resorted to this if we weren't certain the Warners are in some danger."

"So your missus says. Well, he had a little box he kept things in. He brought it out once when I asked him where he grew up."

"But he didn't tell you where he grew up?"

"On a farm. He described it but it could have been a farm anywhere. A dairy farm. And he told me about the canal boats, and trading things with the boys who lived on them."

"You don't know where he kept this box?"

"He went into the bedroom and came back with it. It had things from his childhood. When his wife came home, he hid it. I don't know why."

"What could you see in the photograph?"

"Just a boat on a canal, but he said it was near his home."

We thanked him and he went off. Then we went into the bedroom and I started picking things off the floor.

"What are you doing, Harry?"

"Well, Emmie, I don't know if I should be revealing this to you, but whenever a boy wants to hide something from prying eyes, he finds a loose floorboard."

"What if there are no loose floorboards?"

"He finds a crowbar."

When we actually did find a loose floorboard, and below it an old wooden box, Emmie giggled.

"It's like *Tom Sawyer*, Harry."

14

In the box was an old stereoscopic photograph of a canal. The only caption was written in pen, "Battle Island." On the reverse was written the name of the photographer and "Oswego, NY."

"Where's Battle Island?" Emmie asked.

"I don't know, but there's a branch of the canal that goes to Oswego."

"Where's Oswego?"

"On Lake Ontario. But that's just where the photographer is from. The scene could be anywhere along the canal."

"We need a gazetteer," Emmie said.

We went back over to the Astor Library, where they had several gazetteers for New York State, but only the last listed Battle Island. It was on the Oswego River, just above Fulton.

"Where's Fulton?" Emmie asked.

"Just above Syracuse."

We consulted a railway guide and learned we had two options. We could either take a night train, and arrive in Fulton at seven the next morning, or take an afternoon train to Syracuse, find a hotel, and catch an early morning train to Fulton. We made our way back to Brooklyn in order to pack.

"Oh, let's take a night train, Harry. We can book a sleeping car."

"Have you ever taken a sleeper, Emmie?"

"No, but it always struck me as being romantic."

"Romantic? On a Pullman sleeper, the porter decides when you go to bed and when you get up. There'll be a choir of men and women barking and snorting all night long, loosely accompanied by a half-dozen infants who've somehow learned to bawl in rounds. Then there's the young couple just one berth over in need of no sleep whatsoever. The whispers and giggles go on until about three a.m., and at four the first toddlers begin a sloppy steeplechase up and down the aisle. The extra fare is about the same as a night in a good hotel, and we'll arrive completely exhausted."

"But we'll be the young couple, Harry."

"We'll be the young couple in the comfortable hotel in Syracuse."

Emmie gave in rather easily, and it wasn't long after we boarded the 2:00 express that she suggested we visit the parlor car. Some people facing a journey of several hours bring an engaging book, others a cold deck. I declined to accompany her and made it clear she wasn't to consider me her lender of last resort. I didn't see her again until dinner.

"I've been thinking, Harry. Would all these women ever have agreed to have their husbands murdered?"

"Well, what if they were tricked into it? They went along at first when they just thought the policies were for some sort of fraud."

"But it seems rather a big leap to go from participating in a fraud to killing your own husband."

"What if the wife didn't know that was the plan until after he'd been killed? Now she'd be in a very difficult position. If she went to the police, it would look like she was involved from the beginning. She'd have no way out."

"Mrs. Marquisee found a way out," Emmie answered.

"Yes, I guess she did."

After dinner, Emmie returned to the parlor car. She showed up again about half past nine, just before we arrived in Syracuse. She looked rather down. The conductor and a porter were with her and they were being unusually helpful in getting us off the train.

"Just remember, miss," the conductor called after us.

"What was that about, Emmie?"

"They took my money, Harry."

"Who did?"

"All of them. They said I was cheating."

There was little doubt she had been, of course. But there are times when a family must circle the wagons regardless of where the fault lies. I wasn't altogether sure this was one of those times, but I could only hope the experience would impress her. I said a few comforting words.

"But what did the conductor mean, when he told you to remember?" I asked.

"He told me he never wanted to see me on his train again. It was very embarrassing, Harry. "

"I can imagine so. But at least you weren't kicked off the New York Central entirely."

We found a room at a decent hotel and then found a saloon we had visited on a previous trip to Syracuse. Emmie could be oddly sentimental about such things, and always seemed surprised when the reality didn't conform to her nostalgic visions. This was not the friendly tavern she remembered, but the haunt of working men who were out celebrating the end of their work week.

There were about fifty patrons there, most of them not at their best, and not a single woman. We went back to the hotel and had wine sent up to the room.

The next morning, Sunday the 21st, we caught an eight o'clock train to Fulton. Fulton was a small town and we spent a good deal of time finding a stable where we could hire both a carriage and a driver. The driver was an older fellow and we were told he was familiar with the rural area north of Fulton. And he was, in a vague kind of way. The Oswego River and the canal ran together and we ventured up the western side. As soon as we left the village of Fulton, the valley was nothing but farms. The driver knew most of the places, but the further north we got, the less sure he was. Somewhere above Battle Island, we asked at a nearby farm and were told there was a Warner farm in Volnay, on the opposite side of the river. We went up to Minetto, where there was a bridge, and the driver suggested we stop for lunch. I began to suspect he knew the whereabouts of our destination all along, but saw us as a source of ready cash that should be made the most of.

Eventually, we came upon the farmstead we'd been told belonged to a fellow named Warner. We saw a man moving about the barn and Emmie went off to make inquiries. After what looked like an animated conversation, she came back.

"What did he say, Emmie?"

"Well, he first asked me if I was the lady who wanted to kill his son. I assured him I had no such intention, and he asked if I might change my mind. He offered to supply me with a shotgun and said there was little chance I'd get caught as neither he nor his daughter-in-law would have any objection."

"A little rural humor, I imagine. So they are here then?"

"Oh, yes. He said to just go up to the house."

Mrs. Warner greeted us at the kitchen door. She was a young woman, of medium height, with a very round face. We introduced ourselves and told her why we had come.

"Oh, I know about the danger. A man came by last week. He told me we'd better leave New York, as several people had already been killed. Seems the thing had gotten a little out of hand."

"What thing is that?" I asked.

"Well, this insurance thing, of course. Isn't that why you're here?"

"Yes, but we weren't sure how exactly you were involved."

"I don't want to be confessing to anything."

"Mrs. Warner," Emmie said, "I assure you, we will not betray your trust."

"Well, I'm not sure I did anything wrong, anyway."

"I'm sure not," Emmie said. "No doubt you were merely coerced into joining the scheme."

"You talk just like her!"

"Just like who?" I asked.

"The lady who came with the plan."

"What was the plan?" I asked.

"Well, first I should tell you how it all started. Why don't you sit down." She poured us some coffee and offered us doughnuts. "You see, a friend of mine took me to one of these poolrooms. Only you don't play pool, you bet on horse races. And I won, twenty-two dollars. So of course I went back the next day. I lost my twenty-two dollars and then some, with three races still to go. And the man there said, 'If it's just a temporary shortage, we may be able to advance you some money.' And I said, 'Well, as it happens, my husband died just yesterday and I'm due to get $5,000 insurance any day now.' He said that was all fine then and he let me play on credit. I kept going back, and some days I won and some days I lost, but mostly I lost. At the end of a week, I owed him almost four hundred dollars. It didn't seem real. I mean, where would I ever get four hundred dollars?"

"Where indeed?" I said.

"Then the man became rather angry and said I had better come up with the money. I told him I didn't have it, that my husband was still alive. And he said, 'Then maybe you should kill him.' But, of course, there was no insurance policy for five thousand dollars. So killing him then would have just been a waste of time."

Emmie and I exchanged glances.

"Yes, what would be the point?" Emmie said.

"Well, a week or so later a man came by and made some threats about it, but you can't get blood from a turnip. Then one day this young fellow comes, I forget his name. He was much more pleasant. I told him all about how I got into the mess, and he was very understanding. He said that if I paid just part of the money I still owed, I think he said two hundred dollars, he would forget the rest. This seemed fair, but I still didn't have it. Then he put me on a payment plan. Each week he came by and I'd give him a dollar or so from the house money. And then the lady came by."

"What was her name?" I asked.

"She never said. But she talked just like your missus. Only, not as friendly. She had a way of making you feel ignorant. Do you know what I mean?"

"I know exactly what you mean," I said. "What did she look like?"

"Oh, she was very nice looking, tall, and blonde, I think. But she had this cold look."

"What did she propose?"

"Well, she said she had taken over my debt and now I needed to pay her. I told her I couldn't, but she insisted we could find a way. First she asked me how much my husband made each week, and if my family had money. She seemed to realize I had no money to give her. Oh, here's Dickie."

A husky sort of young fellow had entered the room. She introduced us to her husband and he sat down with us and ate a plate of doughnuts.

"I was just telling them, dear, about the lady who came by. Well, since I had no money, she said there is always life insurance. I said we had no life insurance. She said that would be no problem, but the question was, would I be willing to do in my husband. I said I suppose I might be. And she said we could always make the insurance policy for a little more than I owed, then I'd have some money to set up for myself. Well, that seemed a nice idea." She turned to her husband. "More doughnuts, dear?"

"No, I need to get back to the workshop." Mr. Warner excused himself and went back out of the house.

"He's a tinkerer. He's trying to make a machine that will milk cows. He sees himself as a sort of Thomas Edison. Now where was I?"

"The lady generously suggested you might benefit from your husband's life insurance," I said.

"Yes, that's right. A week or so later, a man stopped by with some papers. An application form, I think. He said a doctor would need to come by, and we needed to pick an evening when my husband wasn't at home, and he would take Dickie's place. I thought this was becoming kind of exciting, like in a book. Well, the next week, this man came back, in the evening. And then the doctor came. He examined the man who was pretending to be my husband and said he was very healthy, and then he signed some forms and left. Then the other man left."

I took out the photograph of Huber and showed it to her. "Was that the man?"

She got up and went into another room and came back holding a pair of eyeglasses. She put these on and studied the photograph. "Yes, it very well may have been."

"Were you wearing your eyeglasses when he came by?" I asked.

"No, no. I only wear them if I have to read something. He filled out the form, asked me some questions, and then had me sign my husband's name for him."

"So you might not be altogether sure what any of these people looked like?" I asked.

"No, not exactly. But I'd recognize the voice of the lady, I think."

"Please go on. The doctor and the man posing as your husband had left."

"Well, a couple weeks later, that lady came back. She said, 'You need to take care of your husband soon.' And she gave me a tin of rat poison. I said, 'How am I to get him to eat rat poison?' And she explained how I could put it in his dinner each day. Well, how could I be sure I wouldn't eat some? So I didn't do that. She came by again, maybe just a week ago now. I think it might have been the Saturday before we left. She was even more unfriendly. When I told her I wasn't sure about the rat poison, she became very angry and said it didn't matter how I did it, but if I didn't do it soon, it would be done for me. Well, up until then, I had tried to be agreeable. But now she went too far."

Her husband returned and began looking in a cupboard. "Have you seen that funnel, dear?"

"On the shelf above," she answered. "Well, I mean, if someone is going to kill my husband, I think it should be me. Don't you agree?"

"I do indeed," Emmie said. "I made the same argument myself just a week ago."

"You did?" Mrs. Warner seemed surprised. And her husband gave me a look of utter amazement.

"You mean there're two of them?" he asked. "Good God."

"How did you leave things with this lady?" I asked his wife.

"Well, she said she would leave it to me, but to do it soon. I decided then I had made a mistake. I mean, going along with this insurance thing. I wasn't sure what to do. I didn't think I could go to the police, and I didn't want to have to explain it to Dickie. I wasn't sure he would understand. But then that gentleman came by last Tuesday. He said that Dickie and me were in danger and that the best thing would be for us to leave town, and not tell anyone where we were going. So I sent a note to Dickie, saying I was sick, just to get him home. And we left for here."

She then gave us the address of the poolroom and vague descriptions of all her visitors. Afterwards, her husband motioned me outside.

"You know everything she says is nonsense?" he asked.

"Even the descriptions?"

"No, they're probably mostly real. But all the talk of killing me—she just didn't realize the other people were serious. She's always saying things like that."

As confused as Emmie's doings made me, I had to admit Richard Warner had it worse. We went back inside, where old Mr. Warner had joined our wives.

"I could make it look as if he was killed by his own machine," the old man was saying.

"All right, dear," his daughter-in-law agreed.

Mrs. Warner started to stand up, but sat down quickly and looked a little ill.

"Are you all right, dear?" her husband asked.

"I don't know. Lately I've been feeling a little odd."

"I know what it is," the old man said. "She's having my baby."

"I think he might be right, dear," she told her husband.

"Are you sure?" he asked.

"No, not certain," she said.

"It's mine," the old man said.

"How will we know that until we see it?" Mrs. Warner asked him.

The old man thought on that for a bit and then observed, "There'd be nothing odd in him looking like his brother there."

"Assuming Dickie is yours," Mrs. Warner retorted.

He thought about that for a while. "Well, the next one will be mine."

"Yes, dear," his daughter-in-law agreed. Then she leaned over toward Emmie. "He's a little daft."

Before we left the farm, I made sure they realized they really were in some danger, given that Mrs. Warner could identify all these people. Or at least, they would believe she could. Then we went out and woke the driver and set off for Fulton. There wasn't much to do between dinner and our 9:30 train, so we took a stroll about Fulton.

"What an odd family, Harry."

"Yes, it makes you wonder just what sort of child they'll have."

"I'd been thinking, we should have come with more photographs," Emmie said. "But I don't suppose it would have been much use."

"No, I noticed she had to feel about for things, like the cups when she poured the coffee. I don't think she sees well at all. But her descriptions might still be helpful. The mysterious lady seemed reminiscent of someone near and dear."

"Elizabeth? I suppose it did sound rather like her. But I still don't think she'd have anything to do with murder. And how did this lady, whoever she is, become the debt collector for the poolrooms?"

"Assuming Mrs. Warner's account is creditable, there seems to have been a series of different collectors. First, the threatening thug, probably in the employ of the poolroom operator. Then the fellow who offered to let her off for part of what she owed. And finally, the lofty lady. That second fellow may provide the answer. He sounds like a traditional debt collector, the kind who buys debts at a discount."

"So the poolroom operator, realizing his thug wasn't up to the task, sells the debt to the second gentleman. And then he hires the lofty lady?"

"I imagine it's something like that. It would help to know the bookkeeping arrangements of a poolroom."

"The poolroom she mentioned was one of the ones Elizabeth took me to."

"Well, that could be useful."

"Elizabeth said it was owned by Minden."

I wanted to take the train as far as Syracuse and spend another night in a hotel. But Emmie insisted she have her way this time, and we booked a sleeper through to New York. Just as I predicted, we arrived at half past seven in need of a good night's sleep.

15

After we brought our things home, I told Emmie I'd need to go see Ratigan.

"Are you going to tell him about the Warners?"

"Of course, at least that we found them."

"But don't tell the police where they are, Harry. You wouldn't want her husband's brother to be born in Sing Sing, would you?"

"No, no. Who'd want to break up that happy home?"

I crossed the river and told Ratigan about Mrs. Warner and her account of her various visitors.

"Have you ever heard of gambling debts being taken on by debt brokers?" I asked.

"No, but lots of things go on in this town I find hard to believe."

"Anything new on Anna Farrell?"

"No, she hasn't been near her old place. I'd say she either left town or has fallen through the cracks."

"What do you mean by fallen through the cracks?"

"There's a lot of people down on their luck, barely getting by. They've pawned everything they can. They just kind of disappear, until they're found dead somewhere."

"Have you learned anything else about Osborne?"

"Nothing notable. But we might learn more when we can talk to people at Sovereign."

I walked down to the Bureau and called Tibbitts. He agreed to meet me for lunch at the place on Thames. Keegan came in a while later and I told him about our weekend excursion.

"It doesn't sound as if that solves anything," he said.

"It confirms what we already suspected: the scheme was to enable wives to pay their gambling debts by insuring their husbands, and then knocking them over. But we still don't know who all was involved. When do you think we can get into Sovereign's offices again?"

"Soon. There's someone who wants to meet with you. Perhaps this evening. He's out in Brooklyn, too."

"Does he have a name?"

"Mr. X for now. He may be taking charge of Sovereign—at least that's what he's trying to do. I'll see if I can set something up. Check in with me before you go home this evening."

Then I went off to Thames Street. Tibbitts was late, which only increased my displeasure with him.

"What was all that about last Thursday?"

"I thought you saw through that," he smiled. "To tell you the truth, I don't know myself. The old fellow that bartender described, someone you know?"

"Yes, someone who was out at Aqueduct on that afternoon."

"Yeah?"

"I saw him there myself."

"I never get to go to the races."

"But who put you up to it?"

"What's it matter?"

"I'd like to know what I'm up against."

"Is that why you wanted to meet?"

"Yes. If I'm going to be led around by the nose, I'd like to know who's doing the leading."

"I'm not sure that it had to do with you, more likely the other party. Let's leave it at that. Are you still trying to get to the bottom of the Sovereign case?"

"Yes."

"They aren't."

"How do you know?"

"Same way I knew about it in the first place. Are you going to be able to clean it up?"

"Does it matter to you?"

"Sure, I need to know when to cover my shorts," he smiled.

"You've shorted their shares?"

"Sure. Haven't you?"

"No, maybe I ought to."

"Probably too late. The question now is when to cover the shorts. How's the lady Custis working out?"

"She's moved in."

"You're kidding," he stopped. "That was fast."

I smiled. "It turns out she went to school with my wife, and she insisted."

"She been any help?"

"Well, some, I guess. What made you bring her into this? Was that your idea or someone else's?"

"That was all mine. To be honest, I just wanted her to keep an eye on you. She didn't have anything better to do, and she owed me a favor. But since then I haven't heard from her."

"Didn't have the hold on her you thought you had?"

"Oh, I would have found her quickly enough."

We split up and I took a long walk back to the Bureau. On the way, an amusing notion occurred to me. I walked over to Ratigan's office and interrupted his lunch.

"I just had a thought," I began. "Suppose, just hypothetically, you heard about a scandal at some large company that they were trying to keep a secret. And you had some control over what would be revealed, and when.

Could you make a very large sum shorting the stock without exposing yourself?"

"You could have, but I'd say you're too late now."

"No, seriously."

"I am serious. Hadn't you shorted it already?"

"No, had you?" I asked.

"Just a little," he smiled. "But I already covered."

"Well, let's get back to the hypothetical. Suppose that the man in question isn't a foolish insurance investigator, but a shrewd financier. How much could he expect to make?"

"That would depend on the company and the nature of the scandal. With a company the size of Sovereign, in an industry where integrity is so important, I'd say a lot. There's no question a lot of money's already been made."

"And it would be even more profitable if you could string it out?" I asked.

"Sure, the longer the questions go unanswered, the lower the price will go."

"Well, I had a thought on the way over here," I said. "More money has been made shorting Sovereign's shares because of this scheme than the scheme itself could have made."

"I suppose that's true. And if the fellows who are short are really clever, they'll go long just as it all comes out in the newspapers."

"But why wouldn't the price of the shares fall even further?"

"Well, it could. But usually people's imaginations are worse than the reality. Plus, if you're short a huge block, you want to cover your position when there are still a lot of people wanting to sell."

"And to cover your position, you have to buy?"

"Yes, and there is nothing worse than having a huge short position when things turn around and the market is buying. Each time you buy, you raise the price some. If there are a lot of people short and they all have to buy at once, things get really ugly."

"So if a fellow shorted the stock before anyone else knew about the situation, and then when he knew it was about to become public, he bought shares, partly to cover his short position but a lot more besides, he would make an incredible fortune."

"That was what Jay Gould and his friends specialized in. It's frowned on a little more today, so it would need to be done with more discretion. But you can be sure it goes on all the time," Ratigan said. "You think someone has been doing this with the Sovereign stock?"

"The insurance scheme itself made $15,000 on Barclay. Even if they collected on all four policies, it wouldn't have made more than $30,000. And there were a lot of people involved, each expecting a share. Maybe they expected to get a lot more, but someone who timed the share prices correctly would have none of the risks and could make just as much money."

"More. Maybe even gain control of the company. But if they engineered the insurance scheme, they would still have that risk."

"Yes. But maybe they were able to control it without being directly involved. I shouldn't tell you this...."

"That someone's planning a takeover of Sovereign?"

"How'd you know?" I asked.

"Just a hunch. Their share price has actually risen some the last few sessions, even though a lot of new shorts have entered the game. But you don't need to tell me any more."

"I think you already know more than I do," I said. "Is there any way to find out who made sizeable gains over this?"

"I can ask around. It won't be definitive, but I can get a pretty good idea who the big fish were."

I went back to the Bureau and stopped in to see Keegan.

"All right, Harry. It's on for this evening. The man's name is George Koestler. He lives just below Prospect Park...."

"On Albemarle Road," I finished for him.

"You know him?" Keegan asked incredulously.

"I met his daughter. I assume it's his daughter. She was a childhood friend of William Huber's. Which means her father must have known Huber."

"Well, just a coincidence in this case. Koestler has taken control of a large block of Sovereign shares. The board is going to meet in the morning and sometime around noon tomorrow he will be taking temporary charge of the company."

"Then we can get back inside?"

"Yes, absolutely. But this evening, Koestler would like you to tell him how you see things. He'll need to release a statement tomorrow and it will need to be as detailed as possible."

"I'm a little short of details."

"Well, better to paint the picture too dark than be seen as covering up anything now. It will be imperative that the public, and Wall Street, believes this is behind them. He'll be expecting you at nine."

When I arrived home, Elizabeth informed me that Emmie would be home late, as she'd found employment.

"I don't suppose I could be made privy?" I asked.

"Not by me. Emmie's been a little closed-mouthed. What happened on your trip?"

"Nothing really." I thought it best to change the subject. "How's your romance with Edward Howell progressing?"

"Oh, that's off. I found out his family money gave up the ghost years ago. Besides, I think I reminded him too much of his wife."

Elizabeth made dinner again that evening and I realized what a loss it would be if she were to be arrested. She seemed to be in something of an irritable mood, so I chose a conversation topic she couldn't take offense at. I asked her what Emmie was like in school.

"Well, she was quite different in some ways. She was very studious. She didn't live in the houses. So she wasn't a part of the push."

"That must have been too bad."

"She complained about it, but I was never convinced she really minded. She had a very low tolerance for all the frivolous chatter and affectations. But I don't remember her having this fascination with murder and gambling. Is that all due to your marriage?"

"No, vice versa, I think."

About half past eight, I went off to the Koestlers. I was led into the library and not long after George Koestler came in and introduced himself. He was an affable fellow of about fifty, and if I were asked to guess his occupation, it would not be cutthroat financier. He gave me a drink and in a while his wife came in. Lucy Koestler was significantly younger than her husband, not older than thirty-five.

"There is a need for extreme discretion, Reese," Koestler said.

"Yes, of course," I assured him.

"I've asked Lucy to help with the preparation of tomorrow's communiqué and it's necessary she be abreast of the facts."

"What *are* the facts, Mr. Reese?" Mrs. Koestler asked.

"Well, I'm not sure how much you've been told already."

"Only the vaguest account," Mr. Koestler interjected.

So I started at the beginning of my being called in and went through what had transpired. When I finished, Mrs. Koestler, who'd been taking notes throughout, gave her summation.

"It sounds as if you've made a muddle of it, Mr. Reese."

"Now, dear," Mr. Koestler said.

"Well, to be honest, I've mainly worked on fire insurance cases in the past. But we do have operatives from Newcome's on it. And the police are of course involved." I left Emmie off the list. "But I'm afraid you're correct in thinking we have a lot to find out."

"Perhaps we should put off our takeover," Koestler said to his wife.

"The problem is," I said, "Redfield has put the lid on us learning anything about what Osborne was doing."

"So you're counting on the takeover to gain access?" Koestler said.

"Yes, precisely," I said. "But I don't think it's likely that this involved more than the one person inside Sovereign."

"And William Huber, of course," Koestler said. "So you believe that with Osborne's death, the scheme is ended."

"Yes, at least as far as Sovereign is concerned."

"But that's all that matters for tomorrow. You can work on filling in the details afterward."

"Do you think that's wise, dear?" Mrs. Koestler asked.

"Unavoidable, I'm afraid. Once we make our announcement, the police will look foolish for not having uncovered anything themselves. But it will be important that we stay one step ahead of them."

He asked his wife to type a letter that instructed Sovereign employees to cooperate fully with my investigation. She did, and handed it to me.

"Don't let anyone see that until the takeover is completed," he said.

As I was leaving, he told me that he would be at Sovereign after noon the next day and to keep him regularly posted. Outside, I met Sally on the path to the house.

"Looking for me?" she asked. She seemed noticeably less perky than usual.

"Yes," I said. I wasn't sure how far I was meant to take the discretion. "I was just wondering if you had any news?"

"About William?"

"Yes."

"No. I would have telephoned you. Is that really why you came?"

"I was passing by, and just thought I'd check with you."

When I arrived home, Emmie was there speaking to Elizabeth and it seemed things weren't quite as light as they had been. They stopped when I entered.

"Where have you been?" Emmie asked.

"I might ask you the same." Of course I might, but there was little point. "I will tell you this, there will be some excitement tomorrow in the insurance trade."

"Does it take much to excite the insurance trade?" Elizabeth asked.

"Frankly, no," I conceded. "Nonetheless, developments could be interesting. But I mustn't say anything more about it."

We went in to bed, while Elizabeth stayed up reading.

"You seemed to be taking Elizabeth into your confidence," Emmie said. "Does that mean you agree she had nothing to do with it?"

"I'm afraid not, dear. Just a little test."

"I don't like that, Harry. It makes me feel as if you're spying on her."

"Are you so sure she isn't spying on us?"

About an hour later, I heard Elizabeth moving about. She was making a phone call. I heard the word Sovereign, but nothing more. The next morning, while we were alone at breakfast, I asked Emmie about her new employment.

"I'm trying to find out who the second man was."

"The second man?"

"The second man who visited Mrs. Warner. The one you conjectured was a debt collector. But I won't say any more until I find something out."

When I arrived at the Bureau, I called Tibbitts first thing.

"I have some news I thought you'd be interested in, but maybe you already heard it?"

"About Sovereign?"

"Yes. Did you know?"

"No, what is it?"

"There will be a takeover announced at noon. I'm told that anyone short might want to cover by then."

"Thanks, Reese. I owe you one." He hung up without saying anything else.

I took that to mean Elizabeth hadn't telephoned him the previous night, though perhaps he was just playing his hand close. I couldn't think who else she would have called. Then I let Ratigan know about it and he sent a couple operatives round with the idea I would take them into Sovereign as soon as we had access. We needed to talk to everyone who had worked with Osborne and try to find out about any unusual meetings or movements—did he leave early one day, come in late, etc. We spent the morning planning.

At exactly noon, Koestler went in with his people and took control. His communiqué was released to the financial press at the same time, and at about 12:10, I went in with the two operatives Ratigan had sent. I went immediately into what had been Osborne's office. His replacement as chief of the Claims Department had taken it over. I introduced myself and told him why I was there.

"Have you come across anything unusual among Osborne's effects?" I asked.

"Nothing personal. I thought perhaps his wife had gone through the office and taken those things."

"But anything related to the job that struck you as unusual? Any files out of place?"

"Not that I've noticed."

"Would you mind going through them and just look-ing for anything that catches your eye?"

I also gave him the cards Emmie had found and asked if he could find the policies on Warner and Marquisee, and check with the agents named. Then one of the operatives from Newcome's came in.

"I think you might want to meet this fellow." He led me out and introduced me to Eugene Donigan, Osborne's brother-in-law.

"I had a feeling something was going to happen," Donigan said. He was in his thirties, and had a kind of careless look.

"Why?" I asked.

"Can we go somewhere else?"

"Sure, we can find an office to use," I suggested.

"Maybe out of the building?"

"All right," I agreed.

We went out to a chop house and ordered lunch.

"You suspected your brother-in-law was involved in something?" I asked.

"I knew he was afraid of something."

"Why? What did he say?"

"Nothing, really. But he told me to take Ellen out of town."

"Ellen is your sister?"

"Yes, and his wife."

"We were told there was an illness in the family, that's what sent you both to Cincinnati."

"That was just an excuse."

"But you must have had some idea why he was sending you away."

"He said he'd done something he shouldn't have. That there was some danger. He was pretty upset."

"Didn't that seem out of character? He sounds like a straight-laced guy."

"Yeah, he was. That's why I took it so seriously. I assumed it was some shuffle at work."

"What sort of shuffle?" I asked.

"Just some paper thing, where money ends up going to someone it shouldn't. Every day they write dozens of checks for claims. If someone in his position wanted to make some money, it'd be pretty easy."

"Yes, but pretty easy to get caught, too. And he seemed like the cautious sort. There is another possible explanation. Maybe he came across someone else working a scheme and wanted to uncover it."

"Yeah, I thought of that, too," Donigan said. "But why wouldn't he tell someone else in the company?"

16

After lunch, I went out to Brooklyn to meet Osborne's wife. The maid let me in and led me to the parlor. A little while later Ellen Osborne, a short, stout woman, appeared. She was dressed in mourning and looked older than I expected, but that may have been due to the circumstances. She was the picture of distress. She told me much the same story as Donigan, but offered none of his conjecture.

"Do you have any idea why your husband wanted you to leave town?"

"He wouldn't say exactly, but he was very upset. I didn't want to make him more so, so I followed his wishes. That's really all I know."

"Did he know he had a bad heart?" I asked.

"Yes. It didn't trouble him much, but he had to avoid strain."

"Had he been meeting with anyone new recently?"

"I don't know what you mean."

"Well, did he have to go places in the evening?"

"No, nothing out of the ordinary. Do they think he did something wrong?"

"Yes, I'm afraid it looks that way."

"That would be so unlike him." She looked away, maybe to keep me from noticing she was crying. Then she excused herself with a whisper.

When I arrived back at Sovereign, one of the fellows from Newcome's pulled me aside. He told me a co-worker of Osborne's had seen him having lunch the

Monday before his death down at Delmonico's on Beaver Street. This co-worker thought it was notable because Osborne never dined extravagantly. He also described the fellow Osborne was with and he sounded suspiciously like John Huber. I telephoned Huber and he said he'd be in a meeting uptown until seven and then was heading to his parents'. I suggested we meet briefly at the Carleton, which would be on his route home. He agreed. I spent another hour speaking with people at Sovereign and not finding out much else. Then I went and met with Ratigan.

"Can you check up on John Huber? William's brother."

"You think he's involved?"

"Well, I believe he met with Osborne the day before he died. And he's the one who discovered his brother's body."

"I thought that was definitely suicide?"

"Yes, so I was told."

I gave him the relevant facts and he said he'd put someone on it right away. Then I used his phone to track down the doctor who performed the autopsy on William Huber. His name was O'Hanlon, and he happened to be at Brooklyn's morgue on another job. I caught an L across the bridge and then walked down to Willoughby Street. It was about half an hour before Dr. O'Hanlon came out of the examination room. I introduced myself and explained my interest in Huber's death. I also made sure to mention that powerful interests were behind my investigation. He didn't seem terribly impressed.

"I don't suppose there's any chance you might have made an error in the report on Huber?"

"What sort of error?"

"The location of the head wound?"

"I don't even remember."

"You testified the wound was on the forehead. Could it perhaps have been on the back of the head?"

"What difference would that make?"

"Well, a wound on the forehead would be consistent with Huber hitting his head on the desk after being rendered unconscious by the gas. But a wound on the back of the head might mean he'd been rendered unconscious by another party. Then that party turned on the gas."

"If I said it was on the forehead, I'm sure it was."

"Perhaps the body can be exhumed."

He looked more annoyed than frightened at my threat.

"Look—this is how it went. It was a busy day. I completed my finding and sent it on. When the police sergeant on the case saw my report, he told me I had it wrong. I had it that the wound was on the back of the head. He said it was on the front of the head. Then he had the boy's family corroborate that. I assumed I had just made an error and wrote out a new report."

"Without checking the corpse?"

The doctor began walking out of the room, but turned and said over his shoulder, "By then he'd been buried."

Whether O'Hanlon was simply easily persuaded or outright corrupt, I had no way of knowing. But I'd never met a doctor so willing to be second-guessed.

From the morgue, I made my way over to Williamsburg. The sequence of events the night Huber died had always been vague. John may have arranged to pick up his brother at his office and accompany him to the family home. He might have knocked him out then, turned on the gas, and later made sure he'd be the one who discovered him—just in case there were any loose ends that needed attending to. The note found with the body simply said, "Tell Mother I'm sorry." William could have written that for a thousand reasons, and at any time. But I couldn't imagine what John's motive would have been. Or how he could convince a police sergeant to cover up the crime. Perhaps the wound really was on the forehead.

I was at the Carleton by seven, renewing acquaintances and whatnot. Huber came in a while later and we sat down at a table. I decided to play my hand close.

"Have you learned anything?" he asked.

"I was hoping to learn something from you," I said.

"What do you mean?"

"How did you meet Sanford Osborne?"

"I knew there was something odd about that."

"About what?"

"He telephoned me, about a week ago. We met for lunch. He said the people at Sovereign felt this 'problem'—that's the word he used—this problem could be dealt with quietly. And he suspected my family probably felt the same way. I told him that of course we didn't want William's name to be stained. Then he suggested that I go to William's office and pull any of the recent Sovereign policies I saw."

"How recent?"

"Beginning last December. I told him I would, but it might be a couple days before I got out there. He said it needed to be sooner. So I told him I might have a friend who could get them. I asked what we were to do with the files and he said he'd pick them up. And that I should have my friend call him when he had them. Then I went up to the office and telephoned Sally. She agreed to go over right away and get them and then to call Osborne."

"Did she get them?" I asked.

"It was a couple days before I got ahold of her again. She told me she had gotten the files, and phoned Osborne, but he never showed up to get them. She asked me what she should do with them and I told her to burn them."

"Burn them?"

"Well, I assumed the purpose in taking them was to destroy them. And by then, I'd read of Osborne's death. Was he really involved in some scheme?"

"Osborne? It looks like it," I said.

"Actually, I meant William."

"Well, I can't think of another explanation. He seems to have written policies he knew were fraudulent. What he thought would transpire later, I don't know. Maybe he just thought they were for people who couldn't get insurance otherwise."

"Yes, I'm sure it was something like that. Even so, it would look bad."

"There's something else I wanted to ask you. How well do you know the Marquisees?"

"I know about Mrs. Marquisee, if that's what you mean."

"But both William and your father had dealings with her husband."

"We knew them in the past. I remember the two of them visiting the house long ago. Since then, I'm sure father has done some business with him, and that's probably how William got him as a client."

"But you wouldn't know why Mrs. Marquisee would kill herself?"

"No. Though I remember hearing they didn't get on well. Mr. and Mrs. Marquisee, I mean. But I don't know if there's really anything to that."

"I don't suppose you'd know if she gambled."

"No, I'd have no idea," he said. "Is that all? I should be going."

"There is one other thing. It seems there was some mix up with the report on William's autopsy. The first one indicated the wound was on the back of the head."

"Did it? But then it was corrected." He stood up and looked at his watch. "I really need to be going. You can call me if there's anything else."

Then he left for his parents' and I telephoned the Koestlers and asked for Sally. She was out. I decided to see if I could get into the Frauenverein on the chance she was there. Mrs. Demming was downstairs and greeted me.

"Did you come to pick up Emmie?" she asked.

"Emmie?"

"Oh, dear. Did I let the cat out of the bag?"

"That's all right, I'm used to Emmie's surprises."

We went upstairs and I saw Sally at a table with some other girls. Mrs. Demming led me up to a room off the mezzanine that looked like a bookkeeping department. Emmie was there working an adding machine.

"Oh, hello, Harry. I won't be finished here until eight."

"Shall I await you downstairs?"

"Yes, all right."

As I left her, I saw the "bartender" who had identified Demming as meeting with Osborne at the saloon on First Avenue manning the faro bank. I went down and pried Sally away from her friends and we sat at another table.

"I was just speaking to John," I said.

"Yes? About what?"

"About your visit to William's office."

"I was afraid that's why you were at the house last night."

"Did you destroy the files?"

"Yes. John said I should."

"How is it the girl at Huber's office didn't recognize you?"

"Why would she? I just waited until I saw Mr. Huber go off somewhere. I told her I was from the insurance company."

"And then you called Osborne?"

"Yes. He seemed relieved and told me to keep them until he came to meet me."

"Meet you where?"

"At a friend's house," she said.

"Where was this friend's house?"

"Here in Williamsburg," she said. When it was obvious that hadn't satisfied me, she added, "On Rush Street. But it had nothing to do with them. It was just a convenient place to meet."

"Is it a green house?"

"Yes, how did you know that?"

"Just a guess," I said. "But Osborne never came?"

"No. Then John told me that Osborne was dead and that I should burn the files. But that would have taken forever, so I just put them in the trash."

"Did you look at them first?"

"Yes, when I took them. John had said to take anything with Sovereign after last December first."

"But you didn't notice the names on the policies?"

"No, I was doing it as quickly as possible."

"How many do you think there were?"

"I don't know, eight or nine—less than a dozen."

Emmie came down and joined us. She mentioned she had seen a Koestler on a list of Smith alumnae. Sally confirmed it was her stepmother.

"She's disappointed in me for not wanting to go off to school. But I really can't see the use."

On the way home, I told Emmie all about the autopsy report and Sally being the one who picked up the files in Huber's office. Just before we went up to the apartment Emmie asked if I had told Elizabeth I'd be late.

"No, I didn't think to. Why?"

"Well, I think she may have had dinner waiting for you. I told her how much you enjoyed her cooking. I hope she isn't upset."

Emmie's hope was in vain. I tried apologizing for my faux pas. But it was not in Elizabeth's nature to forgive freely.

"Oh, you can eat it cold," she snapped.

"Elizabeth, Harry didn't mean to offend you," Emmie tried consoling her.

"You aren't any better. You both are treating me like a pariah. You think I've done something, and you haven't even told me what it is. I can understand him not trusting me, but you've known me for years. You really are unfair, Emmie."

Emmie began leading me toward the door.

"Maybe you should go for a walk, Harry."

"Will you be all right, Emmie?"

"She gets this way. Catamenia," she whispered.

"Catamenia?" I asked.

"The curse, you yap," Elizabeth clarified.

I went for a walk. I found my way to a saloon on Atlantic Avenue I'd visited before, but it lacked the camaraderie of the Carleton. After about an hour of listening to fellows complain about their jobs, their wives, and Roosevelt's mess in the Philippines, I went home to see if the storm had subsided. Emmie and Elizabeth were sitting on the settee speaking in whispers.

"I'm sorry I called you a yap, Harry."

"Oh, that's all right."

Then I went off to the bedroom. Emmie came in about half an hour later.

"Tomorrow Elizabeth will go with you to see Mrs. Warner," Emmie announced.

"Tomorrow?"

"I told her what happened. She insists on showing us she wasn't involved in this."

"Why can't you take her up there?"

"I have my job, Harry."

"Have you learned anything yet?"

"Yes. I've learned I never want to be a bookkeeper. But I think I may know how to find out our mystery gentleman's name."

"How?"

"I'm not at liberty to say just yet."

"Be careful, Emmie."

"Don't worry, Harry," she assured me. "You'd better get to sleep dear, you're catching an early train tomorrow."

"I hate early trains."

"But this way you'll be back Thursday morning. I telephoned and checked the times. You can catch the early train tomorrow morning, meet with Mrs. Warner in the afternoon, and then catch the night train home."

"Travel by two unpleasant trains with a severely sarcastic woman suffering from catamenia. Just to meet with an eccentric who dreams about homicide. If you don't mind, Emmie, I'll plan my next excursion myself."

"All right, Harry."

The next morning, I called Ratigan from the station and told him about the autopsy report and Sally's taking the files. Then Elizabeth and I boarded the Empire State Express. We spent the morning alternately dozing and reading and Elizabeth proved herself a reasonably pleasant traveling companion. About one, when the rush was over, we went to the café car for lunch.

"You know, if you had any questions about my doings," Elizabeth began, "all you had to do was ask."

"Tibbitts hadn't painted a very flattering picture. And I found it odd that you were living out in Williamsburg. Whose idea was it for you to move out there?"

"Tibbitts's, of course. He wanted to give you the illusion I had some connection to this case you're investigating."

"Why?"

"He wanted me to keep an eye on you. And I suppose he assumed the more you suspected me, the more I would see of you. Something like that."

"Did he tell you why he wanted you to keep an eye on me?"

"No, our relationship is purely for his convenience. He did me a favor, as I suspect you know. But had I known the price of it, I wouldn't have accepted. He's a man devoid of human emotion."

I took that to mean he was a man Elizabeth wasn't able to manipulate. It was about three when we got off the train in Fulton. We hired a carriage and arrived at the Warners' sometime before five. Old Mr. Warner greeted us, this time offering a choice of weaponry to do in his son with. When I declined, he directed us to the house.

"What a peculiar sense of humor," Elizabeth commented.

"And he's just the prologue," I told her.

Mrs. Warner was at her station in the kitchen, and welcomed us in her usual friendly manner. At first, she mistook Elizabeth for Emmie. A natural mistake, excepting that Elizabeth was several inches taller, and very blonde. She served us some tea and biscuits.

"I'm so glad you stopped in—we don't get many visitors here. Certainly not like New York."

We agreed it wasn't. Then we all prattled on a bit, until Elizabeth cleared her throat. I brought the conversation back around to Mrs. Warner's homicidal plans for her husband, and her various visitors.

"You see, what we wanted to ascertain, Mrs. Warner...," I tried.

"He wants to ask you if I am the woman who visited you with this plan," Elizabeth said.

"Oh, you are much like her," Mrs. Warner said. "Let me see." Then she went and got her eyeglasses. "Yes, I suppose you are. Aren't you?"

"No, I am not, you silly fool!" Elizabeth explained.

"But Mrs. Warner, you weren't wearing your eyeglasses when you met this woman, were you?" I asked.

"No, why would I be?"

"Yes, exactly," I said. "Perhaps we might try another approach. Suppose you sit facing the other direction, while Miss Custis speaks to you. Then you only have her voice to go by."

After several minutes of this, I asked Mrs. Warner the verdict.

"No, I would say it's not the same lady. But she

sounds very like her. And she does have that temper. You really shouldn't let things upset you so, dear."

Elizabeth apologized and we had another round of tea and biscuits.

"Do you have plans to return to New York, Mrs. Warner?" I asked.

"If we're sure it's safe. At least, I want to. Dickie would rather stay here and tinker. But I worry about his father."

With good reason. Elizabeth and I went back to Fulton and had dinner.

"Should I be relieved that that bedlamite has cleared me?"

"That bedlamite is the only person who seems able to identify the mystery lady. So I would say yes."

"Then you no longer suspect me?"

"No, we can forget about that," I said. "But I do need to ask you one question. When I alluded to the takeover at Sovereign Monday evening, you realized what I was talking about immediately, didn't you?"

"Of course, wasn't I meant to?" she asked.

"Well, yes. But who was it you telephoned with the news later that evening?"

"It suddenly occurred to me we would want to cover our short position. I called our stock broker."

"Who exactly is 'we' in this context?"

"Emmie and I, and I presume you. Don't you ever talk to your wife?"

"Frequently, I just rarely learn anything. I wonder how we did."

"Quite well, I imagine."

"I didn't even know we had the resources to make such a wager."

"I suppose that's why Emmie wished to keep it from you."

"She's really a wealthy heiress?"

"Frankly, I have not been made privy to the source of her funds. But I would guess she came by it through her own efforts."

"Yes, no doubt," I agreed. "That's what worries me."

17

Thursday morning, April the 25th, Elizabeth and I arrived home in time to have breakfast with Emmie. We told her Mrs. Warner's verdict and ours was a happy home. Emmie and I arranged to meet for lunch and then I went in to see Ratigan. He was on the telephone when I arrived, but motioned me into his office a little while later. I told him about my meeting with the Koestlers and the second trip to the Warners'.

"Koestler was the name I came up with," he said. "He was shorting heavily, then last week he started covering. And then went long in a big way. He timed it perfectly."

He handed me a sheet that had various dates and the number of shares in each transaction.

"That's probably not complete. He was using several brokers."

"Were there any other notable names on the list?"

"The fellows who always have their ears to the ground. But there were dozens in on it. Probably everyone who knew. Except you, of course," he smiled.

"Well, I was mistaken on that point. It turns out we *had* shorted it, or rather, my wife had."

"Your wife? She takes care of the finances?"

I didn't like his tone. First I was a sap for not having shorted the stock, now I was because my wife had.

"Have you found out anything about John Huber?" I asked.

"Nothing worth bringing up. Do you really think he's mixed up in this?"

"I can't figure that out. Maybe the doctor did just make a mistake."

"But then there's the episode with the girl picking up the files," he said. "That's quite a coincidence. George Koestler is making a big play for Sovereign while his daughter is involved in a scheme to defraud it."

"I think she and Huber were just naïve, trying to protect the memory of William."

"But you can't be sure they've told you the truth."

"No, I can't," I agreed. "Have you learned anything else about Osborne?"

"He left the office abruptly on Friday morning—that was the 12th. He didn't return until after one o'clock. Then a while later he left again, his brother-in-law, Donigan, going with him."

"I was there, in the Claims Department, Friday afternoon and didn't see either of them. When did Donigan and Mrs. Osborne leave for Cincinnati?"

"That evening," Ratigan said. "And Mrs. Barclay and her sister left the next day for Europe, and Anna Farrell disappeared about the same time. Maybe Osborne was warning them Friday morning?"

"That seems reasonable. Maybe all your sniffing around spooked him."

"You didn't call us about Osborne until Saturday afternoon. Maybe it was just your own sniffing around."

"Maybe," I said. "But I really hadn't done that much sniffing around Sovereign's offices before then. And why did he send his own wife out of town?"

"Could the warning have come the other way around? Maybe one of the widows warned him. Had you been sniffing around them?"

"No, but my wife had." I explained about Emmie's

recent charitable work with the Widows Aid Society.

"Sounds like you're married to a loose cannon," he observed.

"It feels that way."

I then told him what John Huber had said about the Marquisees' marital problems.

"That fits with what we learned from the neighbors. But if it was like that, why'd she kill herself?"

"You mean, why not just do him in? Maybe she thought she'd get caught."

"Still not a reason to kill herself."

I had to admit he was right, but I didn't have a better explanation. I walked down to the Bureau and handed Keegan the list of Koestler's trades.

"I suppose you already knew about it," I said.

"Not in this detail. How'd you get this?"

"Ratigan, over at Newcome's. Koestler seems to have timed things particularly well."

I went into our office and found a telephone message from Koestler marked urgent. I phoned him and he instructed me to report to his office at Sovereign. When I arrived, he kept me waiting for twenty minutes.

"I thought you were going to stay in contact," he said.

"I needed to check something out of town."

"What did you learn?"

"Nothing, really. Just eliminated a suspect."

"Well, try to have this wrapped up before the 30th. That's next Tuesday. There'll be another board meeting and we need to lay out all the facts then."

I assured him I would make every effort to do so. Then I went down to see the fellow who'd replaced Osborne. He hadn't been able to find the policies on Marquisee and Warner.

"Any idea where they could be?"

"Not really, unless they were simply misfiled. I have a girl looking for them."

"What about those two agents, on the cards for Warner and Marquisee?"

"You were right, they knew nothing about those policies."

I went out and saw Donigan at his desk.

"I was wondering, just when was it Osborne asked you to take your sister out of town?"

"That Friday we left."

"But what time of day?"

He looked at me as if he were waiting for me to answer for him. I could see why he depended on nepotism for his employment.

"It was Friday evening," he finally answered.

"But you were both out Friday afternoon."

"Yes, that's right. After lunch sometime, he said to me, 'We need to go.' I figured he had something he didn't want to tell me here. We both went out to Brooklyn to his place, and that's when he told Ellen and me."

"And then you left on an evening train?"

"Yeah, me and her and the two kids."

I went off to meet Emmie for lunch and recounted the morning's events, and the various theories.

"I don't think the scenario whereby one of the widows warned Osborne is plausible, Harry."

"No, it does seem rather unlikely," I agreed. "Anna Farrell is too callous to bother warning anyone else, and Mrs. Barclay too dimwitted. Osborne must have gone off to warn them, and then had his wife leave town. Possibly it only occurred to him later that she might be in danger."

"But why did he wait until the following Tuesday to notify Mrs. Warner?"

We puzzled over that while we ate.

"There seems only one likely explanation, Emmie. Osborne didn't know about Mrs. Warner on Friday."

"Which means he wasn't one of the conspirators," she said. "But perhaps was protecting someone?"

"His brother-in-law. Why else did he leave town as well? Mrs. Osborne could have taken the train herself."

"Then, after they had left, Osborne spotted the cards that had been changed. He realized there were more people involved than Donigan had told him."

"Yes," I said. "Osborne must not have found them until the next Monday. He hid them under his blotter, then met with John Huber and arranged to have the Sovereign files removed from William's office. And on Tuesday went off to warn Mrs. Warner and Mrs. Marquisee, not knowing the latter was already dead. I'd better call Tibbitts."

"I suppose I won't be able to come along this time."

"I'm afraid not, Emmie."

I phoned Tibbitts and he started to thank me for the stock tip.

"There's something else. I think we may finally have someone worth arresting." I told him about Donigan and we arranged to meet in the lobby of the Sovereign building.

He arrived with another fellow and the three of us went upstairs. Donigan wasn't in.

"I'm afraid I may have tipped him," I admitted.

"You think he left town?"

"Maybe."

"Where's he live?" Tibbitts asked.

I got his address from the department head and then Tibbitts and I went off, leaving his colleague behind in case Donigan returned. When we came upon his boarding house on West 24th Street, there was a fellow on the stoop.

"Have you seen Mr. Donigan recently?" I asked.

"Just left."

"You wouldn't know where?"

"Maybe to catch a train."

"Did he say so?"

"No, but he was carrying a bag, and headed to the river."

"The North River?"

"That's right."

"How long ago?" Tibbitts asked.

"Ten minutes maybe."

"The ferries, at 23rd Street," Tibbitts said.

Tibbitts found a cab and about five minutes later we were at the 23rd Street terminal. The boats left there for the Erie and Pennsylvania depots in Jersey City. A boat for the Erie was just pulling out into the river. Tibbitts suggested we get on the next boat—bound for the Pennsylvania—which was leaving just a few minutes later. We looked over the boat but Donigan wasn't on it. When our boat landed we ran up to the Erie depot, about a half mile up from the Pennsylvania's. But the train that the Erie boat had met was gone. It was the 2:45 express to points west, including Cincinnati.

"I guess this is my fault," I said.

"You never know when a bird will fly," Tibbitts said. "Besides, that train's an express—he can't get off before Binghamton. Let's go over to the office and call someone up there."

We went back across the river and Tibbitts took me to the detective bureau. We composed a long cable to the police in Binghamton and Tibbitts sent it off. The train wouldn't reach Binghamton until almost nine that evening.

"Not much else we can do but wait," Tibbitts said. "I can call you when we find out something."

"There is one other thing," I said. "Remember you said you owed me one?"

"Sure."

"How about releasing Elizabeth Custis?"

"She's free, isn't she?"

"Come on, you know what I mean."

"All right. I can't say she was much use anyway," he said. "Now we're even."

From there I went back to Sovereign to report to Koestler. I told him about Donigan's flight.

"So there were two people here involved?" he asked.

"I don't think Osborne was in on it. He just came upon something that made him realize Donigan had been. Then, out of familial duty, Osborne covered up for him."

"And you're waiting to see if the police in Binghamton can apprehend him?"

"Yes, I'm hoping he'll be able to give us some names."

"Well, remember—it needs to be cleared up by Tuesday."

Back at the Bureau, I gave Keegan the same report. He seemed distracted and barely interested. Then I went back out to the Osbornes' house in Brooklyn. Mrs. Osborne answered the door and led me into her parlor.

"I'm afraid your brother has fled, Mrs. Osborne."

"I see."

"Your husband was covering up for him, wasn't he?"

"I don't see much point in talking about it now."

"Don't you think you owe it to your husband to clear his name?"

"Would that clear his name?"

"I think it would make his actions more understandable."

She didn't see it that way. Evidently, she was more concerned with protecting her brother. I went on back to the apartment, where Elizabeth was once more preparing dinner, and took a nap.

The two of us ate alone again and I told her of my conversation with Tibbitts. She thanked me, but the topic of her subjugation obviously embarrassed her so I recounted the rest of the day's events. It was only then that I realized how little she really knew about the case.

"It seems far too complex," she observed.

"I think the reason is that we aren't simply seeing the unfolding of a single conspiracy. However it started, it evolved by new players acting on it, and exploiting it. Now there are so many intertwined threads unraveling it's almost impossible to follow them."

"Especially since most of your witnesses are dead or gone—or insane."

Emmie came in just before nine and I told her about Donigan. Then we waited. It wasn't until ten o'clock that Tibbitts finally telephoned.

"Donigan's dead. They shot him," he said.

"Who shot him?"

"One of those cops in Binghamton. It sounds like they made a show, held up the train, and he must have realized what was happening. He got off and tried to make a run for it."

"Why would they shoot him?"

"Because we told them to stop the guy."

I hung up and gave the two women the news.

"What fools," Elizabeth said.

"All it would take is one fool," I said.

"Maybe it wasn't so foolish," Emmie said. "Someone certainly benefits."

"Not the cop in Binghamton who pulled the trigger," I pointed out.

"Are the police in Binghamton so incorruptible?" Emmie asked.

Her friend answered with a noise that seemed to indicate skepticism.

"Have you learned anything about debt collection, Emmie?" I asked.

I almost forgot," she said. "I did find something, but it was rather disappointing. It was a list of what appeared to be outstanding debts to Minden. I didn't recognize any of the names, however."

"How many names were there?" I asked.

"Two dozen perhaps. It was the amounts that were notable. One man owes over $13,000."

"I don't suppose you jotted down any of the names?" Elizabeth asked.

"No, I didn't. You need to direct your stratagems elsewhere, Elizabeth."

"Oh, I have other avenues."

"Are you sure no one saw you snooping about, Emmie?" I asked. "Maybe you should give up this job."

"This is our best chance to find the debt collector," she said. "It stands to reason that if someone came up with a scheme to broker gambling debts, they'd approach Minden. I'm certainly not going to give up now, after a week of working that wretched adding machine."

The next morning I went to see Mrs. Osborne. Emmie came with me, and I was glad of it. While we waited in the parlor, we could hear children in the house. It was not Mrs. Osborne who came to us, but a sister. I insisted we speak to Mrs. Osborne. She brought her in and we all sat down. I gave them the sad news about their brother. They spent some time comforting each other. Then Mrs. Osborne looked at me angrily.

"He'd be alive if you'd left him alone," she said.

"Perhaps," Emmie said. "But if you and your husband had taken him to the police when you learned of the scheme, they'd likely both be alive."

"I never knew what it was about. My husband told me nothing, and Gene led me to believe he was covering up for Sanford. It was only on the train back I realized how foolish I'd been. By then he was dead."

It was obvious Mrs. Osborne had nothing else to tell us, so we offered our condolences and left.

"Her husband certainly was an ass," Emmie observed. "If he had told her what he'd learned about her brother, she probably would have agreed that he needed to tell the authorities. By trying to shield her, he just made things worse. You wouldn't be as foolish as that, would you, Harry?"

"No, dear. I'm perfectly willing to turn in your relatives. But keep in mind, Osborne's motives may not have been purely altruistic."

"How do you mean?"

"Well, he secured the position for his brother-in-law, and I'm sure vouched for his character."

"And he would have been held responsible for something he knew nothing about?"

"He would have been at the mercy of his superiors, who may not have been of the merciful sort."

We stopped by the apartment, where the packers were at work. Elizabeth said she would not be preparing dinner so I told Dorothy I would be dining out. Then I went off to see Ratigan and told him about Donigan. From there I went down and gave Koestler the news. He wasn't upset.

"It's probably for the best," he said. "Justice has been done."

I didn't quite believe he cared all that much about justice, and pointed out it would make the investigation that much more difficult.

"Then let's end the investigation right now," he said. "Some things just aren't worth explaining."

He thanked me, and shook my hand. That was to be the end of it. I went out for lunch and then over to the Bureau and told Keegan about Koestler's decision.

"Well, I might have something else for you," he said. "Be in the office tomorrow at nine and be ready to travel."

"For how long?"

"You'll be back Monday."

I asked what it was about, but he wouldn't say. He did, however, tell me to bring along all my notes on the case. I went up to Ratigan's office and asked him to wrap things up, for the second time. I walked around a bit and ended up on the ferry to Williamsburg. I wasn't happy about having to close the case, but I'd adjust. Emmie would be a different matter.

18

When the boat landed in Williamsburg, I wandered over to the Carleton. I joined some fellows playing poker and tried to forget about insurance schemes and stock manipulations. By about the fifth round, I'd achieved my goal. And by the time I went off to meet Emmie I was feeling more than a little chipper. It took some cajoling at the continuous card game before I was granted entrance to the Frauenverein's inner sanctum. One of the ladies made reference to a boiled owl.

Once upstairs, I saw Elizabeth and Edward Howell sitting with Sally and Charlie Sennett. I sat with them while I waited for Emmie. A little later, I may, or may not, have upset someone's drink, but Sennett left soon afterwards. I was relieved when Emmie finally came down. She took one look at me and suggested we go home for the evening. On the way, I told her about Koestler calling things off.

"Well, I suppose he's welcome to do as he wishes," she said.

Her breezy tone troubled me. "Look, Emmie, I don't want you working at that place any longer."

"All right, Harry."

If I hadn't been in the state I was in, I would have recognized that there had to be something behind her ready acquiescence. When we got in I told her about Keegan mentioning a trip.

"How would you like to come along, Emmie?"

"Does it have to do with the case?"

"Apparently—I was told to bring my notes, and that I'd be back Monday."

That was the last I remember of Friday evening. The next morning we breakfasted and left together for the Bureau. Emmie was curious enough to want to find out the nature of the trip and she too was prepared to travel. I sat her down in our room with Little and Cranston and went to talk with Keegan.

"You know how Koestler gained control of Sovereign," Keegan began.

"By playing the movements of the share price."

"Yes, exactly," Keegan confirmed. "And as you noticed, his trades were well-timed."

"As if he knew ahead of time what would be revealed."

"Yes. For instance, he was shorting shares even before we heard about the problem. And he shorted another large block just before that fellow Osborne's body was found. Maybe this was just coincidence. There are other reasons the share price was vulnerable. Nonetheless, there are those on Sovereign's board who have concerns."

"What is it you want me to do?" I asked.

"I've arranged to meet with several of the board members on Sunday. Some will be coming down from Boston and so I've offered to host the meeting at my cottage in Newport. We have the dates of Koestler's trades. What I want you to do is to prepare a scenario of the events involved, back to the very beginning. Then we'll be able to compare the two."

"All right. But why would I need to travel to do that?"

"Well, there's a second part to this, and it's more in the nature of a favor. The cottage is closed up, and I don't want to call the agent there to have him open it. What I'd like you to do is to take the morning train, and you can work on your scenario on the way. You'll arrive in Wickford about three and then take the boat to Newport. You'll need to pick up food and wine. I have to stay in town this evening and will be catching a late train. Tomorrow the others will be arriving about one."

I'd never been invited to Newport before, so I accepted. He gave me a detailed list of victuals to purchase, and just then Emmie entered the room.

"So where are we off to?" she asked.

I hadn't mentioned the possibility of Emmie accompanying me to Keegan yet.

"Oh, you're welcome to come along, my dear," Keegan said. "But I'm afraid you might have to play hostess."

I could see Emmie wasn't keen on that idea, so I added that it would be at his cottage in Newport. We didn't get many invitations of the sort, and the novelty was enough to sway her. After we left Keegan, I explained the nature of the mission. We caught the ten o'clock train and settled in to the task. It took quite a bit of time to turn my notes into discrete events, and then to choose the ones relevant to Keegan's purpose.

Our chronology had just over a dozen entries:

January 2nd: Policy written on Barclay by Huber.

February 12th: Barclay found dead.

February 14th: Claim on policy received at Sovereign, okayed for payment.

February 28th: Policy written on Farrell.

March 1st: Policy written on Marquisee.

March 5th: Policy written on Warner.

March 13th: Huber takes his life.

March 15th: Perkins begins looking at Huber's policies.

March 22nd: Farrell found dead.

March 25th: Claim made on Farrell policy, payment delayed pending inquiry.

April 2nd: Redfield contacts Keegan.

April 3rd: Investigation begun.

April 13th: Mrs. Barclay sets sail with her sister. Anna Farrell disappears.

April 14th: Mrs. Marquisee found dead.

April 16th: The Warners leave New York.

April 17th: Osborne's body found in river, fell off ferry previous afternoon.

April 25th: Donigan flees, is killed by police.

We went into the dining car for lunch and looked it over again.

"This doesn't really tell us anything, Harry."

"Oh, I wouldn't say that. It tells us there was something going on. And that both Barclay and Farrell were probably murdered."

"Because they died so soon after the policies were written?"

"Yes. They succeeded with Barclay, and if they had waited another month or two, they might have gotten away with Farrell as well. It was only Huber's suicide that got Perkins to start paying attention. But he would have forgotten about it at some point."

"Why do you think they waited until after Barclay's claim was paid to sign up others? To make sure they could get away with it?"

"I imagine so," I said. "Maybe that's when they got Donigan involved, figuring he could get the other claims approved without eliciting notice."

"But Huber's death put the kibosh on it," Emmie said. "I suppose we can infer then that his death was unplanned—even if it was murder."

"Why do you say murder?"

"Well, if he wrote these other policies after Barclay was dead, he had to know the nature of the scheme. Which makes the idea he was misled unlikely."

"Yes. Though he may have been doing it under duress."

"Perhaps."

After lunch Emmie insisted we tally all the other clues we had, for our own purposes.

"Well, we know Mrs. Warner gambled," I began. "And Mrs. Barclay, according to Elizabeth."

"And Mrs. Marquisee."

"That was just a rumor I heard."

"Don't you remember, Harry? I told you last night. One of my colleagues at the Frauenverein told me she had seen Mrs. Marquisee there several times."

"I don't remember much of last night. Did you tell me anything else?"

"Not that I recall."

"Was there anything you didn't tell me?"

"That's rather vague, Harry."

"I was just curious why you were so willing to leave your post as bookkeeper."

"Oh. Well, the truth is, I was fired. Bannon saw me in his office."

"That was taking a risk, Emmie. You told me you'd be careful."

"Well, he didn't become violent or anything. He just suggested I wasn't cut out for the work."

"Amenable fellow. But back to the matter at hand:

William Huber also gambled. And according to one rumor, he owed a lot."

"And Mr. Minden also seems connected."

"Yes, his places feature prominently. And there's one other clue there."

"What's that?"

"His faro banker played the part of the bartender who claimed Demming was on First Avenue. Given Tibbitts's part in that, I assume he's under the influence of Minden, at least indirectly."

"I imagine," Emmie said, "that Minden, or Bannon, might have come up with the scheme to clear up debts."

"I don't think so. It would have been too risky for them to have involved themselves. The cops and the politicians can be bribed to turn a blind eye to all the poolrooms and casinos. But murder is something else entirely."

"Well, what if they found one of the debtors was in a position to orchestrate the scheme?"

"Huber?"

"He may not be the innocent you seem to believe he is, Harry."

"I guess that's possible."

"And perhaps Donigan was also a debtor, and among the other debtors there's someone willing to perform the murders to clear his own debt."

"Yes, all that's possible."

"And then there's Koestler," she said. "Mr. Keegan seems to suspect he's involved."

"I'm not sure what exactly Keegan suspects. These pillars of finance seem to stand for all sorts of behavior, things anyone else would find reprehensible. Then every once in a while they jump on one fellow as having gone beyond the pale. But his machinations rarely seem any different from those of his accusers."

"But setting aside all that," Emmie said, "Koestler will have gained the most?"

"Yes. And there are other clues that point his way. For instance, his daughter was a childhood friend of Huber's, which means he must have lived in Williamsburg and known the Hubers. And perhaps the Marquisees as well."

"That might just mean he heard about the scheme and exploited it."

"There's something else. The description Mrs. Warner gave of her visitor, the woman we thought might be Elizabeth, also describes Sally's stepmother, the current Mrs. Koestler."

"She's that young?"

"Maybe thirty-five. But she speaks in the same manner. And just as caustically. And remember, Mrs. Warner sees people as a blur."

We arrived in Newport about four and immediately set to work procuring provisions. Then we hired a wagon and went off to locate Keegan's cottage. It's important to keep in mind that a cottage in Newport is not the three-room affair you might be picturing. It was more like a large suburban house. But compared to the opulence of the local mansions, it ranked as just a cottage.

We prepared the house, ate a simple supper, and then ventured forth. Emmie's taste ran toward the lively, so of course we had to go down to the harbor. We entered the most congenial-looking place on the Long Wharf. But just as I had hoped, five minutes was enough to satisfy even Emmie. It's an established fact that saloons near naval stations attract excessively rambunctious crowds and the White Swan was no exception to the rule. I suggested we go back to the cottage and open a bottle of Keegan's wine. But before I could convince Emmie, we ran into Mr. Cobb, the oysterman whose wagon we had hired that afternoon. He was headed to a party at one of the lesser mansions to replenish stocks. Emmie insisted we accompany him, for the ride, she said.

I was not at all surprised that when we arrived at our destination she broached the idea of entering the house uninvited. She was not dissuaded by my protests, or Mr. Cobb's. But when she failed to coax the kitchen help into collusion, and had eyed the large fellow manning the main entrance, she agreed something could be said for a quiet evening at Keegan's.

He showed up about 9:30 the next morning and immediately put us to work preparing for the luncheon party. I knew Keegan was an epicure, but until then I never knew he could cook. The three gentlemen meeting Keegan arrived with their wives about one, two having come by yacht from Boston. Emmie and I served, and ate our own meal in the kitchen. I can't say I enjoyed playing servant, but the meal was a noteworthy one. Afterwards, the women separated themselves and I sat with the men to give my synopsis. While I recited my chronology, Keegan interjected with the dates of Koestler's trades. He must have learned of others not on Ratigan's list, as there were many more trades, through several brokers. But there were several sizeable trades that were notably well-informed, or at least appeared so. Though Koestler was already short Sovereign before the first of the year, his first large trade occurred on March 15th. This was just two days after Huber's death, and simultaneous with Perkins' initial investigation of Huber's policies. Then there was

another trade on March 22nd, the day Farrell's body was found, and a very large one on the 25th, the day Perkins learned of the claim. The day Keegan was called in, April 2nd, there was another large trade. The last, and largest, occurred on the morning Osborne's body was found.

"Well, we can assume he had someone working on the inside at Sovereign," one gentleman pointed out. They all agreed this was a certainty, but saw nothing particularly improper about it.

"Yes, apparently whenever this Perkins fellow raised his concerns with his superiors, one of them was giving Koestler that information promptly," Keegan summarized. "That would explain all the trades but the one on March 22nd. Can you come up with an explanation for that, Reese?"

"No, I don't see how anyone would know the significance of Farrell's death until Perkins saw the claim."

Emmie had just entered with a tray of port and immediately joined the conversation. "Perhaps Mr. Perkins was the informer, and he recalled seeing the name when he looked through Huber's files."

Our guests seemed rather taken aback. "Ah, my wife, gentlemen."

"I imagine Mrs. Reese may be right," Keegan said. "But perhaps she'd like to join the ladies?"

She left the room, but I doubted sincerely she'd gone off to commiserate with the other wives about the servant problem.

"It is possible Perkins read about the death in the morning papers and remembered the name. But in my notes, I have that he learned of it when the claim came in."

"But is that simply what *he* told you?" gentleman number two asked.

"Yes, that's true," I admitted.

"Let me ask you this, Reese," gentleman number three began, "does it seem plausible Koestler was involved in this episode? Or merely an observer? You see the distinction?"

"If I needed to guess, I would say he merely made use of it. But there are some curious coincidences."

As I was speaking, Emmie had entered with a tray of coffee. In leaving, she passed near me and whispered, but loud enough for the others to hear, "Don't forget to mention Mrs. Koestler."

Of course I had no intention of mentioning Mrs. Koestler. That would necessitate explaining all about Mrs. Warner and was a matter of pure conjecture.

"What about Mrs. Koestler?" Keegan asked.

"It's nothing, really. One of Emmie's fancies," I said. Then I forced her bodily from the room.

The meeting broke up not long afterward and the gentlemen and their wives went off to enjoy the afternoon on their yachts. Emmie and I spent the remainder of the afternoon cleaning up while Keegan read the newspapers.

"Why didn't you tell them, Harry?"

"What was I going to say, Emmie? 'I think Mrs. Koestler may be part of a ring that murdered men for their life insurance. I base this on the fact she bears an auditory resemblance to a woman described by an eccentric I met on a dairy farm.' I believe that's known as slander."

"I suppose you're right," she conceded.

But that evening, when we sat down to another meal of Keegan's preparation, Emmie told him all about it.

"I think Harry was right to leave it unmentioned, my dear."

"Well, we'll know one way or another soon enough," Emmie said.

"I hope you aren't planning to kidnap Mrs. Koestler and take her to the Warners' farm," I pleaded.

"Oh, it won't require anything as silly as that," she said.

The evening was spent with me reading and Emmie teaching Keegan how to cheat at cards. On the train back to New York the next day, they formed a syndicate and found some others to play bridge with. The firm's financial statement revealed just how lethal a team they were.

19

We arrived at the apartment shortly after five Sunday afternoon and found it empty—not just empty of people, but completely empty.

"I didn't realize they'd finish the move this quickly," Emmie said.

Then we trooped down to the Margaret. Just before we were to enter the new apartment, Emmie stopped.

"Harry, there's something I haven't told you."

I was back in Emmie-land. "There's much you haven't told me, isn't there, Emmie?"

"Yes, perhaps. But I'm referring to something in particular. Do you remember admonishing Dorothy about her little amorous adventure?"

"Did I admonish her?"

"Well, you made some reference to intentions," she said. "You see, it seems both Dorothy and Jim wanted desperately to marry."

"Emmie, I'm sure it's a romance worthy of Laura Jean herself, but is there a reason I should hear about it out in the hall?"

"If you'll allow me to finish. As I said, they wanted desperately to marry, but they had nowhere in which to set up house."

"They're living in our new apartment?"

"In the servant's room," Emmie clarified. "We had no use for it."

"All right, Emmie. Can we go in now?"

We did so, and found ourselves amidst chaos. Elizabeth and Dorothy were unpacking boxes and Jim was moving things about as instructed. Emmie introduced him to me and he seemed like a nice fellow. Not someone I'd invite to share my home, but a nice fellow. Emmie and I put our things away, and when we came out, Jim was leaving for his work on the night shift at the Atlantic Avenue ferry docks.

"There's something I'd like to speak with you about, Mr. Reese. Tomorrow, when all the women aren't about."

His tone wasn't particularly friendly now. I wouldn't call it menacing exactly, but leaning in that direction.

"Oh, dear," Elizabeth said, looking after him.

"Oh, dear?" I asked.

"I'm afraid young Jim is anxious about leaving his wife here with you home."

"Me? He'd never even met me before."

"No, but he has read your literary effort. And that was quite enough."

"What literary effort?"

"Your little notebook listing the attributes and abilities of various young women."

"I'd forgotten about that." This was the bit of reading I had prepared for Emmie's snooping eyes. I'd lost track of it a couple weeks back and assumed Emmie had it.

"You really shouldn't have left that about, Harry," Emmie said.

"Well, you can explain to Dorothy that it was simply a joke," I suggested.

"How would I know that, Harry?"

"Mr. Bagley also seemed to have been concerned by it," Elizabeth said.

"Who on earth is Mr. Bagley?" I asked.

"Your new janitor."

"Oh, yes. How did he come by it?"

"Well, when the movers came across it, they wanted to share it."

"Where is it now?" I asked.

"Safe with me," Elizabeth said. "You need no longer worry about it."

"May I have it back?"

"I think not. It may come in useful."

"Is there anyone who's not party to it?"

"Well, I don't believe Mrs. Warner's seen it."

"Mrs. Warner?"

"Oh, has Mrs. Warner arrived?" Emmie interjected.

"Yes, yesterday evening," Elizabeth answered. "She wasn't feeling well, so she's lying down in your third bedroom."

"Emmie, why is Mrs. Warner resting in our third bedroom?"

"I asked her to come down for a visit. We'll need her to be nearby if she's to help us spot the mystery woman. And you couldn't expect her to stay alone over on First Avenue."

"It's convenient we rented such a large apartment," I said.

"Yes, isn't it, dear?"

Emmie suggested I dine out that evening, as things were so disordered at home. I concurred and went off to the Carleton. There weren't many of the fellows about when I arrived, but a few stopped in during the course of the evening. I never found the opportunity to mention the expansion of my harem, but someone else brought up the subject of William Huber's love life.

"I never learned his secret," one fellow confessed. "I

mean, he was good looking, I guess, but it was something more. He knew how to charm them."

"Yes, but he worked at it," another fellow pointed out. "I overheard him on the telephone to a girl once. You should have heard him crooning, 'Oh, Eliizaaa, I miss you so.' Seemed a lot to suffer for a woman."

"Was the name definitely Eliza?" I asked.

"No, more like Eliizaaa," he smiled.

"Did you hear her last name?"

"No, he seemed past that point with her. Why are you so interested in the girl?"

"I think I might know her," I said.

"Well, if you have to speak to her like that to get anywhere, I'd stay away."

We all laughed, and the only thing else I learned is that the conversation on the phone had taken place quite a while back, the previous fall, he thought. Even in my partially inebriated state, the idea that the Eliza Huber was wooing was Eliza Barclay seemed unlikely. At the time, she was carrying on with Howell. And from what I'd heard of Huber, he was quite the Lothario, and probably had the roll of names well covered. Eliza wasn't particularly unusual.

When I went into our room that night, after first mistaking Mrs. Warner's for ours, I told Emmie about the episode.

"Harry, that changes everything. It means Huber had a reason for wanting Barclay dead."

"You're jumping to the conclusion it's the same Eliza."

"And you're resisting the idea because it would mean Huber wasn't as innocent as you imagined."

"Well, there's also the fact Huber's dead, and Koestler has taken us off the case."

But I knew she was right, and by morning I had to agree there could be something to it.

"I have to go in to the Bureau, Emmie. But I suppose you could try to check the story," I said.

"I'm glad you agree, Harry. I thought I might see if I can find out anything from the Howells' maid, or the people who work in the building."

"We tried that, remember?"

"Yes, but I thought I'd come with greater resources this time. What sort of bribe do you think they'd be expecting?"

"We already know the doorman is bribable, but the price for intimate details may run high."

"I'm willing to pay what the market demands. But I'll need Huber's photograph."

I found it for her, then we joined our guests for breakfast.

"You know, it smells just like the country here," Mrs. Warner observed.

"A farm, you mean," Elizabeth said. "Harry rented an apartment across from those giant stables."

"Elizabeth dear, the residents of the Margaret request that you not refer to the Riding and Driving Club as stables," Emmie told her friend. "It usually isn't this bad, but they had their big show last weekend. The cleaning up seems to be taking some time."

There wasn't a lot of eating after that. Emmie and I agreed to meet for lunch and then I went in to the Bureau. Little and Cranston felt our tome was ready for the printer and I was in no position to argue the point. Cranston was heading to a new job in Boston the next morning and they had planned a dinner to celebrate the event. We spent the morning on some final preparations and sent off our manuscript just before noon. Then I went to meet Emmie.

"Did the doorman come across?"

"He did, but I don't think it was worth the price. I gave him ten dollars, and showed him the photo, and he assured me he'd seen Huber there. But I had a feeling that he would have told me anything he thought I wanted to hear."

"Yes, that's always a danger."

"I had better luck with the maid."

"So she was bribable, after all?"

"Well, in her defense, she hadn't been paid in two weeks."

"So you brought the account up-to-date?"

"Yes. She was quite grateful. I showed her the photograph and she also said he'd been by repeatedly. But I was more careful this time and didn't mention his name, and she was able to provide it."

"How many times had she seen him?"

"Oh, at least a dozen, she thought. Starting back before Christmas and until February sometime. But she wasn't sure when the last visit occurred."

"You know, Emmie, this explains Huber's connection to Barclay's wife, but it muddles up everything else."

"How so? You mean, how did he meet the other women?"

"Yes, that. And also the story of Howell having an affair with Eliza."

"I asked the maid if that story was true and she said it was. She hadn't noticed anything between them, but Mrs. Howell herself told her about it. Harry, I think this also means you misread Huber's character. He was in on it from the beginning."

"I made a judgment about his character based on the fact he killed himself, apparently out of guilt. If he was ruthless enough to be behind the scheme, why would he feel guilty for it?"

"So you agree it wasn't suicide," she said.

"I didn't say that."

"But what about the head wound? What if it *was* on the back of the head?"

"Oh, I don't doubt it was."

"Well, then...."

"Well, then, what?" I asked.

"Oh, never mind." Then she changed the subject. "What are your plans for the afternoon?"

"An outing. We're celebrating the completion of our magnum opus. What will you be doing?"

"Trying to speak with Edward Howell."

Then she was off and I went to join the boys for another trip out to Aqueduct. It was the first warm day of spring, so it was impossible not to have a good time. We didn't arrive back at the Bureau until late in the day. There was a message from Emmie, so I telephoned her.

"Did Howell tell you anything?" I asked.

"He didn't seem to be in at his firm. No one was sure if he was just working out of the office or was out of town. One gentleman suggested that if he wasn't at home in the evening, I should check at the Harvard Club. I thought maybe you could do that this evening, Harry."

"I'm afraid I've allowed my membership to lapse, Emmie."

"Oh, you don't need to be a member. Just tell them Edward Howell expects you and they'll lead you right to him. I won't be home until late—Elizabeth and I are going to an alumnae event."

"What about Mrs. Warner?"

"Oh, we'll bring her along. It's a friendly crowd."

The boys and I went out to a saloon, and then on to Sherry's. The only thing that marred the event was Little getting all bleary-eyed. When we had said our good-byes, I went off to the Howells' apartment. The maid told me Howell hadn't arrived home and she had no idea when to expect him. So I went to the Harvard Club and did as Emmie instructed.

"I'm afraid Mr. Howell hasn't arrived. Perhaps you'd like to wait in the guest parlor?"

"Yes, please."

As it happened, some friend of Howell's overheard this exchange and said he would escort me. He was an affable fellow and by the time we approached the room where guests were relegated we'd established a certain rapport.

"Oh, you don't want to wait in here. Why not come upstairs and play a few hands of cards?" he suggested.

I agreed. He brought me up and introduced me to a couple of his friends and we sat down to play. Unfortunately, it wasn't until we'd been playing for an hour that I learned we were playing for money. The subject had been spoken of in a sort of Cambridge cant, as gambling was strictly against the rules. Eventually, I managed to turn the conversation to Howell, but it was only the one fellow who knew him well.

"I've noticed he's been sampling the cuisine while his wife's away. I saw him with another blonde just last week. That makes two since his wife set sail."

I alluded to Howell's exile at the club and this fellow confirmed he had stayed there for a period earlier in the year. But then he was cautioned by his partner, an older fellow, that perhaps a little discretion was in order, and the subject was changed to the coming boating season. They all were avid yachters, as was Howell, I was told. It wasn't a conversation I was able to contribute to with any firsthand knowledge, but I did tell the story of Emmie's uncle. He had been a yachter who faked his death at sea—a lake, really. Once I assured them he wasn't a Harvard man, they wanted to hear all about it. By the end of the evening, my partner and I had lost twenty-eight dollars each. And this was real money, since I was no longer on an expense account. Thankfully, my drinks were charged to Howell.

It was past midnight when I arrived home. Emmie and friends had gotten in just before me.

"Did you talk to Howell, Harry?"

"No, and his friends took me for twenty-eight dollars. But they were very pleasant about it."

"Well, we learned something."

"Some juicy gossip about those not in attendance?"

"Perhaps I didn't mention it, but Mrs. Koestler is on the alumnae committee."

"Did you say hello?" I asked.

"Emmie did much more than say hello," Elizabeth explained.

"It was necessary to draw her into conversation for our little test," Emmie said.

"And to draw her ire, apparently," Elizabeth added.

"Well, we needed Mrs. Warner to hear her when she was somewhat irritated. It didn't occur to me she would be that sensitive on the subject."

"I see, you wanted Mrs. Warner to tell if she was the mystery woman," I said. "And was she, Mrs. Warner?"

"No, she seemed a little too old, and even too angry.

Is there something about college that makes girls angry?"

"It's difficult to say," I said. "Some believe it's simply that angry girls are attracted to college. What was the subject that upset Mrs. Koestler?"

"I merely asked if there were many drawbacks to having an older husband," Emmie said. "Her reply was rather intemperate."

"Yes, but most amusing. The woman is a master at a certain form of rhetoric," Elizabeth agreed. "But I managed to assuage her anger."

"How was that achieved?" I asked.

"Well, I told her Emmie was a little soft in the head, of course."

"And she accepted that explanation?"

"Oh, readily. But it was Mrs. Warner who genuinely saved the situation."

"Dare I ask how?"

"By stating her views on a wife's prerogative to murder her husband. Though there was no formal vote, I would say the motion was easily carried."

"So a good time was had by all," I said.

"Yes, even Mrs. Koestler had a smile by the end of the evening," Elizabeth said. "And I was roundly thanked for bringing the night's entertainment in the form of my two companions."

Soon after, Emmie and I went in to bed.

"I'm sorry your test didn't work, dear," I said.

"Oh, I didn't really think it was Mrs. Koestler, but I felt we had to find out."

"Is Mrs. Warner returning to the farm tomorrow?"

"Of course not, Harry. We still haven't found the mystery woman."

"Well, given we now know Huber was involved with

Mrs. Barclay, perhaps it was her, or more likely her sister."

"Why her sister? Mrs. Barclay is tall and blonde, isn't she?"

"Yes," I said. "But it's rather difficult imagining someone of her mentality executing a plan like this. What did Mrs. Howell look like?"

"Not terribly tall, though taller than Mrs. Warner or myself. She had brown hair, almost chestnut. And she was pleasant enough, but I suppose I could picture her speaking crossly to Mrs. Warner."

"Perhaps Mrs. Barclay presented herself, and her sister acted the ventriloquist?"

"Or perhaps they visited serially and Mrs. Warner conflated the two?"

"It's too bad they're in Europe," I said.

"Oh, I expect they may be returning soon."

"What does that mean?"

"I'd rather not say for now. Good night, Harry."

20

The next morning at the Bureau, Little and I began packing up our research material. This was Wednesday, May 1st. Keegan sent for me about ten o'clock and told me Koestler wanted to see me right away. I walked over to Sovereign and found Koestler looking decidedly disturbed.

"Sally is missing," he said.

"For how long?" I asked.

"She never came home Monday night. No one's seen her since."

"Have you called the police?"

"Yes, of course. Yesterday. But I want you to look into it, too. It must have something to do with this whole affair."

"You don't think she might have just eloped? Or maybe is having a fling?"

"She wouldn't leave that way. She may be a little wild, but she's a decent girl."

"But what's the connection to the scheme?"

"Maybe there isn't one. Or maybe someone wants some leverage with me. Whoever was behind this scheme doesn't know what my intentions are. Maybe he wants to make sure I don't pursue it any further. You agree others must have been involved?"

"Yes, absolutely," I said. "I just don't know who exactly."

"I think one of them wants to make sure I leave him alone."

"So he abducted your daughter?"

"Yes, or had someone else do it."

"Then it's ironic. You dropped the investigation last week, and only are calling me back because Sally's missing."

"Yes, but he didn't know that."

"No, I guess not. Can I call in Newcome's again?"

"Of course. If you need to hire someone, go somewhere, whatever, just do it. And keep me abreast."

"Can you see if you can get Tibbitts assigned to it?"

"Remind me, who's Tibbitts?"

"The police detective."

"Who should I call?"

"Someone in the central office. I don't know how these things work. But when you're running a big company, the police are supposed to jump for you."

"Yes, all right. I'll do that right away."

"There's something else I learned last week. I hadn't thought it worth mentioning before." I told him about Osborne's request for Huber's files and John Huber relaying the request to Sally. "I assumed it was all about helping a dead friend who'd been foolish. But now it looks like Huber may have been more directly involved."

"That doesn't mean Sally knew anything about it."

"No, certainly not. Still, since this involves her directly now, I thought I should tell you about it."

I had him provide me a list of names of Sally's friends and also suggested he contact his wife and let her know I'd be calling at some point. Then I left him and went up to see Ratigan.

"This is the third time you've opened this case," he pointed out.

"Maybe the third time's the charm," I said. Then I

told him about Sally's disappearance and what else her father had told me.

"And Koestler thinks some big gambling interest has tempted away his daughter in order to convince him to drop the case? You don't get to be a big gambling interest if you're that much of an idiot."

"Well, it's a little hard to swallow. Maybe there's some other connection he's decided to keep to himself. But I do think that in finding her, we might solve the rest of it."

"Does he care about that?"

"No, not really. The first thing is to find the girl."

"Any ideas?"

"Yes, she's been hanging out with a gambler named Charlie Sennett." I described him, and related what Demming had said about him.

"Any idea where he lives?"

"No, but I'd guess over on that side of the river. I hadn't really thought him important until now. All I really know is that he has an unsavory reputation and knows a lot about women's fashions."

"I guess that's useful knowledge in some lines. All right, I'll put some fellows on Sennett, and check with her friends."

"The cops are supposedly working on this too, but I haven't spoken with them yet."

"Well, we won't count on them for much."

I used his telephone to call John Huber and he agreed to meet me for lunch at Delmonico's. When I arrived, he was waiting for me.

"What's so important? Is it about William?"

"No. Sally Koestler seems to be missing."

"Sally? Since when?"

"She never came home Monday night."

"Frankly, I'm surprised that's a notable event." His initial sound of concern had melted away.

"So you think she's just having some little adventure."

"If that's the euphemism you want to use."

"You don't paint a very flattering picture of the girl. You seemed friendly the evening I spent with the two of you."

"Yes, and the next evening she would have been just as friendly with someone else. I'm sorry. I shouldn't speak ill of her."

"But you don't think this is something to worry about?"

"Well, you met her. Were you surprised to hear that one night she didn't make it home?"

"It's two nights now," I said. "Look, even if it is just a lark, it would still be a good idea to find her, don't you agree?"

"I might, but I very much doubt she would."

"Let's follow our own instincts. When was the last time you saw her?"

"That evening with you. I've telephoned her a few times, but she seems to have a full social calendar."

"She did pick up those files."

"Yes, but that was all arranged over the phone. We didn't meet."

"So I don't suppose you'd have any idea where she might be, or who she might be with?"

"No, not really."

"Do you know Charlie Sennett?"

"No. One of her dance partners?"

"Yes, it would seem so." His denial seemed sincere.

"There is one thing I've learned about William."

"What's that?"

"He was having an affair with Eliza Barclay, the wife of the first victim in the insurance scheme."

"William saw a lot of women."

"Well, it was during the time the policy on Barclay was written, and when he died. And that was before the other policies were written."

"I see what you're getting at," he said. "I'm not sure I believe it."

"But you're not sure you don't?"

"No, unfortunately, I'm not sure I don't."

"Last week, when I brought up the bruise on William's head, you implied the final autopsy report was correct. You're sure it was on his forehead?"

"Well, I wasn't sure. I found him on the floor, dragged him to a window and called the hospital. I also called my father. The doctor and my father arrived about the same time. The doctor pronounced William dead. Then my father called the police. A sergeant came by just a little while later. I explained what I had found and then they took William away. The next day, the police sergeant read my statement back to me. I had thought I had said the wound was on the back of the head, but he had it on the forehead. He said that's how he remembered it, and my father also. Well, I'd been pretty upset, and I didn't think it mattered much."

"It's quite a coincidence that both you and the coroner made the same mistake."

"Yes. But that's what happened."

"When you mentioned the note William left, you said it was on a slip. As if it was torn from a larger piece of paper?"

"Perhaps. Yes."

He looked at his watch and prepared to leave, but I stopped him. "There's something else. Sally told me that on the night of your birthday, your father became upset when your mother asked why William hadn't come home with him."

"I don't remember that. But it may just be I'm used to it. It doesn't take much to upset him these days."

I thanked him and went up to the Bureau. There was a telephone message from Tibbitts waiting for me. He had been directed to take over the investigation of Sally's disappearance and asked me to meet him at his office. When I arrived, he told me all that had been done so far was to check with Sally's friends. I asked if Charlie Sennett was on the list.

"No. So the first order of business is to find this Sennett?" he asked.

"Yes. I saw him with Sally Koestler on the other side of the river."

"Where'd you see him?"

"Ah, do I need to be precise?"

"What?"

"Well, I wouldn't want to get any friends in trouble. It was a gambling parlor, of sorts."

"Look, we aren't going to raid the place."

"Do you know the Hotel Le Roy?"

"Minden's place?"

"Yes, one of them. Well, beside it...."

"Yeah, I know. The German ladies' clubhouse, what-do-you-call-it."

"Yes, I saw Sennett in there a couple times with Sally Koestler."

"Well, let's start there."

We took the cross-town horse trolley down to the Grand Street ferry and on the other side rode the L down Broadway to the Le Roy. We went up to the second floor. Tibbitts spoke to a man and then we waited. About five minute later, Bannon entered through what turned out to be a steel door. Apparently, another route to the Frauen-verein next door.

"We're looking for a fellow named Charlie Sennett," Tibbitts said. "Know him?"

"Yeah, he's a small-time bookmaker."

"Seen him today?"

"No, I see him in the evenings sometimes."

"Any idea where he lives?"

"He's local, Brooklyn somewhere."

"Will you check around? This is important. People are squawking."

"About what?" Bannon asked.

"Do you want to tell him?" Tibbitts asked me.

I couldn't see why not, so I told him about Sally Koestler. He agreed to telephone if he learned anything and we left the Le Roy.

"Where to next?" I asked.

"We'll see what they know at the Lee Avenue station. This is their beat."

We walked a half dozen blocks to the precinct house and Tibbitts stopped outside.

"Listen, they aren't going to like us in their territory. Just go along with whatever they say."

We went in and Tibbitts spoke to a sergeant.

"I need to speak with the captain," was his only response. He came back with his superior.

"What were you doing at the Le Roy?" the captain asked Tibbitts.

"Sorry, just trying to save time. I've got people breathing down my neck."

"From now on, when you cross into the 59th, you check with me."

"All right, I will," Tibbitts assured him.

"Tell him what you know," the captain told his sergeant and then left us.

"Not much," the sergeant said. "Sennett is a bookie. He circulates around these parts."

"Where's he live?"

"Grand, past Union. Check with Stagg Street."

We left and I remembered the green house on Rush Street, all of a block and a half from the precinct station. I told Tibbitts about it and we walked over. He knocked and a woman opened the door and looked us over.

"Police," Tibbitts said.

"We're paid up."

"Not with me. We're looking for a girl, Sally Koestler. Short, blonde."

"Never seen her."

"We'll see for ourselves."

We went upstairs and Tibbitts roused the occupants in a manner that can only be described as abrupt. There were a lot of high-pitched protests and we found three girls and two men. But Sally wasn't there.

"That wasn't what I expected," I said as we left. "She seemed a little wild, but...."

"You never know with people," Tibbitts said. "But it doesn't mean she was working there. She may have met someone there. You can be sure they'd rent a room to anyone needing a place."

It seemed odd it could operate so close to the police station, but I kept that observation to myself.

We walked over to Stagg Street. "I should tell you, I'm persona non grata at the Stagg Street station. Sergeant Corwin suggested it might be better if I avoided his precinct."

"I know Corwin. We'll be okay," he reassured me.

When we arrived, Tibbitts asked for Corwin and was told he was out. Then we spoke with another sergeant named McNamara. We explained Sennett's connection and he agreed the expedient thing to do was to go up to his house on Grand Street.

"Do you know much about him?" Tibbitts asked as we walked.

"Sure, he's been around for a few years," McNamara said. "He's smarter than most, knows how to keep his nose clean."

"Did you ever see him with a little blonde?"

"No. But that doesn't mean much."

Sennett was out. The landlady was against letting us in but eventually she had to relent and led us into Sennett's sitting room. There were some drawers open in the bedroom, but nothing made it clear if he had skipped or just happened to be out.

"When was the last time you saw him?" McNamara asked the landlady.

"Just a while ago."

"Did he leave with anything?"

She thought for a bit and then said, "No."

"Did he ever bring a young blonde girl around?" Tibbitts asked.

"Mr. Sennett never brought any girl around."

McNamara grunted and we walked back to the station.

"Do you think she really saw him today?" I asked.

"Who knows? We can find out when he was last around," McNamara said. "But if he heard you're looking for him, we won't be seeing much of Sennett for a while."

"If he isn't with the girl, why bother hiding?" I asked.

"All he knows is some cops want to find him. He can probably think of a dozen reasons why."

"Would he be out at Aqueduct this afternoon?"

"No, he works the street. Makes the rounds of the saloons, has all his regulars."

As we neared the precinct house, I saw Corwin and a patrolman lead Jacob Marquisee inside.

"That was Marquisee they just took inside," I said.

"You know Marquisee?" McNamara asked.

"I was looking into his wife's suicide," I said.

"Or murder," McNamara corrected. "The daughter came in this morning and swore out a complaint against her father."

We went in and McNamara led us to Corwin. He eyed me warily, but greeted Tibbitts with a slight bit of warmth.

"What's the story?" Tibbitts asked.

"The daughter came in this morning. Marquisee was living with her. Last night he said something about his wife getting her due. I already had my eye on him."

"You suspected he had killed her?" I asked.

"I suspected something. There were marks on her neck."

"That didn't come out at the hearing," I observed.

"It wasn't what killed her. The doctor thought she might have made them herself, when the arsenic took hold of her," he clarified. "You still think this is connected to the Huber kid?"

"I'm sure of it. Huber wrote a policy on Marquisee that Marquisee never knew about."

"So the wife had a big policy put on her husband, then planned to kill him," Corwin said. "Only he found out and killed her first. Nice match, those two."

"She gambled, and I think the money from the policy was meant to cover a debt she had. Huber had something to do with setting up that scheme. I don't suppose you ever had any question his death was a suicide?"

"It looked like it, even had the note. I don't see how anyone else could have arranged it. Not many people would sit still waiting for the gas to kill them."

"But wasn't there a head wound?" I asked.

"Just a bump on the head. The doctor said it looked like his head hit the desk when the gas rendered him unconscious."

"Both John Huber and the doctor remembered it differently. They both noted it was on the back of the head. At least until you convinced them otherwise."

"His father swore it was on his forehead."

"What did you see?"

"I left it to the doctor."

"But then told him he was wrong."

"Conrad Huber carries a lot of weight. I've known him a long time."

There didn't seem to be much point in pursuing it further, so I dropped the matter. Tibbitts told him about Sally being missing and her association with Sennett. And I told him of the connection between Sally and Huber. Then I gave them my number at the apartment and went on home. From there I telephoned Ratigan and told him what I'd learned about Sennett.

"I have a couple fellows looking into him. They've

basically found out what you know, but no sign of him yet. And I have a couple others looking into who else the girl might be with. Did Huber tell you anything?"

"He said he hadn't seen her in weeks and I believed him. He's soft on the girl, but I think he runs a little slow for her."

"That's what we heard. Frankly, some of her 'friends' didn't speak too highly of her conduct."

"Did any of them know about Sennett?"

"At least one girl mentioned him. But it sounds like he might have been one among many."

I told him I'd check again after visiting Mrs. Koestler. While I was cleaning up and putting on a new collar Emmie came in. I told her about Sally, the search for Sennett, and Marquisee's arrest. She was especially attentive during my description of the house of assignation.

"It's a relief that you've been put back on the case, Harry. But you don't think Sally's disappearance has anything to do with the scheme, do you?"

"It probably does. But you sound disappointed. Doesn't it fit into your solution?"

"No, it doesn't. How did you know I had a solution in mind?"

"Just an educated guess." Then I told her about my conversations with John Huber and Sergeant Corwin about William's head wound. She smiled. "I take it that fits in with your scenario?"

"Yes," she confessed. "What are you getting duded up for?"

"I'm to pay a visit to Mrs. Koestler."

"Perhaps I should go with you?"

"After your performance the other evening? That

would seem ill advised. I'm hoping she hasn't connected the two of us."

"Oh, she knows you're my husband."

"Well, I'd rather not remind her of it."

I made it to the Koestlers' at about 4:30. The girl showed me into the study, where Mrs. Koestler was attending to some correspondence. All she had to do was look at me and I was ready to head back out the door. A dog rushed in and began sniffing me enthusiastically.

"You must have stepped in something," my hostess conjectured. She led the dog out of the room and then we both sat down.

"I imagine you're here about Sally," she said.

"Yes, Mr. Koestler has asked me to look into it. He seems to think she may have gone off with a man."

"Have you narrowed it down yet?"

"Narrowed it down?"

"Well, I believe she had quite a number of... let's say, 'admirers.'"

"You don't think much of her conduct, I take it."

"Do you?"

"That's not really my place."

"No, I suppose not. What was it you wanted to know?"

"Well, you already told me some. I had the impression your husband was somewhat blind to Sally's behavior."

"Yes, he was. I hope now it's clear to him. And you assumed I would have a better sense of where the truth lies?"

"Yes, exactly. But I also hoped you might have some idea who she could be with, and perhaps weren't comfortable making the supposition to your husband."

"That's very astute of you. But I'm afraid I have no idea," she said. "When her father and I first married, Sally and I were fairly close. But in the past two or three years I seem to have made her all the more rebellious. I suppose it's my fault, for wanting her to be someone she isn't. So she felt she had to make a point of asserting herself. Now I try not to intrude. She's still very close to her father."

"Do you think it's likely she's with a man?"

"Yes. She's a simple girl, and it would be easy for someone to turn her head."

"I had gotten that idea. Is there someplace she might have wanted to go to? Someplace she vacationed?"

"She's fond of the ocean, and actually a good sailor. But I don't know if that helps much."

"Do you own a boat?"

"No, but many of her friends' families do."

"Do you think she could have had much money with her?"

"No, not much. Her father doesn't spoil her, and she's not a greedy child."

I thanked her and she wished me luck. The girl led me back out and on the stoop I encountered Elizabeth. I imagine I looked a little shocked to see her. As she walked by she whispered that she'd been invited to tea.

21

When I arrived home, I told Emmie about my conference with Mrs. Koestler.

"Do you think Sally would elope with Sennett?" she asked.

"I wouldn't have thought so. She just seems out for a bit of fun."

"But he'd have a motive to persuade her," Emmie said. "Her father's money."

"I doubt Sennett's foolish enough to think Koestler is going to welcome him to the family. If he's with Sally, I'd imagine he just sees it as a bit of fun, too. Maybe not realizing how seriously her father would take it."

"Or maybe she isn't with Sennett at all."

"Yes, there's a good chance of that," I agreed.

"You don't suppose Sally could be the mystery woman?"

"She's blonde enough, but nothing like tall."

"But maybe Mrs. Warner just didn't realize where she was standing. If someone is standing closer to you, they look taller."

"Assuming Mrs. Warner's eyesight is particularly poor."

"Well, she mistook Elizabeth for me when she arrived."

"And at the farm," I said. "But Sally also lacks the cultured tone and the caustic tongue."

"Yes, but I'll wager you she can do a pretty convincing imitation of her stepmother."

"Probably a safe bet," I agreed. "What was Elizabeth doing over at the Koestlers'?"

"I have no idea."

That evening, Emmie treated the household to dinner and the theatre. Mrs. Warner wanted to see Clyde Fitch's *Sapho*, which had received much notoriety the year before because of the insinuated infidelities of its heroine. But Elizabeth, who'd seen the play, explained it was exceedingly dull and not half as scandalous as the Old Testament. So we went instead to the vaudeville at the Orpheum, where Rose Coghlan was headlining. It was a diverse lineup. Mrs. Warner particularly enjoyed the elephant act.

At seven the next morning, Koestler phoned and told me to get over to his house immediately. That was Thursday, May 2nd. I hurried over and was told the maid had found a satchel on the porch that morning. It was empty, but for a letter addressed to Koestler. It was written in clumsy block printing and it said:

Koestler,
We have your daughter. No harm will come to her provided you follow our instructions precisely.
You are to put $25,000 in this bag. It must be in ten and twenty dollar bills, and you must use this bag. The money must be delivered by a woman. And she must not be accompanied or followed. Any interference will mean the worst for your daughter.
At 10 a.m. you will receive a telephone call with further instructions.
Remember, you are being watched.

"Have you called the police?" I asked.

"No, I didn't want to take the chance."

"Will you pay it?"

"Of course—I have no choice."

"Do you have someone to deliver it?"

He looked over at his wife.

"Of course I will, dear," she said. But there was a decided lack of enthusiasm.

"Can you think of anyone else?" he asked.

"Well, I have a houseguest who might be willing. I believe Mrs. Koestler knows her. Elizabeth Custis."

She nodded and her husband asked me to summon her. I telephoned the apartment and Emmie answered. She refused to wake Elizabeth until I told her what it was about. But, of course, that was that.

"I'll be right over, Harry."

I hung up and turned to the others. "Miss Custis was unavailable, but my wife is willing to take on the task. In the meantime, I should at least call in Newcome's."

"All right," Koestler agreed. "But don't have them come to the house. In case it is being watched."

I phoned Ratigan and he agreed to round up half a dozen operatives. But until we knew where the meeting would be, he would keep them near him.

"You'll need to call the cops, too," Ratigan said. "We may need them."

I hung up and told this to Koestler and he agreed to let me call Tibbitts.

"Call me as soon as you hear," he said. "We can't depend on the local precincts not to muck it up, but I can have a few boys ready."

Then Emmie was shown into the room, with the dog nipping at her heels.

"Alfred's attracted to scents," Mrs. Koestler said.

"He's particularly fond of Violettes Russes."

"Alfred?" Emmie asked, looking at Mr. Koestler.

"The dog—he's named for Lord Tennyson."

I gave Emmie the ransom note to read and Koestler began making arrangements with his bank.

"I'll go and get it myself," he said. "At least I'll be doing something."

"All right," I agreed. "I'll go along, too."

He had a carriage waiting. We arrived at the bank well before opening time, but were immediately ushered into an office. The cash was assembled and placed in the bag and we got back to the house about half past nine.

"I have an idea, Harry," Emmie said. "We can use Alfred."

"Use him for what?" Koestler asked.

"Well, as Mrs. Koestler mentioned, he is very fond of a particular perfume. We did a little test while you were out. Not even raw meat distracted him from it."

"You're suggesting wearing this perfume and having the dog follow you?" I asked.

"No, what good would that do? There's only one reason they supplied the bag. Think of the green goods game, Harry."

"The green goods game?" Mrs. Koestler asked.

"Yes, where the gang is selling counterfeit money, but it really isn't counterfeit," Emmie explained. "They put the real bills into a bag like this one, and then, when the mark's attention is diverted, switch it with an identical bag that contains nothing but old newspapers. That's why they sent this brightly colored red bag—so it would be conspicuous."

"I see what you have in mind, Emmie. If we scent the bag, the dog won't be misled by a duplicate."

"Yes, but it's the money we want to follow. We should scent that. You could lead Alfred, Harry."

Emmie opened the bag and doused the cash. The phone rang at exactly ten and I answered it.

"Do you have the money?"

"Yes, here in your bag."

"And a girl to deliver it?"

"Yes."

"All right then. She is to go alone to Jenning's Café. It's on Front Street, near Moore."

"Down by Whitehall?"

"Right. She is to take a table there and await further instructions. And she's not to be followed."

I immediately phoned Ratigan. He said he would have his men down there, ready to follow any red satchels. Next I phoned Tibbitts.

"They must be planning to use the crowds at the ferry terminal to get away," he said.

"I guess that would make sense."

"I'm going to bet on it. I'll put my boys at all the opposite points. When he gets off, we'll follow him from there."

I explained to Emmie how to get to Jenning's Café.

"You'll leave the house first, Emmie. But go up in the car, cross the bridge, and come back down."

"Wouldn't it be quicker to take a ferry, Harry?"

"Yes, I'll leave the house after you and take the boat from Hamilton Avenue. That way I should get there before you. But just to make sure, take your time. Try not to get there before eleven. If you see me hovering about, be careful not to look long."

"All right, but remember, Alfred will go for the bag as soon as I'm near."

She went off and then I left about five minutes later. I had some difficulty waking Alfred when the boat docked, but we were on Whitehall at about 10:45. Ten minutes later I strolled up to Front Street and walked past the café, then waited about a block down.

I saw Emmie come up. She was a little early so made a show of losing her direction. Or perhaps she was genuinely lost. Either way, she went into the café just at eleven. About five minutes went by and then a fellow emerged with the red bag. He went down Moore to South Street and then entered a saloon. I positioned myself just north of it. A minute later he emerged, but instead of going south, toward the ferries, he walked right past me. The dog took no notice. Then another fellow emerged, with an identical bag, and he was followed by two more. All with identical bags and each headed in a different direction. But it wasn't until a fellow emerged from a chandler's, next door to the saloon, that Alfred took an interest.

I assumed Ratigan's men would be following the bags, so I let Alfred lead me after our man down to the ferry landing. We boarded the Jersey Central boat that went over to the depot in Jersey City. Tibbitts would have a man at the other end, but he'd be looking for the red satchel, and making a point of remaining inconspicuous. It was then I realized Emmie was standing beside me.

"Which is our man, Harry?"

"He's at the far side, in a grey jacket."

"With the seaman's cap?"

"Yes."

"They were very clever, weren't they?"

"You saw the four bags leave the saloon?"

"Yes. And then I saw you head to the ferry," she said.

"I suppose now that we have him spotted, Alfred will be more of a hindrance than a help."

"It would seem so, but he might come in useful again before this is over."

We arrived in time for the express to Philadelphia. Our man got on and we followed. Unfortunately, the conductor found Alfred objectionable and he and I were sent to the baggage car. There was only one stop before Philadelphia, in Elizabeth. I made out a note addressed to Tibbitts, telling him what train we were on and giving him a description of the man we were following. When we arrived in Elizabeth, just at noon, I got off the train with Alfred and handed the message to a cop. Along with a dollar, just to be safe. He wasn't insulted.

Then I saw our man, followed by Emmie, getting on another train. I followed. Once more into the baggage car. We were on a local that ran along the Jersey shore. I made out another note to Tibbitts and at Perth Amboy gave it to another cop with another dollar. Alfred spent the next half hour inspecting the contents of the car. At Little Silver, just past Red Bank, I saw Emmie on the platform.

"He's just ahead there, Harry."

He had left the station and was headed down a quiet road. There was no way for us to follow him without him noticing, so we waited until he was far ahead. Alfred seemed to be following a scent, but every now and again was distracted by some noise in the field beside the road. Eventually, we saw a few buildings ahead, and we seemed to be entering a small village. Alfred led us to a cottage, and then laid down.

"I hope this means he's inside, and not simply that Alfred has had a long day," Emmie said.

"We need to get help, Emmie. But first let's get out of sight."

We went up and around a corner to a spot where we could watch the cottage without being obvious.

"Shall I stay and watch, Harry?"

"No, I'll wait here with our friend, you see what you can find in the way of law enforcement."

I saw Emmie go off and enter a store of some sort, and then cross the street to another building. Then she returned.

"I telephoned the local police, Harry. But they seemed rather thick-headed."

"Are they coming?"

"Yes. But only after I told them there was a reward. Is there a reward, Harry?"

"Not that I'm aware of. Perhaps they'll be satisfied in being virtuous."

"Yes, perhaps."

It was a good hour before they appeared, three men in a wagon. I told the chief about the kidnapping and the possibility there was a wealthy captive. Just then two men emerged from the house. One was the man we'd been following, the other was Charlie Sennett. Alfred ran straight for them and the cops and I followed.

"Where's the girl?" I asked.

"She isn't here," Sennett said. "Leave us alone or you'll never see her."

"You tell us where she is, or you'll never see tomorrow," the chief said.

"We never had her," the other fellow confessed.

We found the money stuffed in their various pockets. Then we looked through the cottage. But there was no sign of Sally. We all got into the wagon and rode into

Red Bank. I wired the news to Tibbitts, Ratigan, and Koestler. But since our prisoners had decided not to talk, there was little to do until Tibbitts showed up about six. He arranged to have the money and suspects turned over to him and then we all headed back to Jersey City on the train—Alfred, myself, and the money he refused to be separated from riding in the baggage car. From the depot, Emmie and I took the ferry back to Brooklyn.

"Sergeant Tibbitts seemed to think that man was telling the truth," she said. "That they never kidnapped Sally."

"Perhaps Sennett just heard she was missing and thought he'd take a chance. If you hadn't thought of the dog, Emmie, they would have made it. That was very good."

"Thank you, Harry. But we still wasted the entire day."

"Well, maybe not. Sennett may know something about Sally."

"Why do you think that?"

"Would he bother to arrange such an involved scheme if he wasn't sure she wouldn't be returning? What if she had just turned up at home this morning? All these preparations would have been wasted. And if he was caught, he'd be facing a few years in Sing Sing."

"Yes, I see what you mean."

"He must have seen it as a one-time chance to clean up and go off to a new life somewhere."

It was after nine when we arrived at the Koestlers. I told them what had transpired and asked if they had heard anything on Sally.

"No, nothing," Koestler said.

I set the money on a chair and Alfred jumped up and laid on it. Then Emmie and I went home. First thing the next morning, I went over the bridge to check in with Ratigan.

"We've learned one thing: Sally Koestler was very active socially. Every one of her friends mentioned some other friend, and they all remember her with some other fellow. A few saw her with Sennett. Some remember her with William Huber a while back. Apparently that was pretty serious for a while last fall. But she also was seen with older men. We've started to check with her relatives out of town. Angry girls often run to a friendly aunt."

"It's hard to even picture Sally angry, but that's an idea."

"We also have photographs now and can check the stations, steamship lines, etc. But it would help if we had some idea where she might go."

"Apparently she likes the ocean. Sailing particularly. And her stepmother said many of her friends have boats."

"All right, that's something. Anything else?"

"There is one other thing. Would you be able to find out where Eliza Barclay and her sister are right now?"

Ratigan looked back at a stack of notes. "The *Hohenzollern* would have docked in Gibraltar on the 22nd. All right, we can find out."

From his office, I went down to the Bureau. Keegan was in, so I briefed him. Then I phoned Tibbitts and mentioned my theory that Sennett might know something of Sally's whereabouts.

"Yeah," he agreed, "that makes sense. The other fellow is Sennett's brother. He'd been in the green goods game. He just rounded up the boys, that's why they set it up so fast. I'll see what I can find out from Sennett."

I went home for lunch and told Emmie about Sennett's brother being in the green goods business.

"But how is it you're so well informed on the subject?" I asked her.

"Oh, one reads about these things."

Elizabeth and Mrs. Warner joined us. But I noticed Dorothy wasn't about.

"I'm afraid we lost Dorothy, Harry," Emmie said. "Jim felt the situation untenable."

"He was convinced you were deliberately avoiding him," Elizabeth added.

"Avoiding large dockworkers who have grievances is a sort of hobby of mine. I'm quite good at it," I said. "By the way, Elizabeth, do you remember being in the Frauenverein last Friday with Edward Howell?"

"I wasn't with Edward Howell. When I came in he was sitting with Sally Koestler. Then Sennett arrived, and not long after, you came in."

"Do you mean Howell was there with Sally?" Emmie asked.

"Well, only that they were sitting together," Elizabeth said. "At the time, I thought Howell had come looking for me. But I suppose they could have come in together. They did seem to know each other."

"Why do you think they knew each other?" I asked.

"That first night he and I went to the Frauenverein, he knew her name before being introduced. You were there."

"I missed that. Was going there your idea or his?"

"I believe it was his."

"And last Friday, did you leave the two of them together?" I asked.

"Yes, but I thought Sennett had come there with Sally and would be returning."

"What is this Frauenverein you talk about?" Mrs. Warner asked.

"A sort of German Don't Worry Club," Emmie told her. "We must take you sometime."

"Does Howell have a yacht?" I asked Elizabeth.

"He said he had some sort of boat he sails. Why?"

"Apparently Sally has a love of sailing."

"I was told Howell was away on some sort of business," Emmie said.

"But maybe that's just what he led them to believe."

I telephoned Ratigan and asked that he look for Howell, and find out about his boat.

"All right, where will you be?"

"I'm going over to search his apartment," I said.

"I'll send some boys over to help."

22

I hung up and discovered my dutiful wife at my side. We made our way to the Howells' apartment and Emmie introduced me to Mary, the maid.

"I don't suppose you've heard from Mr. Howell?" Emmie asked.

"No, ma'am."

"Well, if you don't mind, we'd like to look around a bit."

"All right, ma'am. I was just putting my things together."

She left us and I led Emmie to the study I had been taken to on my first visit.

"What should we look for, Harry?"

"We'll know when we find it. If you see anything about his boat, give a holler."

There was a large desk and several bookcases. The desk held all sorts of letters, ranging from the personal to the mundane. Then there were files on the family's finances and various legal matters. In the midst of which, Emmie found one on his boat. It included a description, invoices for docking it, travel itineraries, all we'd need.

"We should get this to Ratigan," I said.

"Oh, wait." She handed me a page from the folder. "He sold it a year ago."

"That doesn't mean they aren't on a boat."

There was one last drawer and it was locked.

"Maybe Mary knows where the key is?" I said.

"I'll ask her," Emmie said. She went off to check

with the girl and I began going through the shelves, looking for anything behind books or between pages. Emmie came back armed with a claw hammer.

"I'm afraid Mary has never seen the key," she said.

Then she took her weapon and began hacking the front of the desk with her usual determination, but accompanied by a savagery I'd not seen her exhibit previously. I made a mental note not to leave any claw hammers lying about our own apartment. She eventually had the drawer open, but not without significant damage to the desk and the near total destruction of a lamp that had the poor sense to be nearby. The colorful leaded glass of the shade was scattered about and the noise had gotten the better of Mary's curiosity. She came in and looked at us both.

"I'm afraid the lamp fell, Mary," Emmie told her.

"I'll just clean it up, ma'am."

"Oh, I wouldn't bother about that. You go back to your packing."

"Yes, ma'am."

The drawer held little, and nothing that seemed worth the devastation Emmie had wrought. When I pointed this out, she said, "It's his own fault, Harry. If Howell hadn't misrepresented the contents by locking the drawer, none of this would have happened."

We spent the next half hour going through the rest of the apartment and found nothing.

"It's odd there are so few photographs," Emmie said. "Not even a wedding photo of the Howells."

"Maybe they don't look their best in photographs."

"Or, more likely, she destroyed them due to his philandering."

Not long after, a couple of Ratigan's operatives

showed up. We told them where we had looked already, but they said they'd go over everything again. They seemed surprised when I explained that the destruction in the study was my wife's work. Then Mary came out with a couple bags and put them by the door.

"Mary, if you're looking for a new position, we have a need for a maid," I said.

She looked at me quizzically, and then at Emmie.

"That's already been arranged, Harry."

We went downstairs and I sent the doorman to hire a cab.

"Mary, when exactly was the last time you saw Mr. Howell?"

"Monday. Just after I gave him the telegram."

"What telegram?"

"The one that arrived Saturday evening."

"Why hadn't he seen it before then?" I asked.

"It came to Mrs. Howell, so I put it on her dressing table with the other mail waiting for her. But then I thought it might be important and I ought to bring it to Mr. Howell's attention. But he came in late that night. And I didn't think of it again until Monday morning. That's when I brought it to him. He looked at it and said it seemed like they had made a mistake, it wasn't sent *to* Mrs. Howell, but *from* her. Then he left the table and went into his room. I didn't see him go out."

"Did he pack a bag?"

"I hadn't noticed then, but I believe he must have. Some of his things seem to be gone."

"I don't suppose you saw what was in the telegram? Maybe he left it behind?"

"No, of course I didn't look at it. I think he put it in his pocket."

The cab arrived and Emmie took Mary to her new quarters while I went down to see Ratigan. I told him about the telegram and asked if we could find out anything about it.

"Probably, they log everything. It's just a matter of finding the right person to ask." He made a brief phone call instructing someone to look into it and then a girl came in and handed him a slip of paper. "We've heard from London. The two women left there on the 26th for Liverpool."

"Liverpool? Why would they go to Liverpool?"

"Maybe to catch a boat." He went into another room and came back a minute later. "The *Etruria* sailed on the 27th for New York by way of Queenstown."

"Why would they book a boat to Europe if they didn't plan on staying even a week?"

He began reading from the report he'd been handed. "From Paris, they booked a room in London for three weeks. Then, after they arrived there, Mrs. Howell received a message from her husband and said she needed to return home immediately." He looked up. "At least, that's what she told the hotel."

"I wonder what message he sent her?"

"Maybe that he was planning to leave with Sally Koestler?"

"Why would he do that?" I asked. "Besides, it seems like it wasn't something he'd planned in advance. He got that telegram and skedaddled."

"Maybe he was warning his wife about something, and she was responding to that. It must have occurred to you that this isn't necessarily an elopement. Sally may think that's what it is, but maybe he sees her as a hostage."

"Yes, I had thought of that. But would we even be looking for him if she weren't missing?"

"Well, there's also the chance they see her as a liability. Maybe she knows something."

"I make it a habit to put unpleasant thoughts out of my mind," I confided. Then I handed him Howell's boat file. "I thought it might offer some clues. He sold the boat, but he could have borrowed or rented one. Apparently he's sailed up and down the coast several times."

"All right, I'll start on that."

I used his telephone to call Tibbitts and told him about Howell.

"Do you think Sennett will be any help?" I asked.

"He'll talk, he knows what he's facing. Let's see if he comes up with Howell, too."

Then I told him about the boat idea.

"If I were going to run off and didn't want to be found, I'd use something anonymous," he said. "I'd take a crowded train to a crowded city."

"But maybe the boat was a necessary lure for the girl. I don't think she'd elope with someone just to slink off to a Philadelphia flophouse."

I hung up and then Ratigan took a call.

"That was one of the boys at Howell's. They found something. It sounds like someone was blackmailing Eliza Barclay. I told them you'd be over."

I went back up to the Howells' and was shown a crudely printed letter addressed to Mrs. Barclay:

> *I know your husband was killed. You will receive your claim. I only want a little part of it. I'm sure we can come to an arrangement. I will contact you again.*

They had found it in a book in the Howells' bed-room, but nothing else. I took the letter back down to show Ratigan.

"It must have been from Donigan," he said. "He just made a guess it was murder."

"Maybe he recognized Barclay's name from the bucket shop fiasco. It must have made the papers. Or maybe he was a patron. That combined with the recent policy and the convenient accident was enough to give him the idea that Barclay was murdered for the insurance money."

The girl came in and handed Ratigan another slip.

"The telegram delivered to the Howells' Saturday came from Liverpool. It read: 'Returning on *Etruria* New York on fourth.'"

"Why would that have caused him to run off?" I asked.

"Maybe he hated his wife. It happens. I've checked, the boat's due in tomorrow, late afternoon or evening."

"But she was only coming because he wired her."

"Maybe he wasn't the one who wired her. Is there anyone else who might have?"

Unfortunately, someone else did come to mind, but I was damned if I was going to say as much to Ratigan. "I'll have to think about that."

I headed home and found Emmie making dinner. We were alone. Mrs. Warner had decided to move back to First Avenue, Elizabeth was out, and Mary had asked leave to visit her sister in Paterson.

"Have you learned anything, Harry?"

"Yes, several things. For instance, why you seemed to think Mrs. Barclay and her sister might be returning soon."

"So it worked? I knew it was a good idea."

"I'm sure you did, Emmie. But do you mind telling me just what you wired?"

"Well, it was the day you came back from visiting Mrs. Warner with Elizabeth. I'd been thinking of the likelihood of the mystery woman being either Mrs. Barclay or possibly Mrs. Howell. So I thought I'd find out."

"How did you know they were in London?"

"Elizabeth. Apparently Howell had told her his wife's plans for an extended stay there."

"What exactly did your wire say?"

"'Situation dire. Return soon.'"

"How did you sign it?"

"I didn't. You see, even if I had guessed correctly they were involved, I couldn't be sure who else was."

"Well, you succeeded in inducing their return. But there were consequences you didn't anticipate."

"Howell's wire was from his wife?"

"Yes, they arrive tomorrow. It seems as soon as he heard about her return, he took off with Sally."

"I was afraid that's what it was," she said. "But he must have already planned to leave before she returned. He told Elizabeth he didn't want to see his wife again."

"I imagine most married men in dalliances say something similar," I said. "Might I ask, Emmie, that before you embark on any other initiatives, we consult?"

"All right, Harry. At least as far as this case is concerned. But you need to confide in me as well. What else did you learn today?"

I told her of the note and our suspicion it was from Donigan.

"But why would she leave that lying about?" Emmie asked.

"I was thinking about it on the way home. I wonder if she saved it to return the favor. Donigan thought it was anonymous, but who else would have seen the claim and could assure her it would be approved?"

"So she wanted to be able to blackmail him in turn. We *are* speaking of Mrs. Howell, I assume?"

"Yes. I think she has to be the one behind it. Dear Eliza isn't clever enough, and Edward Howell's reaction to her telegram would seem to indicate he's either running from her or following her instructions."

"Couldn't William Huber have been running the scheme? At least in the beginning?"

"If he was running it, he had no reason for suicide at all. I think it had to be someone else's plan. Mrs. Howell wanted to extract her sister from the sorry match to Barclay. Eliza was willing to go along. Huber must have taken some convincing, but he wanted Eliza."

"Why are you sure Huber would require convincing?"

"Well, if for no other reason, because of the suspicion it would arouse. And apparently it did, hence the note from Donigan."

"But having gotten away with it, why not just give some money to Donigan and be done with it? Why the other policies?"

"Greed. I imagine they thought Donigan could be used to their advantage. If they had someone on the inside who could make sure the claims went through, they could do the same thing again. I think she convinced Donigan he would make more money by joining the conspiracy than from blackmail."

"That still leaves the question of how they got the names of Missuses Farrell, Warner, and Marquisee," Emmie said.

"If Eliza had a large debt, that was both an impetus for the scheme and a conduit to the person who managed the debt. Maybe the same debt collector who visited Mrs. Warner."

"And having successfully used the insurance scheme once, they thought they could use it again to help others to clear up their own debts?"

"And make a sound profit for themselves," I said. "But how could they know which women might be willing to do in their own husbands?"

"Well, both Mrs. Farrell and Mrs. Marquisee had seemed to dislike their husbands enough, and Mrs. Warner gave that impression."

"But how could anyone have counted on that?"

"Yes, I imagine there are *some* women, even among those with gambling debts, who would resist the idea," Emmie agreed. "That note from Donigan wouldn't be enough to convict someone, would it?"

"I can't see how. All it proves is someone was trying to blackmail Eliza Barclay. They've left very little evidence at all."

"You forget, we have Mrs. Warner, Harry."

"Mrs. Warner was perfectly willing to name Elizabeth as the mystery woman until she protested. I imagine a reasonably talented defense attorney could convince her his client is innocent as well."

"Perhaps you're right. Then we need someone to confess." She thought a bit. "The gentleman debt collector?"

"It's too bad you didn't learn anything about him during your time at the Frauenverein."

"We could try again," Emmie said. "If we go in while they're busy, I'm sure I can get back into Bannon's office."

I wasn't particularly keen on the idea, but I would have been even less so if Emmie had tried to execute it on her own, which I knew she would do if I declined. We arrived at the Frauenverein sometime after ten and found that business was brisk.

"This is perfect, Harry."

"What do you have in mind, Emmie?"

"Well, now everyone upstairs knows me. I'll just go in as if I'm working and look around."

"But you already looked around and didn't find anything. And what if Bannon sees you again?"

"I thought you could handle that."

"I'm not sure Bannon is anxious to renew my acquaintance, either."

"You'll think of something."

We went upstairs and Emmie peeked into the bookkeeping room. "Bannon's not there now. Just keep him from going in, Harry." And then she vanished inside.

I bought some chips and made some small bets at the craps table and then moved on to roulette. It'd been half an hour when Bannon showed up. I stopped him.

"I was wondering if I could have a word," I said. He wasn't looking particularly conversational, but I tried to kindle his interest. "It's about your debt collection agency."

He just waved a thumb: "Out."

When I didn't make a move, he snapped his fingers and pointed to me. Two fellows showed up. Big fellows. Big enough, anyways. They turned me around, but I looked back and saw Bannon headed toward the bookkeeping room. Action was called for.

"This roulette wheel is rigged!" I yelled. "Turn it over and show them, Mr. Bannon."

Well, as I had mentioned, the place was crowded, and I had everyone's attention, including Bannon's. His fellows were becoming increasingly unfriendly, but I had aroused a certain curiosity in the crowd and a couple of patrons had managed to get to the wheel and overturn it. From the underside, the mechanism for reducing and enlarging the slots was readily apparent. There were three distinct reactions among the patrons: the majority, who had no idea what the underside of a roulette wheel was meant to look like, found it all bewildering. The next largest segment, who had always assumed the game was rigged, were merely amused. And then there were the ladies of the Frauenverein, who were shocked at my bad manners. Outnumbered and without friends, I was forced to retreat down a fire escape and into the street.

"There you are, Harry."

Emmie was standing just beside me.

"When did you get out here?" I asked.

"A while ago, while you were speaking to Bannon. Didn't you see me leaving?"

"No, perhaps you could have said something."

"I'm sorry, Harry. Why'd you leave by the fire escape?"

"Oh, I wanted some air."

Emmie patted her chatelaine. "Well, I found it."

"What, exactly?"

"A reference to a Brooklyn collection agency on Broadway." As we walked she pulled out a slip of paper and read from it: "The Sumner Johnson Agency."

"What was the reference?"

"It was a copy of a receipt. The Johnson Agency paid $1,750 on April 30th."

We went home and there found Elizabeth reading.

Emmie couldn't keep from telling her what she had found.

"Where were you this evening, dear?" Emmie asked her.

"Oh, arranging my next endeavor."

She said no more than that, but it was enough to give me a feeling of unease.

23

The next morning, Emmie and I headed off to the Johnson Agency. It was a small office on the second floor of an auction house on Broadway, just a few blocks from the river. There was a girl at the counter reading a dime novel.

"Making a payment?" she asked.

"No, we'd like to speak with Mr. Johnson."

"Junior or senior?"

"Senior."

"He's dead, I'm afraid."

"Then not him. Is junior still healthy?"

"Too healthy." She got off her stool and went into a little back office, then came out with a fellow about thirty years old. He had a head too big for his body and a bushy head of hair that accentuated the fact.

"How can I help you, sir? And madam, of course." He gave Emmie a particularly unctuous smile.

"We wanted to speak with you about your arrangement with Mr. Bannon," Emmie told him.

"Well, let me see, Bannon, you say. I don't believe I remember a Mr. Bannon. Do you, Kate?" he said to the girl.

"Do I what?"

"Look, we were hoping to avoid having the police involved," I said. "We're only looking for a name. Couldn't we just talk?"

"All right, come back to my office. But I'm not sure what I can tell you."

The three of us entered a tiny room and he closed the door.

"We know that you took on some of Bannon's debts, and that you made payments to him," I said. "We're just interested in four cases: Eliza Barclay, Anna Farrell, Kathryn Warner, and Clara Marquisee."

"I'm not sure those names are familiar to me. And I need to leave to make collections shortly."

"Please, Mr. Johnson," Emmie said. "For your own sake. There's someone very important involved. His daughter is missing. Bannon will not be able to protect you."

"Or the local precinct."

"How can I be sure I can I trust your discretion?" he asked.

"Well, we could have brought the police now," Emmie pointed out. "But why make things unpleasant?"

"Why, indeed," he said. "Okay. Yes, I had those ladies on my roll."

"How much did they owe?"

"I can't remember precisely. Farrell and Marquisee, about two or three hundred each. That Mrs. Warner something more, maybe four hundred. They were making little payments, not even covering the interest."

"What about Eliza Barclay?"

"Well, she was of another class. I believe her debt was upwards of three thousand dollars," he said. "And, of course, that's how I met the other lady."

"What other lady?" Emmie asked.

"She never gave me a name."

"What did she look like?"

"Oh, she was a stunner. A blonde. Looked like a Gibson girl."

"Wasn't that Eliza Barclay?" I asked.

"Oh, she was, too. Indeed. I met her, went around to collect a few times. Then the last time, she paid it in full. Didn't even ask for a discount."

"Then this other lady called on you?"

"The very next day, I believe. She told me she was a friend of Mrs. Barclay's and had helped arrange her payment. Then she asked me if I had many ladies in a situation similar to Mrs. Barclay's—owing money they didn't want their husbands to know about. I said I did have some. And she said her idea would only work if the lady in question didn't get on well with her husband.

"I said, that's most women I see. But she asked me for the names only of ladies I was quite sure didn't care for their husbands. I do speak to my clients, of course, so I was able to give her three names I felt very certain about."

"Missuses Farrell, Warner, and Marquisee?" I asked.

"That's right."

"What did you think this woman's plan was?" I asked.

"Well, she was quite attractive. She would have had no trouble drawing the interest of these women's husbands. Especially if things weren't good at home."

"Blackmail?"

"I didn't use the word."

"But it is what you were thinking?"

"Yes. And then I read about poor Mrs. Marquisee killing herself. I thought, she must have changed her mind and felt bad. But when I read they'd arrested her husband, I was much relieved."

"Relieved?"

"Sorry the poor woman's dead, of course. But relieved it had nothing to do with me."

"You would, of course, recognize this woman who visited you," Emmie said. "Was she tall?"

"Oh, yes. But I would be reluctant to implicate her. She lived up to her side of the bargain, paid off all the debts."

"All of them?" I asked.

"Yes, all of them. She said each of the situations had been resolved satisfactorily and asked that I forget all about the women, and herself. I assured her I would."

"When was this?"

"Well, let me check my records." He went into the larger room and through some files, then came back with a page. "They were all paid April 13th."

"A Saturday?"

"Yes, I believe it was."

"What time of day?" Emmie asked.

"Well, certainly after I did the collecting. But I believe it was later still. Yes, after lunch."

We thanked Mr. Johnson and again assured him of our discretion. Then we walked up Broadway and caught a car home.

"Well, now we know Mrs. Warner was right," I said. "There is a tall, blonde woman involved."

"But not Mrs. Barclay," Emmie said. "I suppose you're thinking of Elizabeth again?"

"It's hard not to. She knew Eliza Barclay. And there's nothing really exonerating her. She may have just bullied Mrs. Warner into clearing her."

"No, I'm sure it wasn't Elizabeth."

"All we need to do is invite Mr. Johnson to tea."

"No, I'd feel as if I was betraying her."

We arrived back at the apartment, where Elizabeth

informed me Tibbitts had phoned. I found him in.

"You were right about Sennett seeing the girl with Howell," he said. "He told me he saw them together twice, the last time on Monday morning."

"Where were they?"

"Leaving Manhattan. On the ferry to Hunter's Point. And they both had bags with them."

Then I told him about Johnson.

"Huh," was his only comment. Then he quickly changed the subject. "Here's another strange bit you might want to know. Marquisee has confessed to killing his wife, but says it was someone else who gave her the poison."

"Who?"

"Some woman. That's all I heard. An assistant D.A. is going to interview him this afternoon. I can set it up if you want to be there."

I said I did and he told me to meet Sergeant Corwin at the Raymond Street jail at two o'clock. I phoned Ratigan and told him about Sennett's seeing the missing pair on the ferry.

"I doubt it was just an excursion to Queens," he said. "Probably headed to the depot there."

"To take a train out on Long Island?"

"Lots of harbors, lots of boats."

I hung up and the three of us sat down to lunch. Emmie related the morning's events and we both watched Elizabeth's reaction.

"So it *was* Cynthia Howell," she said.

"I didn't think her particularly tall," Emmie said.

"Taller than me, certainly," Elizabeth said.

"Taller than you? What color is her hair?"

"Blonde, of course. Haven't we all been assuming it was her who visited Mrs. Warner?"

"I wish Mary were here," Emmie said.

"She is here," Elizabeth told her. "She's in her room unpacking." She left us and returned with Mary.

"Mary, do you remember the first time I visited the Howells' apartment?" Emmie asked.

"Yes, ma'am. When you were working for the charity."

"Yes, that's right. I asked to speak to Mrs. Barclay and you said she was out, but that her sister might see me."

"Yes, ma'am. Then she came out and talked with you. Mrs. Dyer."

"Who's Mrs. Dyer?" Elizabeth asked.

"She's Mrs. Barclay's other sister. Three sisters. And now two of them widows."

"What happened to Mr. Dyer?" I asked.

"Died in the Spanish war, of fever. Down in Florida."

"I don't imagine they staged that," I said.

"I just assumed it was Mrs. Howell," Emmie said. "When did Mrs. Dyer leave?"

"They all left that Saturday morning. Mrs. Dyer went home to Baltimore and her sisters went to the boat."

"What time did they leave for the boat?"

"About eight, I think."

"Mary, I thought you were at your sister's until Sunday?" Emmie inquired.

"It's a small place they have, ma'am. And two babies. And her husband drinks. I thought it would be all right if I came back early."

"Yes, of course."

Mary went back to her unpacking.

"This doesn't really change anything," I said. "It still

CROSSINGS

couldn't have been either Mrs. Barclay or Mrs. Howell who visited Johnson, because he saw the woman after their boat set sail."

"Of course, he may have mistaken Friday for Saturday," Emmie said. "But that will be resolved when Mrs. Howell arrives."

I telephoned the Cunard line and was told the *Etruria* wasn't expected to dock before five. Then I phoned Tibbitts again and asked if he could have Missuses Howell and Barclay detained on their arrival. He said he'd contact the harbor patrol and phone me back when he learned anything. Then Emmie and I left for the jail. Corwin was surprised to see Emmie.

"The D.A. won't like this," he said.

"Tell him I'm a stenographer," Emmie said.

The D.A. arrived and Corwin told him we were employees of Koestler. Then Marquisee was brought in, looking like someone who'd spent the last three days in jail. The D.A. had him sit down and then told him to explain all that had happened.

"It started a few weeks ago. I was having stomach problems."

"Stomach problems?"

"Yes, painful ones. After about a week of it, I went to a doctor. He said it might be something I ate, and to see if it just went away. And it seemed to, right after that. But a week later it started again. I went to see the doctor again and he said maybe it was some paint we were using. I said, I don't do the painting, but he said maybe it came from that anyway. So I started checking on that.

"Then one evening I came home, and there's this lady in the house. She said, 'Clara's very sick.' 'What's wrong with her?' I said. 'She took this poison.' It was rat

267

poison. Then this lady says, 'I think she's been trying to poison you.' I asked who she was, and how she could know that. She wouldn't say, but she said that Clara had an insurance policy on my life and would collect eight thousand dollars if I died. Then she showed it to me. It was just what she had said. 'Clara wanted to use the money to gamble,' she says. I knew Clara took money from the house to bet with. Everything this woman said seemed to be true. Then she said, 'There wasn't enough poison to kill her.' Well, she could see how angry I was. Then she says, 'It might be best if you just do it. Then no one needs to know.' I asked what she meant and she said, 'Use your hands.' Well, now Clara was going through something awful. She was throwing up blood, and I actually felt sorry for her. So I did it. Just to stop it. I barely touched her, but she went limp."

He paused for a bit, looked at each of us, and then the D.A. asked him to go on.

"Well, then this lady says, 'You'll need to put the body somewhere so it won't look like she died here. Maybe in a cellar you're digging.' Then she left."

"Then what did you do?"

"I thought of doing like she said. But there was no way I could do that without the fellows who work for me seeing it. So that night, I took out one of my wagons and carried her from the house. Down to the canal there. She sank when I put her in. But she must have come back up."

"What was the date?"

"The date?"

"What day was it you found this lady in your house?"

"Saturday. Saturday three weeks past."

"The evening of Saturday the 13th?" I asked.

He thought a bit. "Yes."

"The body was found on Sunday the 14th," Corwin said.

"What did this lady look like?"

"She had a dark shawl on, and a hat. She was a good-looking woman, tall."

"But you never saw her other than this one time?"

"That's right."

"When did you move to your daughter's?" Emmie asked.

"The very next day, Sunday. I couldn't stand being in that house."

After Marquisee was taken away, Corwin told the D.A. we were looking into an insurance scheme, so we spent the good part of an hour telling him the story. Then we took a car back to the apartment. Elizabeth immediately went off on an errand. I phoned the Cunard line again and was told the *Etruria* had just reached the bar and would dock about six.

"Now it seems certain there's someone else involved, Harry."

"Yes, it couldn't have been either Mrs. Barclay or Mrs. Howell who visited the Marquisees, since their boat sailed at eleven that morning."

"And, you must admit, it couldn't have been Elizabeth."

"Elizabeth had dinner with us the day before. You saw her the afternoon of the 13th, but not that evening. She may have visited Johnson just before meeting you."

"Oh, you can't see her being that ruthless, can you?"

"Well, I can't see anyone being that ruthless. If Marquisee didn't seem such a dull specimen, I'd think he was making it up."

About five, Tibbitts phoned.

"Cynthia Howell and Eliza Barclay are on the *Etru-ria*. When it docks, they'll be escorted to the customs office. That's the Clarkson Street pier."

I agreed to meet him there and then told him about Marquisee's statement.

"Damn," he said. "I'll see you at the pier."

Emmie and I left for the pier and got there about 5:30. The ship was just now in sight, coming slowly up the North River. We watched it being positioned, and at about six located the customs office. We found Tibbitts and another detective waiting.

"I think the first thing we should do is take her to see Marquisee," he said.

"Yes, that would settle that part of it," Emmie said. "But there's Mr. Johnson, too."

"I'd rather leave him out of it," Tibbitts said. "If Marquisee names her as the woman, that's murder. We don't need to bother about the rest."

Emmie looked at me and I signaled her to let the matter drop. It wasn't until half past six that a customs man brought in the two women. Unfortunately, the "Mrs. Howell" in tow was neither tall nor blonde, and bore a striking resemblance to the woman Emmie had mistaken for Mrs. Howell.

24

Emmie confronted the woman on the matter, and she readily confessed to being Mrs. Dyer.

"You've been traveling under your sister's name?" I asked.

"Yes. But I don't see what concern that is of yours."

"But why do it?" Emmie asked.

"I'd rather not say," Mrs. Dyer said.

"Lady, you just came into port giving a false name," Tibbitts told her. "You'd better have some explanation."

"It isn't anything nefarious," she said. "Cynthia was worried Edward, her husband, was being unfaithful. It was her idea that she would make him think she'd gone to Europe."

"Then spy on him?" Emmie asked.

"Watch him, yes."

"Where is she now?"

"I expect at their home."

Throughout this, Eliza Barclay seemed only remotely interested in the conversation. Tibbitts suggested we all go up to the Howells' apartment and settle the matter. When we arrived, it appeared uninhabited. Mrs. Dyer went into the Howells' bedroom and when she came out, she told us her sister must have returned to the apartment.

"How can you be sure of that?" Emmie asked.

"Her dressing gown is there, and so are her toiletries."

Emmie went in the room and came out. "Those weren't there on Friday afternoon, Harry."

"When you two went to the boat, where did Mrs. Howell go?" I asked.

"The Netherlands Hotel."

"And the maid didn't know of this?"

"No, no one."

"Why was the wire to Mrs. Howell sent here, then?" Emmie asked.

"That was a mistake. Eliza misunderstood," Mrs. Dyer said.

Emmie, Tibbitts, and I went off to the Netherlands, leaving the other detective to keep an eye on the two sisters. At the hotel, we learned that Mrs. Howell had been staying there since the evening of the 13th using her sister's name, Dyer. We were led to the room where her trunk remained along with some of her wardrobe. Also, a telegram sent from Queenstown on the 28th, where the *Etruria* stopped briefly after leaving Liverpool. It read:

Sailing Etruria arrive New York on fourth. First wire sent to apartment in error.

It was addressed to Mrs. Dyer at the Netherlands and signed Cynthia Howell. The three of us sat about the room for a bit.

"Well, this makes things simpler, doesn't it?" Tibbitts asked.

"Yes," Emmie agreed. "And it explains why there were no photos in the apartment of Cynthia Howell. It must have been her who went to see Johnson, and Marquisee."

"Yes, and Mrs. Warner," I said. "I suppose she thought she had a perfect alibi to clean up the loose ends."

"Mrs. Warner!" Emmie exclaimed. "She's home alone."

The three of us rushed off to the Warners' tenement on First Avenue. Mr. Gilbo was standing guard at his neighbors' apartment door.

"What's going on?" I asked.

"Someone tried to kill Mrs. Warner," he said.

"Is she all right?" Emmie asked.

"Yes. A little shaken."

He let us in and we found Mrs. Warner preparing supper for her protector.

"There you are," she said. "You received my message."

"What message?" I asked.

"I telephoned right after it happened. Your new maid took down the message. She seemed like a nice girl."

"Yes, very nice," I agreed. "But I'm afraid we didn't get the message. What happened?"

"She showed up. Angrier than ever. You know, I think she might be a little mad."

"The same woman who came to you before?" Emmie asked.

"Yes, it was her all right. I think she wanted to kill me. If Mr. Gilbo hadn't been passing by, I think she would have."

"When was this?"

"Oh, just an hour or two ago."

"And then she left?"

"Yes, though Mr. Gilbo tried to hold her."

"It was like holding a tiger," Mr. Gilbo elucidated.

"Did you telephone the police?"

"Oh, yes. They came. I told them all about it. Her

coming before, and my meeting you. But I don't think they believed me."

"How odd," I said. "Well, Sergeant Tibbitts believes you."

"Sure I do," he said.

"Do you want to come back to our apartment until she's caught?" Emmie asked. "We do know who it is now."

"I think I'll just stay here, thank you. Now I can wire Dickie about it, me being in danger, and he'll come back. At least I hope he will."

We left them to their supper and outside Tibbitts found a call box. He telephoned the local precinct and asked that they look after her. While he went off to put out an alert on Mrs. Howell, Emmie and I went home for our own meal.

"What do you suppose Cynthia Howell was doing the last three weeks, Harry?"

"Looking for Mrs. Warner and Anna Farrell. And keeping an eye on her husband. And Donigan, I imagine."

"It was a clever idea, switching names like that. If I hadn't sent that telegram, we still would know nothing about it. You see, Harry, sometimes it pays to take little risks."

"If Cynthia Howell finds out it was you who undermined her subterfuge, the risk may not seem so little."

"She'd need to get by you first, Harry."

"Yes, that's just what bothers me."

The next morning, sometime after eleven, Ratigan phoned.

"Howell rented a boat out in Patchogue. They were supposed to go out yesterday, but something went wrong with the boat and the man at the yard told them it wouldn't be ready until Tuesday. Howell told him they'd be staying there in town at the Ocean Avenue Hotel, under the name Channing. They weren't in the room this morning, but they haven't checked out and they left their luggage behind. My man thinks they're still out there, waiting for the boat. If you want to go out, let me know and I'll have him meet your train. The next train leaves Brooklyn at 1:45."

"All right, I'll be on it," I said. "It's definitely Sally Koestler he was with?"

"The description matches. Who else would it be?"

I told him about Mrs. Howell's adventures. Emmie and I packed bags in case we'd be gone overnight and then rode the Long Island Railroad out to Patchogue.

"So now we're looking for Edward Howell and Sally Koestler, and the homicidal Cynthia Howell," Emmie said. "Do you think there's a chance the Howells have been working together this whole time?"

"It's crossed my mind. But what about the telegram? Howell thought it was from her and bolted as soon as he read it."

"But perhaps he knew it wasn't from her," she said. "If he was aware his wife was in town, he may have gone off to warn her that her sisters were returning."

"And Cynthia instructed him to elope with Sally? As a hostage?"

"Yes, something like that."

"When he left with Sally, Cynthia didn't expect to be in need of a hostage," I pointed out.

"It's too bad, really."

"What's too bad?"

"Well, it looks like we may find Howell and Sally out

on Long Island. I was just hoping for a more dramatic ending."

"Like a chase on the high seas? They set sail, hoist the Jolly Roger, and head off for the Caribbean?"

"Well, something like that," she admitted. "But absent the clichés."

"It would make a gripping yarn, Emmie. But I'm afraid too long for our market."

We arrived in Patchogue a little after four. An operative named Kimball met us and took us around to meet Joel Furman, the man who was renting the boat to Howell.

"How did you know to look for Furman?" I asked him.

"A repair bill in that file of Howell's."

The house was on a knoll, overlooking the inlet.

"I rented him the boat last week," Furman told us. "He came by last Tuesday, but I had to rig it and get it on the water. I handed it over to him yesterday, but the rudder shaft had got bent somehow. We had to take it back out."

"Did you know Howell?"

"I did some work on his own boat. He had to sell that, he said."

"When was he supposed to return for the boat?"

"I told him Tuesday. No earlier. Like I told this fellow this morning, Howell said they'd be staying at the Ocean Avenue Hotel, under the name Channing. Mr. and Mrs. Channing."

"And Mrs. Channing was a young girl?"

"Yes, a small thing. Blonde hair, just like this fellow described."

"If Howell left the hotel, would you have someplace else to contact him?" I asked.

"I'm sure I have his New York address if you want it," Furman said.

"No, we've been there."

"Are you working for his wife?" he asked. "She was just here."

"Mrs. Howell?" Kimball asked. "When was this?"

"Oh, maybe two hours ago now. She said she was Mrs. Howell and asked me if I had heard from her husband. I told her no, of course. Then I sent a boy over to the hotel to let 'Mr. Channing' know."

"Did you recognize her?" I asked.

"No, I'd never met her."

I asked him to describe her. It sounded like Cynthia Howell.

"I saw her get on the 3:55 to New York," Kimball told us. "I had no idea who she was, or that we were looking for Howell's wife."

"We thought she'd been in Europe until last evening," I told him.

Then Kimball walked us over to the hotel. Another operative had been watching the place, but had seen nothing of the "Channings."

Kimball asked if he'd seen the boy go inside to deliver a message.

"I did see him go in. He came out and spoke to a lady. But it wasn't this Sally Koestler."

He described the lady, and it was the same one who had visited Furman, and later got on the train.

"She must have suspected Furman was lying and followed the boy," Kimball said.

"Yes, then probably paid him to tell her about it."

Kimball took us into the manager's office.

"Of course, we didn't realize the situation," he said.

"Please assure Mr. Koestler we will cooperate however possible."

"When did they arrive?" I asked.

"Monday. They checked in that evening. We had no reason to suspect anything."

"When was the last time anyone here saw them?" I asked.

"The fellow at the desk saw them go out early, 7:30 this morning," Kimball answered for him.

We left the manager and went back outside.

"Where do you think they went off to?" I asked Kimball.

"I think they just realized if they hung about here all day someone might see them. A lot of people come in from New York on Sunday. I bet they're just laying low somewhere out here."

"Is there a morning train back to New York?"

"There is. Leaves just after eight. But no one saw them go to the station, or get on the train," Kimball told us. "Of course, there aren't a lot of people at the station at eight o'clock Sunday morning. But they didn't buy a ticket here."

"They may have bought tickets on the train," I said.

"Sure. Or they just went somewhere else out here on the island," Kimball said. "Why would he go home to New York if his wife is looking for him?"

"Of course, she's found them here," I pointed out.

"Yes, but they don't know that yet," Emmie said.

Kimball went with Emmie and me to observe who boarded the six o'clock train back to New York. There was no sign of our trio and it was only after it left that we learned it was the last train of the evening. We'd be staying the night in Patchogue. Since both Howell and

Sally had met Emmie and me, it was agreed we should stay at another hotel in town, Roe's, just by the station. Emmie registered us under an alias, Mr. and Mrs. Rawdon Crawley. I wasn't sure I cared for the implication, but doubted the clerk was on to it. Then the three of us went into the dining room for dinner.

"Do you really think they'll be back here Tuesday for the boat?" Emmie asked Kimball.

"Why not? They left before we got here. He doesn't know about his wife being around. Furman said he could get to Cuba in that boat."

"The Caribbean?" Emmie smiled.

"But maybe they do know his wife is around," I suggested. "She could have come in last night. If Howell saw her, it would explain the quick exit this morning."

After dinner, Kimball went to relieve his colleague and Emmie and I went for a long walk on the beach.

25

Having exhausted the opportunities for public entertainment on a Sunday evening in Patchogue, Emmie and I went back to our room. Just after midnight, I turned out the light.

"You don't believe Howell and Sally are still out here on Long Island someplace, do you, Harry?"

"I don't know. Maybe if there's someplace one of them is familiar with—someplace they can hide out for a day or two, until the boat's ready. But I doubt they just went down the island and got a room in another hotel. They must know people will be looking for Sally."

"What about Mrs. Howell? She has the same problem."

"Yes, but I'd guess she went wherever she expects them to be. She seems more interested in tying up loose ends than in getting away."

At five the next morning, I was awoken by drops of cold water being flung at my face. Emmie wanted to talk.

"I was thinking of what you said about Mrs. Howell, Harry. I mean, her wanting to wrap up loose ends. What about Mary?"

"Mary doesn't seem to have had any idea about the scheme. She didn't even catch on to the ruse with the trip to Europe."

"Yes, but Cynthia Howell couldn't know that for sure. What if she found out we took Mary away? She may suspect it was because we thought Mary would tell us something."

"Oh, people pilfer each other's servants every day."

Ten minutes later, I was dressed and downstairs trying to put a call through to the apartment. Emmie insisted we warn Mary of the potential threat. Unfortunately, the lines were tied up—or down, or whatever the excuse du jour was—and it was decided we should head back to Brooklyn as soon as possible. I checked with Kimball to make sure Howell and Sally hadn't returned, and then we boarded the first train of the morning.

"You know, Harry, there's also Mr. Johnson. He knew about the scheme. He's in danger, too."

"The welfare of a debt collector who colludes with poolroom operators and blackmailers is not paramount among my concerns."

"Yes, I suppose you're right."

After that I dozed some, but just around Massapequa I was roused by a thought.

"You know, Emmie, Sally and Howell could be at any of the places we'd checked before."

"Is there someplace you have in mind?"

"The house on Rush Street. Sally has stayed there before, and they make it their business to be discreet. I think we should go there first."

"I don't think I'll rest easy until we check on Mary. Then we can go to Rush Street."

I pointed out that if Mrs. Howell were planning to strike at Mary, she probably had already done it. And if we were heading home to a house of slaughter, later would do as well as sooner. She had to concede my point.

We arrived at the Bushwick station just before eight. The Stagg Street precinct house was only a few blocks away, so we went up there and I asked to speak with Sergeant Corwin. He kept us waiting and Emmie went off to find a telephone. A while later, she returned.

"I spoke with Elizabeth, Harry. Everything's fine."

About 8:30, Corwin finally called us in and I told him about Howell and Sally being out in Patchogue, and her link to the house on Rush Street. Then I asked if he could accompany us there. Before answering, he clipped his first cigar of the day and stuck it in place.

"That's the 59th. We'll have to call them first."

When raiding a disorderly house operating under the protection of another precinct, it's only common courtesy to inform them in advance. He telephoned the 59th and was told everyone was out on parade duty.

"What parade?" Emmie asked.

"The circus," Corwin told her. "Let's see if I can find the captain."

He went off for what seemed like an eternity. While he was out of the room, I telephoned Tibbitts but he wasn't in. Then Corwin returned and said that the captain was out.

"This is absurd, Harry," Emmie announced. "Let's just go ourselves. If we find them, Sergeant Corwin can explain to Mr. Koestler his reluctance to help."

That didn't improve his demeanor any, but he did agree to come along. We walked down Stagg Street and then worked our way to Division Avenue. Here we were met by the crowd. In order to clear a path for the parade, cops were herding people to the sides of the street. Emmie somehow became separated from us and wound up on the other side of the street. It was then that the parade came around the corner. Corwin, suddenly impatient, was trying to lead me down a side street and I considered abandoning Emmie.

But only for a moment. She gave me a pathetic look,

something quite uncharacteristic. I broke through the crowd to the other side and then we dashed back before a line of elephants. As we did, I glanced at Emmie and saw a little smile. She dropped it as soon as she noticed I was looking. But I saw it, alright. At Bedford Avenue, we encountered the parade again. But this was the tail end, with the calliope playing a familiar cakewalk. Soon we were on Rush Street and just below the green house, where several partially dressed women were at the windows straining to see the parade. One of them was Sally.

A fellow tried to stop us from going upstairs, but Corwin easily knocked him to the floor. Sally had seen me and was hurriedly dressing when we entered the room. Howell had obviously just risen.

"That's the girl?" Corwin asked me.

"Yes, that's Sally Koestler."

"Why couldn't you leave us alone?" Sally asked.

"Well, your father wouldn't like that. I'm afraid Mr. Howell might not be the perfect prospect."

"I know he's married," Sally said. "To a madwoman."

"Did he tell you about the murder of Robert Barclay?" I asked.

"He had nothing to do with that, that was his wife."

"Was it?" I asked.

"Perhaps we should leave them, Harry," Emmie said. "But you should know, Mr. Howell, your wife is on the loose, and seems to be in a vengeful mood."

"She doesn't know we're here," Howell said.

"Doesn't she?" Emmie asked. "She knows you left Patchogue. And she knows about this house."

"How would she know about this house?" Howell asked. I must admit, the same question occurred to me.

"Because William Huber brought Eliza here," Emmie explained. "Ask Sally."

Howell looked over at Sally.

"He may have," she said.

"And Mrs. Barclay no doubt told her sister," Emmie concluded.

"There are private detectives waiting for you in Patchogue," I said. "You have no chance to get to the boat. You need to help us find your wife now."

"I have no idea where she is," he said.

"But you knew she didn't sail for Europe?"

"Not until last Monday, when I read the telegram from her sister."

"So you fled because you knew she was a danger to you?"

"You never know with her what she's thinking. But if she had stayed behind and hadn't told me, I assumed she was spying on me."

"Whose idea was it to insure Barclay, then kill him?"

"Hers, of course."

"But she had no trouble getting the rest of you to go along?"

"Barclay was a bastard. I went through all sorts of trouble to get him a job at the firm, and then I found he was pilfering from client accounts. Some of the insurance money had to be used just to make them whole."

"And his wife?"

"She never cared for him. Their marriage was something Cynthia arranged. Both Cynthia and Eliza had lost a lot at the bucket shop he'd been running."

"She had her sister marry Barclay to cover a debt?" Emmie asked.

"It was never stated that simply, but that's what it

amounted to," Howell told her. Sally gave him a look of concern, and he added, "It wasn't my idea."

"Was the insurance scheme your idea?" I asked.

"No, of course not. We found out Barclay had insured Eliza without telling her."

"You thought he would kill Eliza for the money?"

"Cynthia insisted he would. I don't know really."

"And Eliza's need to pay her gambling debts was another motive?"

"Yes. But you can't blame her. She's like a child."

"What about Huber? Did Cynthia have any trouble convincing him?"

"She had to work him down some. He had confronted Barclay about getting a divorce, and Barclay told him he would give her a divorce, for five thousand dollars. He thought of trying to raise that, but Cynthia pointed out they'd be marrying with no home and a large debt. In the end, he agreed to it, too."

Just then, Elizabeth arrived. She was accompanied by a man named Gilbert who she introduced as Koestler's lawyer.

"Who posed as Barclay for the doctor's visit?" I asked Howell.

"I did. We were about the same age, so that was simple enough."

"Who actually killed him?"

"Huber wouldn't do it. Cynthia had to."

"So you and Eliza could both have alibis?"

"Yes. There had never been anything between us. That was all just to divert suspicion."

"And then Eliza received the payment."

"Yes. That was a great relief."

"Until Donigan's message arrived?"

"How do you know about that?"

"It was found in your apartment. We thought perhaps your wife saved it in case she needed to blackmail him."

"That sounds like her. When he sent that note we were all terrified. All except Cynthia, of course. She saw it as an opportunity."

"And so she came up with the scheme to find other women with debts who might be willing to do in their husbands," Emmie said. "Didn't that seem a rather bizarre idea?"

"Yes, of course," Howell agreed. "It did to me and Huber, at least. Donigan insisted it would work. And now we were all accessories to murder. There was no backing out. Cynthia got the names from the debt collector and Huber wrote the policies."

"Who posed as the men for the doctor visits?"

"Donigan, for Farrell and Marquisee, I think. And Huber for the other fellow."

"Warner?"

"Yes."

"And then Huber killed himself. Were you surprised?"

"Yes. Not shocked, but surprised. Most of his objections were to the mechanics of the scheme, the likelihood of getting caught, and so forth. I hadn't noticed him being particularly troubled by the morality of it."

"Do you think he might have been killed?"

"Why? Do you mean by Cynthia?"

"Perhaps."

"No, I remember reading her the story out of the newspaper that morning. She was as surprised as I was. It's the one time she seemed unsure what to do."

"Did you consider dropping the scheme then?"

"Yes, Donigan and I wanted to. Donigan even said he'd give up any claim to the money we received on Barclay. But Cynthia insisted it would be just as dangerous not to proceed. The three other wives now knew about it, she said. Once they'd murdered their husbands, they couldn't tell a soul."

"Who killed Farrell?"

"Cynthia. His wife tried, but she couldn't do it."

"But when payment on Farrell's policy was delayed, didn't you realize the insurance company was suspicious?"

"Well, you showed up. But Donigan thought he could alter some files and cover up the other two policies. And Farrell's wife couldn't tell. It seemed we might weather it. Then I found out Cynthia was still trying to get the last two women to kill their husbands. It was madness. I contacted Donigan, and he agreed. He told Cynthia he'd persuaded his brother-in-law, someone higher up at the insurance company, to help cover up what had already occurred, but if that wasn't the end of it, he would reveal everything. He said his brother-in-law suggested both Eliza and Mrs. Farrell leave town. The next day, Cynthia and Eliza boarded the boat to Gibraltar. Or at least I thought they had."

"Did Mrs. Dyer know anything about the scheme?"

"No, certainly not. She'd only arrived a couple days before."

"Or your maid, Mary?"

"No, I don't think so. We weren't that foolish."

"Do you know what became of Anna Farrell?"

"No. I imagine she left town, too."

Just then Tibbitts came into the room.

"Well, well," he said. "You caught up with them."

"How'd you get here?" Corwin asked.

"I've been following Cynthia Howell. She came over across the river, then I lost her. I called Stagg Street and they told me you were here."

"How'd you find her?" I asked.

"She came back to the hotel, late last night."

"You couldn't just take her in?" Corwin asked.

"I didn't want to. I figured she might have some unfinished business with her husband. And maybe a good idea where he was hiding. We followed her out this morning, but she must have seen us. We lost her at the ferry landing over here."

Then Tibbitts made a lunge toward the bed where Howell was sitting. Howell had pulled out a gun. He stepped back from Tibbitts.

"Do you want to come with me?" he asked Sally.

"She most certainly does not," Elizabeth answered for her.

Then he shot himself. Or tried to, anyway. He fired several times, but the gun appeared to be empty. Tibbitts and Corwin tackled him and took him down to the street. The rest of us followed. Then Elizabeth and the lawyer took Sally home.

"What about Mr. Johnson?" Emmie asked

"What about him?" Tibbitts asked in return.

"He knows about the scheme and he could identify Cynthia Howell."

"His place is just up the street from the ferry landing," I added.

We left Howell with Corwin and went off to Broadway. There were a couple cops stationed outside the door of the Sumner Johnson Agency. Tibbitts preceded us inside, where a sergeant was interviewing Johnson. His girl, Kate, was on her stool reading her dime novel, seemingly unaware of the draped corpse at her feet. Tibbitts asked the sergeant for the story.

"That woman came in here about an hour ago," he began, pointing to the body. "She said she wanted to see Johnson. The girl told her he was making his rounds, but would be back later. The woman said she'd wait. When Johnson came in, she jumped on him and tried to stab him with this," he said, showing us a kitchen knife. "Then the girl picked up that embosser there and crushed the woman's head."

He walked over and pulled back the blanket, revealing a tall woman lying face down. Her carefully coiffed blonde hair was marred by a mass of drying blood. It was a gruesome sight. So much so, Kate took time from her reading to marvel at her handiwork.

"She's dead alright," she confirmed. Then, after a brief smile—a well-deserved expression of self-satisfaction—she went back to her reading.

Tibbitts turned the corpse on its side so we could see the face.

"Is that her?" he asked.

She bore a definite resemblance to Eliza Barclay. But her countenance wasn't quite as benign. In fact, after seeing that determined and decidedly malicious face, it would be difficult to argue that Kate hadn't made the correct choice in the matter.

"We've never seen her before," I said. "But she fits the description. Johnson should be able to tell us."

"He says he doesn't know the woman."

"He's lying," Emmie said.

"Now see here, madam!" Johnson protested.

"This is the woman you gave the names of Mrs. Farrell, Mrs. Warner, and Mrs. Marquisee, isn't it?" I asked.

"I don't recall that episode."

Emmie encouraged the policemen to beat Johnson into a confession, but persuasion eventually succeeded. Later that day, Mrs. Dyer identified her sister's body.

26

It was after noon when Emmie and I returned home. Mary prepared a simple lunch for us, and when we were alone we took stock of the events of the last five weeks.

"After all the scheming, and four murders, only Edward Howell is likely to be punished," Emmie said.

"And Marquisee," I reminded her. "But you can't count Kate's dispatching of Cynthia Howell as murder."

"I wasn't."

"Or Donigan's being shot by a policeman."

"No, of course not."

"Well, let's see. Barclay, Farrell, Mrs. Marquisee, and... Anna Farrell?"

"I suppose she may have been murdered. But you know perfectly well who I'm referring to."

"William Huber? How do you figure it, Emmie?"

"Well, obviously his family is covering something up. I think he was killed by his father, or maybe his brother, or possibly both, to protect the family honor. You do agree it was murder?"

"Not now. First, John as a suspect makes no sense at all."

"He could have confronted William that evening at the office, before going to the house. Knocked him unconscious and left him with the gas on. Then pretended to discover him there early the next morning."

"But he was the one coerced into changing his account."

"Well, his father was always my first choice," she said.

"Now I think you're making the same mistake John did."

"What mistake is that?"

"John went along with changing his statement about the head wound because he was told his father insisted it was on the forehead. I think he feared it was because his father had killed William, perhaps accidentally. And then made it look like suicide by turning on the gas and leaving part of one of William's notes that contained the line, 'Tell Mother I'm sorry.'"

"What other reason would his father have for lying about the wound?"

"When Cynthia Howell enlarged the scheme, William had second thoughts. He wasn't willing to come clean to the police. But I think he did tell his father, who he was sure would help him. In fact, he may have spoken with him that very day. That would explain why his father seemed upset that evening."

"His father might have been equally upset if he had killed William," Emmie pointed out.

"True, but according to the bartender at the Carleton, William was also upset that evening. What if it happened this way: he tells his father, but instead of his usual sympathetic response, he's shocked and angry. This isn't like cheating on a college exam, or losing money in a poolroom. In attempting to gain his sympathy, William mentions how ruthless Cynthia had become. And that he felt in danger himself."

"Do you really think that would make his father sympathetic?"

"No. But it plants the idea in his head. So when William is found dead, his father thinks he may well have been murdered by his fellow conspirators. They could have come across a note somewhere in the office with the line apologizing to his mother. But to solve the murder, the police would have to uncover William's involvement in Barclay's murder. His father thought he could spare his family by insisting it was suicide."

"But Howell was sure his wife hadn't done it," she pointed out.

"Yes, and she seemed the only other likely suspect."

"So what are you saying, Harry? It was suicide, after all?"

"That's my bet. The assumption that William was sitting in the chair when he lost consciousness and fell forward was based on the wound being on the forehead. His father jumped to the conclusion a wound on the back of the head meant he'd been murdered, so he had the reports changed. But maybe William had been standing up, or sitting in the chair but facing away from the desk and fell backwards. Who knows?"

"But the note had been torn from something longer. Which means someone else was involved."

"What if William wrote a longer apology, addressed to his father and mentioning his involvement in the scheme. Then he had second thoughts. The whole point in killing himself was to spare his family the scandal. But what if someone else discovered his body? The janitor, or the office girl. So he himself tore the incriminating part of the note off. Probably burning it so it wouldn't be found. Though I doubt if Sergeant Corwin ever bothered to look for it."

"But you could never prove any of that."

"No," I admitted. "But explanations are often more prosaic than you imagine them, Emmie."

"That's hardly my fault."

"No, it certainly isn't due to any lack of effort on your part," I agreed. And then I asked her a question. "How did you know that Huber had taken Eliza Barclay to the house on Rush Street?"

"I didn't know that at all. I was just trying to frighten Howell into talking. I thought he'd be more afraid of his wife than the police."

"Yes, you were right about that," I agreed.

"I was also right about Dorothy," she said. "You never thanked me for that."

"What about Dorothy?"

"Getting her to leave us. I assumed you realized that when I invited them to live here together, it was with a purpose in mind."

"What purpose?"

"To have Dorothy quit us, of course. You see, I made sure your little notebook would be found by the movers. And I knew they couldn't resist sharing it. So, of course Jim read it."

"You know, Emmie, other people merely let their servants go."

"But this way we haven't embarrassed anyone."

We were both looking forward to a quiet day of recuperation. All the running about, and the violent conclusion, had sapped even Emmie's enthusiasm for adventure. Then, about half past one, Elizabeth showed up.

"I'm here, Emmie, to help however I can," she said.

"Oh, Lord. I forgot all about the bridge academy," Emmie said.

"Bridge academy?" I asked.

"Yes, dear. I've invited a number of ladies to attend. At two o'clock."

"Emmie is going to teach them the finer points of the game," Elizabeth said. "For five dollars a head."

I had a pretty good guess what the "finer points" would entail. But if one afternoon teaching the good women of Brooklyn how to cheat at bridge would be enough to pay the month's rent, I wasn't going to complain. Especially since—with the case over, and our treatise at the printer's—I was now unemployed.

I helped with the setting up and then was promptly exiled. The races at Aqueduct were over. And the Superbas were playing in Boston. So I decided to spend the afternoon at the circus. I was a little embarrassed, a grown man going by himself. But the chariot races alone were worth the price of admission. That evening, Elizabeth made us another memorable dinner. It would be her last meal with us, she said.

"I'm moving in with the Koestlers tomorrow," she announced.

"Moving in with the Koestlers?" Emmie asked.

"Yes, I've been hired as Mrs. Koestler's secretary. Though my real duties will lie elsewhere."

"Dare we ask where?" I asked.

"I'm to look after Sally. Keep her from any more missteps."

"How will you do that?" Emmie asked.

"By befriending her, of course. And if I can arrange to have her marry respectably, Mr. Koestler has offered a substantial bonus."

"But what if you merely manipulate her into a match, Elizabeth?" Emmie asked. "You may be condemning her to a lifetime of unhappiness—or worse."

"That's no problem," I said. "After a few years of this racket, Elizabeth could revive the divorce ring and unwind all the unhappy matches. Zeimer should be getting out about then."

"Oh, do shut up, Harrison."

"I'm sorry, Elizabeth. But before you leave us, there is something I should tell you. You remember the little performance at the Carleton Hotel?"

"Yes, what about it?"

"Well, the fellows there made me agree that if ever our little home should break up, the surplus female would be auctioned off. I'm afraid I signed a contract to that effect."

"How amusing," she said.

I had mixed feelings about Elizabeth's exit. I would certainly miss her cooking, but not at all her acerbic wit. Sadly, unbeknownst to me, the future held another helping of the latter and not a bit of the former.

It had been an odd case, and looking back on it, it's hard not to feel that I was more an observer than a participant. But I suppose most of my cases have wound up that way. In the end, all the deaths could be said to have originated with Cynthia Howell. But the plan could never have gone anywhere without the complaisance of all the rest. It's a source of wonder to me how easily the most hare-brained among us can bend others to their will. But it's not a subject into which I wish to delve too deeply.

Koestler succeeded in having most of the facts kept secret by coercing the District Attorney into offering Howell a deal he would plead guilty to. He would serve no more than five years. Marquisee, who was more an instrument than a participant, couldn't be convicted of murder and would be out within a year. Anna Farrell was never heard from again. The others involved, those not among the dead, all evaded the law. Johnson was too well protected, Mrs. Barclay too convincingly ignorant, and Mrs. Warner too convincingly eccentric, for any of them to be prosecuted.

Between the gains from our stock trades and Emmie's income as a scholar of the card table, we seemed to be well set. A European tour—our long-delayed honeymoon—was being planned. Before the summer was out, we'd have our trip to Europe. Just not the one we'd intended.